I0580972

FAIR COMPROMISES

Science Traveler Series

Book 1

FAIR COMPROMISES

Science Traveler Series

Book 10

J.L. Greger

Bug Press

Bernalillo, New Mexico

Fair Compromises

Bug Press
An imprint of IngramSpark
Bernalillo, New Mexico 87004
https: //www.jlgreger.com
Copyright ©2022 by J. L. Greger
Cover design by Barbara Hodges for Got You Covered Bookcover Design©2022
ISBN (paperback): 9781735421421
ISBN (EPUB): 9781735421438
Library of Congress Catalogue Number: 2022909127

All rights reserved. No part of this book may be used or reproduced in any manner whatsoever without the written permission of the author, except as brief quotations used in critical articles and reviews.
This is a work of fiction. Names, characters, places, and incidents either are the product of the author's imagination or are used fictitiously. Any resemblance to actual persons living or dead is entirely coincidental.

To Bug—my loyal and understanding Japanese Chin, who let me think I was the boss, and

To Elf—the playful and mischievous opposite of Bug. He's teaching me reality.

ACKNOWLEDGMENTS

I want to thank John Byram for editing this manuscript. I also want to thank Barbara Hodges for her patience and creativity when designing covers for my books.

Over the years my fellow writers from the now defunct Oak Tree Press have provided intellectual and emotional support for my writing. I appreciate them as authors, advisors, and friends.

CHAPTER 1: The Victim on Wednesday

Estella Garcia Davis tried to dial her phone, but she wasn't sure which keys were real. She blinked. For a second, there were only nine blurred buttons. The double set of keys reappeared. The best she could do poke at the right button of the last row on the display and then twice strike the first button of the first row. She hoped that was 9-1-1.

When she awoke at eight this morning, she attributed her dry mouth and headache to having one too many drinks after the dismal rally last night. She'd swallowed two aspirin, drained two glasses of water, and tried to call her husband. She hadn't located him and had staggered back to bed.

Now at two in the afternoon, she found it hard to get out of bed. The pounding in her head increased as she remembered last night.

She didn't expect food at campaign rallies to be good, but this food had been a dieter's nightmare. She wondered why the fried chicken was even called meat. Dietitians claimed over fifty percent of the calories in some fast-food fried chicken came from fat. The chicken last night had been greasier than any fast-food chicken but without any crunchiness in the breading. The so-called mashed potatoes could have been used as wallpaper paste, and the gravy was a flavorless attempt at queso sauce. She gulped another glass of water and remembered the one item that she liked—home-canned figs with nuts.

Actually, the food had not been the worst part of the event. She thought tourism, technology, and the entertainment industry were the best future engines of economic development in New Mexico. She knew that would be a tough sell in Clovis. Her campaign manager and her husband had convinced her that she couldn't totally avoid the conservative southeastern part of the state of New Mexico where the oil and gas industries were the chief employers. After all, a senator had to represent the whole state. *But* her husband and campaign manager hadn't faced the hostile citizens who attended the event.

The worst part of all was the snickering reporter from *The Eastern New Mexico News*. He noted her grandfather and father had built the family's wealth by drilling for gas and oil in Texas and New Mexico. Then he had called her "a reformed whore" for selling off her gas and oil holdings during the last five years.

She recognized the reporter was right in a way and had replied, "I learned a lot as the mayor of Santa Fe. One reason I'm running for office is to atone for my family's past mistakes."

There was only one good thing about this rally. At most events, there were several male supporters who rubbed her back, patted her seat, and smashed her against their chests in supposed hugs. They seemed to think they owned a piece of her because they had donated to her campaign. No one had touched her last night.

The ride home from Clovis to Santa Fe had been a long one. Her campaign manager had been taciturn after she complained he should have screened the guest list for the event more carefully. She also couldn't reach her husband Nelson at his hotel room in San Diego, even though it was after midnight. She'd enjoyed a bottle of wine and remembered one of her mother's favorite expressions—"Marriage is a series of compromises until you're ready for a divorce." Estella had adjusted her positions on a number of issues to please her handsome husband who was a conservation activist. Still, he seemed to be finding more and more reasons for unexplained business trips.

The operator finally answered the phone, but she seemed dense and kept saying, "I can't understand you."

Estella was speaking as clearly as she could, but it was becoming tough to swallow.

CHAPTER 2: Sara Almquist on Wednesday in Albuquerque

Sara Almquist's eyes felt itchy. She looked into her bathroom mirror. Her eyelids were red and swollen. The junipers must be pollinating even though it was only late February. Allergy season had begun early.

Sara seldom looked into a mirror because she didn't like to notice the effects of gravity on her fifty-year-old face, but her eyes, if not the lids, were unchanged. They were green with yellow and brown dots.

Her parents had both lamented her "curious" eye color. She suspected her father hoped her eyes would fade to a watery blue like his. Her mother had often stated Sara's face would be more interesting if her eyes "matured to a chocolate brown" like hers. Sara guessed they'd both thought her eye color was *curious* because her eyes color was a compromise between theirs. Compromise hadn't been a regular part of their relationship.

Sara realized she had no right to be critical of them. The current compromise that she and her partner Eric Sanders—whom everyone called "Sanders"—had achieved was less than perfect. When he accepted the position as chargé d'affaires in the embassy in Brasilia, Brazil, Sara had refused a position as a science attaché in the same embassy. The overt reason was the current regime in Brazil was hostile to science and Sara didn't want to deal with unsolvable problems. The real reasons were her Japanese Chin Bug was too old to be transplanted to the tropical climate of Brazil and she wanted to learn whether she and Sanders shared any interests other than work-related problems.

The ringing of the phone distracted Sara from her thoughts.

"Got the perfect project for you."

Sara Almquist thought Paul Carbonne's voice had lost its bounce since he'd become the interim director of the FBI's Albuquerque office. She noticed administrative posts often did that to even the most enthusiastic people. The sheer volume of trivialities seemed to grind out the zest for life from administrators. Of course, it was four-thirty, and this was probably one of his last tasks for the day.

"Are you trying to convince yourself or me? What's up?"

"Got a call from New Mexico Department of Health. A nurse practitioner in Clovis saw four individuals with double vision, headaches, and muscle weakness this morning. She thought her patients had the flu, but around noon four more patients arrived with drooping eyelids, as well as double vision and severe muscle pain. She called the poison control center at the University of New Mexico for advice after she learned that all eight were at the same event Tuesday night."

Sara was already searching on her computer for information on botulism before Carbonne said, "Public health official said this isn't usual barf-and-forget-it food poisoning. It's botulism. You know the Defense Department funded research on botulinum as a terrorist weapon for years."

"*But* botulinum toxin is easily destroyed by heat. It would take real planning to intentionally poison anyone with it." She studied a medical article on her computer. "There is an antitoxin… but it has limits. It only protects nerves from further damage."

"Know that," said Carbonne impatiently. "The poison control center at University Hospital has already sent botulism antitoxin to clinics in Santa Fe and Clovis."

"Why did the Department of Health call the FBI?"

"The event was a political rally for Estella Garcia Davis. She's a candidate for our U.S. Senate seat. A couple of hours ago, Estella Garcia Davis was admitted to a hospital in Santa Fe. Now about thirty others, including Estella's campaign manager Jules Smith, have come to clinics with the same symptoms. At least a hundred more are expected."

"Sounds bad, but it doesn't seem like a criminal case unless the caterer can be shown to be negligent."

"That's what I thought, but Barbara Lewis disagrees. Seems Estella's husband, Nelson, fired the original caterer and hired alternate caterers the day before the rally and then disappeared. The last anyone saw him was when he registered in a hotel in San Diego yesterday evening. When told Estella was seriously ill, Jules Smith said, 'Nelson finally did it.'"

"What do you want me to do?"

"Talk to Barbara. She needs your agreement before she signs off on this incident as an accident."

"Why?"

"No one in the Department of Health has worked on a case of botulism in the last twenty years. As a medical epidemiologist, you'll spot important details faster than she can."

"And?"

"Estella's neurological damage is much more severe than any of the others seen in clinics so far. She's partially paralyzed and in the intensive care unit at University Hospital. She may have been targeted. Only a psychopath risks the lives of two hundred to get at one person."

***

Bug, Sara's Japanese Chin, wagged his plumed tail as he sashayed into the FBI Building on Luecking Place on the northeast side of Albuquerque. Most of the guards recognized and greeted him because Bug and Sara had almost lived in the building last August through October as the FBI tightened the noose on a drug cartel. Besides being a versatile scientific consultant, Sara had been the target of several attacks by the cartel because she was the key witness in trials in which leaders of the cartel subsequently had been found guilty.

Bug sat politely as Sara knocked on the door of Carbonne's old office now occupied by Barbara Lewis. When Barbara opened the door, Sara gasped. The piles of boxes and the coat trees so covered with clothes that they looked like haystacks were gone. Now the office seemed much larger with pale turquoise walls, a bookcase organized with several Acoma style pots in key spots, a single file cabinet, and a black table with chairs.

"I always thought this office was tiny… and a dump. You've performed a miracle."

Barbara bit her lip. "Carbonne is a brilliant detective… and a kind and loving man. However, he was undercover too long." She closed the door. "He had become a slob. His untidiness almost drove me away and certainly annoyed other agents."

Sara thought she knew why Carbonne's voice had sounded spiritless on the phone. Dressing and behaving like a bum had been his way of giving the finger to fellow agents who he described as "cowboys." She guessed he must love Barbara and must want to rise in the ranks of the FBI to have changed. "I guess I'll have to stop by and see his new improved image later."

Barbara shook her head. "He always says you and his previous boss were the only ones who understood him." She pulled a dog treat from her pocket and offered it to Bug. "Carbonne's advice to me after I told him about this case was to do anything necessary to gain your cooperation. He thought a good way to start was to bribe Bug."

It was Sara's turn to bite her lip. "Well, it's true Bug makes most of the major decisions in our household but I don't see why you need my help."

Barbara smiled. "You must be a *little* curious. You agreed to come at six in the evening and not wait until tomorrow morning." Barbara motioned Sara to the black table.

As Sara sunk into a chair, she noticed Barbara alight on her chair with perfect posture while she swung her long black braid of hair to her back. The young woman had gained a lot of poise since the first time Sara had met her. Then Barbara had been a uniformed officer working the bomb squad in a small-town police department. Her turquoise silk shirt and black slacks were much more attractive than a blast suit. In the past, Barbara occasionally slipped into the high-pitched singsong voice of women from the New Mexico pueblos. Sara doubted Barbara would today.

"I figured if I learned the details tonight, I'd sleep better than if I kept anticipating problems as I tried to sleep."

"You will not be surprised by what I tell you. I was assigned this case because most of the male agents felt that the FBI should not investigate a case of food poisoning or worry about a woman who 'should not' be running for a U.S. Senate seat." Barbara opened a file on her computer. "Carbonne gave you the basics of the case. I think someone wanted to kill—or at least silence—Estella Garcia Davis and the public health problem is just collateral damage. However, I know nothing about microbiology and germs like…" She read the words slowly. "…*Clostridium botulinum.*"

"Let's start with the basics. What foods were served at the rally?"

Barbara scanned a computer file. "The menu appears to have been limited to oven-fried chicken, mashed potatoes, gravy made from a canned queso sauce, canned green beans, canned figs, and canned fruit cocktail."

Sara sniffed. "They certainly weren't trying to impress the candidate."

"That is what the campaign manager Jules Smith said, but I will get to him later. Public health officials tried to get samples of the food, but the garbage was picked up at the rally site, the VFW Post in Clovis, this morning before anyone had complained of symptoms. The organizers claimed they pitched all the leftovers immediately after the rally."

"Odd. Isn't it?"

Barbara shrugged. "Health officials doubted the organizers and checked the refrigerators and freezers at the VFW. They were empty. *Then* the organizers—LuAnn and Bo McCarran—admitted they had taken all the leftover to a senior center Tuesday night immediately after the rally. However, the manager of the senior center said only chicken, potatoes, and green beans were used at the site. No gravy. No fruit. All the delivered food was eaten by noon today by seniors."

"Oh great." Sara threw a pencil in the air and caught it. "The health officials have more people to monitor."

Barbara closed a file and opened another one on her computer. "Yes, but the McCarrans are the only ones who had memory lapses. Jules Smith seemed to have lots to say initially to the nurse at the clinic. She said he never stopped complaining about the 'lousy food' at the rally. However, when I tried to question him by phone he claimed he knew nothing about the food service at the rally, could not remember what he ate, and had no idea what Estella ate."

"Maybe he was cautious because you were from the FBI?"

"That is what Carbonne thought. He suggested you pose as a public health worker when you question Smith."

Sara leaned back. "I know you don't care what Jules ate. What do you really want me to pull out of him?"

Barbara brought her hand to her mouth. Sara guessed to hide a smile. "I got a call from a Santa Fe county commissioner late this afternoon—not long before I called you.

"Why?"

"He heard Estella Garcia Davis was hospitalized under 'suspicious circumstances.' Those are his words, not mine. He thought I should know Nelson Davis, Estella's husband, had tried to slug Bo McCarran in a parking lot after a Democratic party committee meeting last week, but Jules Smith had stopped him." She shook her head. "No police report was filed. I checked."

Sara found politics interesting but had decided many years ago that becoming aligned with any party or politician was unwise for a university faculty member in Michigan. She had continued to distance herself from politics after moving to New Mexico several years ago. However, she had served as a judge with no party affiliation for several elections in New Mexico. Thus, she knew Estella Garcia Davis was the mayor of Santa Fe several years back but knew little about her inclinations, other than she was considered a liberal. "Barbara, I don't know Estella's political history and doubt I can effectively question Jules."

Barbara tinkered with her phone. "I thought you might want to be briefed on Estella. I certainly do."

There was a knock on the door. The door swung open before Barbara answered. A transformed Carbonne stood there. His ragged, fairly long beard was now short and neatly trimmed. His long, black, kinky hair was gone. He'd shaved his head. Sara suspected it helped to hide his receding hairline. His slacks and shirt weren't baggy or torn. The sleeves of his shirt were neatly rolled to the elbow and his shirt was open at the neck. His trim, muscular physique was obvious. In general, he was a handsome—perhaps dangerous-looking—man in his thirties. Sara had never thought of him that way before.

He winked at Barbara. "I didn't forget. I was almost at your door when you texted me." He held out his hand to Sara. "Better close your mouth…" He snickered and squatted to pick up Bug. "…because I look a little different."

"I guess you're the same man because Bug recognizes you, but I miss your old comfortable image. I always liked how you faded into the background and worked a scene until you were ready to pounce." She studied Carbonne. "However, I see you're still flaunting FBI protocol a bit. Agents aren't allowed beards unless they're doing undercover work."

"Sara, you never change. That's why I want you to do your 'mean mama' role on both Jules Smith and Nelson Davis, if we ever find him. You can get past their facades. The only thing everyone agrees on is Estella has bad taste when selecting advisors. I'd guess that reflects Estella's lack of self-confidence. On the rez they would say Estella is a fry-bread girl who falls for any Chooch who notices her."

Barbara winced. "Do not be unkind."

Carbonne looked slightly chastised. "Here's what we have on Estella. Her grandfather was a wildcatter who struck it rich in the gas and oil fields of southeastern New Mexico after World War II. His son continued in his father's wild ways and married late in life a doyenne in the art world of Santa Fe."

"So, Estella is rich and pampered."

"Yeah, she was propelled into politics when her galleries in Santa Fe were threatened by a decline in Santa Fe's role in the art world. Thus, she became an ardent supporter of plans to draw the entertainment industry to New Mexico and anything that promoted tourism, but she expressed little interest in conservation or the rights of Native Americans. About six years ago—right after she was elected mayor of Santa Fe—her mother died and Nelson Davis, a nature photographer, breezed into New Mexico. Nelson and Estella quickly became an item even though she was ten years older than him. Suddenly, she began speaking out against fracking. The only problem was her money came from the oil and gas industry more than from art. She got a lot of bad press and announced she wouldn't run for reelection about three years ago."

Sara snorted. "You've given me a colorful rendition of Estella's bio, but it's all second hand. You moved to New Mexico two years ago."

Barbara giggled. "Thanks for cutting the chief down." Her lips straightened from a smile to a straight line. "He's made Estella seem incompetent and a bit sinister. On the Acoma pueblo, and I assume other pueblos in New Mexico, Estella has been considered a sympathetic politician for years. She certainly gave artists fair compensation for the pots and weavings sold in her galleries. She also lobbied for tax breaks for the development of wind and solar farms on pueblo lands. Granted she's made more decisive statements about Indian rights during the last three years. Moreover, she lost an infant son three years ago."

Carbonne looked down. "I'm used to talking to male agents and forgot myself. What I said still holds true. Estella started getting rid of her oil and gas holdings and investing in clean-energy projects, like wind farms, after she teamed up with Nelson Davis. She announced her candidacy for the U. S. Senate seat at the opening of a big wind project three months ago. People involved in the gas and oil industry and most police in southeast New Mexico think she's a puppet of her husband. Her campaign manager Jules Smith, who has worked for Estella on and off for the last eight years, has hinted to at least one county commissioner that he'd like to find a new job before her campaign blows up."

"I get the picture. You think Jules Smith knows or suspects dirt on Estella and Nelson and dislikes them enough to talk if coaxed. However, it will ruin his career if he gets caught telling tales about his boss. No politician wants to hire a tattletale because most have dirty secrets. That means motherliness will not be enough to coax Jules to talk. It will take a bribe or a threat. What can I offer him?"

Barbara looked at Carbonne, who nodded. "The nurse practitioner who examined Jules thought he was faking the symptoms of botulism poisoning. He claimed he saw two of objects even when one eye was closed. That doesn't happen in botulism poisoning."

Sara shrugged. "I've nothing scheduled this week. I'm game."

Carbonne peered at Sara. "What's Sanders up to these days?"

"He's on an expedition in the upper Amazon with several scientists studying the decline of amphibian populations."

Carbonne laughed. "We both know Sanders doesn't care about frogs or even conservation. He's there because he wanted an excuse to view something else in the upper Amazon."

Sara busied herself with petting Bug as she responded. "As the chargé d'affaires for the embassy in Brasília, he's had to broaden his interests."

"Yeah, right." Carbonne frowned. "I'm surprised you aren't down there monitoring the collection of specimens."

"I always thought frogs were disgusting." Sara decided to end the conversation. "As you two are learning, it's not easy to maintain a close personal relationship with a co-worker."

CHAPTER 3: FBI Agent Barbara Lewis and State Health Official Mopsy O'Hara on Thursday

Barbara knew Carbonne was right. She needed Sara's help because the state health official assigned to this case—Mopsy O'Hara—was as incompetent as her name suggested. What type of adult woman goes by Mopsy? The name suggested a naughty, cute little girl. Barbara had only talked to Mopsy on the phone, but she doubted Mopsy was little or cute. Mopsy often gasped for breath like a severely obese person when she spoke on the phone.

When she wasn't panting, Mopsy spoke in high-pitched, short sentences. Barbara was ashamed of being judgmental. Many of the older women on the pueblo spoke in a sing-song voice and used only short sentences, but none had as high a pitch as Mopsy. Barbara had worked hard to rid her voice of high tones and speak in the slow, deep cadences of the men of the pueblo after she'd decided in college that she wanted a career in law enforcement. No one took seriously a police officer who squeaked.

Although Mopsy's voice was irritating, her most annoying habit was her disorganization. She seldom finished a coherent sentence without long pauses as she slammed open and shut file drawers and took calls from her ten-year-old son.

Late yesterday afternoon, Barbara had finally told Mopsy to do her job and figure out the source of food contamination at the rally. Barbara had her own problem—finding Nelson Davis. No one had admitted seeing him since Tuesday afternoon when he checked into a hotel in San Diego. Hotel staff, at her request, had checked Nelson's hotel room this morning and found his luggage and clothes were gone.

Barbara had stopped by the intensive care unit in University Hospital at eight this morning. She hoped Estella might provide clues to her husband's whereabouts but found Estella was now on a ventilator. She was another dead end for locating Nelson.

***

Mopsy O'Hara left home at four-thirty in the morning because she wanted to talk to the McCarrans at their home in Clovis. She felt she had a better idea whether she was getting an honest answer if she looked people in the eye as she questioned them in their homes. Besides, Barbara Lewis had made it clear the FBI thought she—Mopsy—was responsible for determining the source of the botulinum contaminated food at the rally.

Mopsy almost laughed as she thought of Barbara's dedication to her work and strict discipline. Barbara reminded her of herself before a rocky marriage and her son's illness.

Mopsy hadn't left for Clovis on Wednesday afternoon because she didn't want to leave her son at home alone overnight. He was a responsible boy, but his health was fragile—as would be expected for a boy undergoing chemotherapy. Hence, she arranged for a college student who lived next door to stay with her son from four-thirty this morning until he left for school at seven-thirty. One good thing about living in a small decrepit adobe home near the University of New Mexico campus was it was easy to get babysitters at reasonable prices. Although she had a theoretically good job, money was always limited since her husband decided he couldn't cope with a sick son and divorced her.

Her plan to talk to the McCarrans in their home failed. Neither of the McCarrans was at home when she arrived in Clovis at seven-thirty. She found LuAnn at the couple's equipment rental shop and learned Bo had left for Lubbock at seven-fifteen to pick up six outdoor heaters.

"Bo always turns off his phone when he drives but he'll call me when he gets there." LuAnn fluttered her heavily mascaraed eyelashes. "Are you fixin' to figure out what happened at the rally Tuesday night? Mebbe I can help until we get customers. Here's a stool."

Mopsy struggled to take a deep breath before she pulled herself on the stool and leaned over the counter. "Let's… start simply. What did you eat Tuesday night… at the rally?"

LuAnn stared blankly at Mopsy.

After she stopped coughing, Mopsy said, "How did you avoid getting sick?"

LuAnn's eyes widened. "That's simple. When Bo told me who was doin' the cookin,' I knew the food would be bad. I made cheese sandwiches for Bo and me before the event."

Mopsy felt hopeful for the first time this morning. LuAnn looked like a painted doll without a coherent thought but maybe the makeup was a mask. "Do you know… who prepared the food for the rally?" She held

J. L. Greger

her breath because yesterday a Curry County health official had been unable to get an answer to that question from anyone.

"Shor' can. Let's see…" It took LuAnn five minutes, but she identified four women in a local Baptist church who had prepared the chicken, potatoes, beans, and gravy. During the process, Mopsy learned the potatoes were prepared from a dried mix and the gravy was canned queso sauce diluted with water.

LuAnn concluded her comments by saying, "I know Bo thinks I'm bein' silly, but it don't make sense that people got botulism 'cause nothin' was home canned, except the figs. I saw the cooks pour the beans and the queso sauce—they called it gravy—from big cans they got from a wholesale food store in Lubbock. I looked. The cans weren't dented."

"Mmm." Mopsy thought LuAnn didn't need more of an incentive to keep talking.

"I finished two years of college in home economics before I married Bo. I had a foods class where the professor talked a lot about food safety. That's why, I made the churchwomen heat the beans and gravy in big pots at the VFW for almost an hour. Bo thought it wasn't enough, but it should have been."

Mopsy tried to clear the phlegm in her throat by swallowing hard. "I agree with you. It doesn't make sense." She paused. "Why did you take the food to the senior center if you thought it was bad?"

"They always need food there and the cook there can do wonders with anything. I called her at the senior center as soon as I saw the churchwomen haulin' the food into the VFW. I told her there would be lots of leftovers, but the chicken would be inedible as cold fried chicken. She asked if I could bring the food to her after the rally was over. She figured she'd pull the skin off right away and make a casserole with the cooked meat, the potatoes, and cheese sauce on Wednesday morning." LuAnn frowned. "But after she tasted the cheese sauce Tuesday night, she pitched it because she thought it would taste funny no matter what she did."

"What about the fruit cocktail?"

LuAnn thought for a second. "The churchwomen took the fruit cocktail home. I figured it didn't matter because the cook at the senior center served canned fruit cocktail on Monday. The seniors wouldn't like it twice in one week."

Mopsy couldn't believe how easy this was. LuAnn had explained why no leftovers had been found at the VFW. She stifled a giggle as she thought of the elaborate plan devised by Barbara to collect the McCarran's garbage this morning before the garbage truck arrived. Obviously, it would yield no evidence. None of the food from the rally had been discarded by the McCarrans.

Mopsy also wondered why local county health officers had claimed the McCarrans were uncooperative. If LuAnn had been part of a plot to poison people, she was the most talented storyteller Mopsy had ever met. She emailed her sentiments to Barbara while LuAnn waited on a couple renting a tent, tables, and chairs for their daughter's wedding.

After they left, LuAnn chirped. "Sure hope that reception ends early. It can get chilly after sundown, but they didn't want to pay for any heaters. We'll have plenty of 'em when Bo gets back." She shrugged. "Bo should be callin' soon."

Mopsy hoped Bo wouldn't call during the next ten minutes. She wanted to ask a few more questions of the talkative Luann before her husband perhaps cautioned her to talk less. "One more thing bothers me. What happened to the home-canned figs with nuts?"

"They were served with a whipped topping mix. Don't think any was left." I know Estella ate a big bowl and asked for more."

"Who brought the canned figs?"

LuAnn stopped smiling. "Don't know. Well, I saw her, and her fake red hair—but I didn't know her. She seemed to think she had made one of Estella's favorite dishes. Kept goin' on about her great figs." LuAnn sniffed. "All that proved was neither she nor Estella has good taste. Bo and I hate the feel of canned figs in our mouths. Gummy and gritty."

The phone rang. LuAnn said, "Bo, I've had the nicest chat with a lady from the state health department. She agreed with me I was right to make the women cook the beans and gravy for an hour." She listened for a minute. "Oh. Bye."

She didn't look at Mopsy as she said, "I guess Bo won't get back for a couple of hours. You'll have to talk to him tomorrow."

***

Barbara sighed when she read Mopsy's emails and decided she had underestimated Mopsy. Barbara had been less successful at turning up clues than Mopsy.

No one using Nelson Davis's name had boarded a plane or rented a car in San Diego. Police had circulated a picture of Nelson among personnel at the airport, car rental agencies, taxi stands, bus stations, and even trolley stations in San Diego this morning. No one admitted seeing Nelson. Barbara had obtained a list of all cars rented in San Diego on Tuesday and Wednesday, which had already been turned in at rental

J. L. Greger

agencies in New Mexico and west Texas. FBI staff in Albuquerque had reached twenty of the twenty-seven drivers who rented these cars. Three of the renters had given suspicious answers or seemed extremely nervous about answering routine questions. They might merit a follow-up visit from an agent if Nelson wasn't found soon.

She cursed silently when she remembered that San Diego was only about twenty miles from the Mexican border. She called the U.S. Customs Office in San Diego. They had not scanned a passport or driver's license for Nelson Davis during the last week.

CHAPTER 4: Sara Meets Dubious Characters

"Mr. Smith—may I call you Jules? I'm trying to determine the source of the food poisoning at the rally in Clovis." Sara noticed beads of sweat on Jules's forehead as he swiped his longish blond hair back from his face. Sara thought the temperature in the room was warm but not uncomfortably hot. Perhaps this man had a guilty conscience. "I'm recording all my interviews because I'm a lousy notetaker, but the Department of Health was desperate for help." After she tinkered with a small device on her lapel, she flashed a broad smile. "Don't be nervous. Tell me what you ate at the rally."

"I'm not nervous."

"Oh, you have sweat on your forehead. Well, it's all right to be scared, but don't worry I'm only interested in about the food at the rally."

Jules almost perfect pale complexion reddened slightly. "Why are you wasting your and my time? Everyone knows that botulism is caused by improperly canned nonacidic foods. It has to be the beans or the cheese sauce."

Sara was glad she'd seen Mopsy's notes on her interview of LuAnn McCarran. "It's probably not the beans. No one at the senior center who ate the leftover beans has become ill."

"That's because they cooked the beans more at the senior center."

"How do you know that?"

He looked at his hands as he twisted a ring on his right hand. "Makes sense."

Sara patted his hand. "Yes, it does, but the cook at the senior center made a salad with the beans by adding onions and vinegar and serving them cold."

"Acid kills botulinum toxin."

"My, you know a lot about botulism." Sara leaned back and stared at him. "Why don't we get back to my question. What did you eat at the rally?"

"I don't remember." Jules's voice was sharper than before.

"Now, now, Jules. Let's not be testy. Did you taste the chicken? The beans? The gravy?"

"I don't know."

Sara straightened in her chair and her voice lost its matronly tones. "You told the nurse practitioner at the clinic that the food tasted terrible. So, you must have tasted something."

Jules stared at her.

Sara thought she could remove his defiant stare. "The nurse practitioner in the clinic thought you were pretending to be sick. You pretended unsuccessfully to have double vision. Why?"

Jules stood. "This is entrapment."

"Sit down or I'll call the FBI. They're involved now in this case. It will be easier for you if you admit to me what you know."

Jules opened the door and saw a uniformed police officer. He closed the door and sat down.

"I know nothing."

"What do you suspect?"

Jules flushed and sat silently for several seconds apparently thinking. "I... I heard Bo and Nelson arguing about the menu for the rally... about a week before the event. It didn't make sense. It was so unimportant. Bo claimed the caterer wouldn't serve homemade food that she didn't prepare. Something about state food safety regs. Nelson snorted and repeated his demands. Bo reiterated his comments several times. Finally, Nelson looked like he was about to punch Bo. I stopped him but couldn't get him to cool down. Typical Nelson."

"What happened next?"

"Nothing, except on the day before the rally, Bo told me the caterer quit after Nelson cursed her out. Bo was panicked because at the last minute he'd have trouble getting enough food for the rally, but then Nelson called and gave him the names of women who would bring the food."

"Did either man give you the caterers' names?"

"No. Nelson only said, 'Don't tell Estella.' But then he assured me everything would be fine. He even noted one woman would bring canned figs with nuts made according to Estella's favorite recipe."

"That's a nice story but why did you fake symptoms of botulism?"

"Bo called at noon the day after the rally and said several people from the rally were sick and complaining of double vision. I... I realized then I didn't feel right." He blinked. "Anyway, the best way to put a positive spin on a disaster is to get the facts… and be sympathetic. You know that's my job as a campaign manager."

Sara's half-smile turned into a frown as she peered at Jules. "But how did you guess the food poisoning was due to botulism? Did you major in microbiology or food science in college? Or work in the food industry?"

"No. I've taken courses on history and political science ever since I worked on Estella's first campaign for mayor almost eight years ago."

"How do you know so much about botulism, then? Do you do home canning? Or did you watch your mother or grandmother can?"

Jules suddenly straightened from his slouch. "It's common knowledge."

Sara remembered Barbara had suggested she'd be less threatening if she didn't reveal her actual employer was the FBI. "Jules—lets concentrate on the business at hand. What did you eat, or at least taste, at the rally?' You must have tasted something."

Jules twisted the ring on his hand. "You didn't see the food. It was easy to skip it."

"Mmm. I understand, but I would think you'd taste a bit of the food so you could file a grievance against the McCarrans or the caterers." She noticed he was staring at his red finger as he continued to twist the ring on his right hand. "That is, unless you thought the food was unsafe?"

He stopped twisting the ring.

Sara surmised that she was getting close to the truth. "What would make you think the food might be unsafe?"

"A feeling."

"How did you get that feeling?"

Jules had returned to fiddling with his ring.

Sara decided Jules was hiding something and it was time to bluff. "What did Bo—or Nelson—say or do?" She noted he stopped fidgeting when she said Bo and coughed when she said Nelson. "You know FBI agents will question you about Estella's campaign. If you tell me everything now and I alert them, you'll be seen as a cooperating witness, not a suspect."

He noisily exhaled. "Nothing specific. Nelson kept saying that we needed to make Estella appear more sympathetic to voters." Jules shook his head. "That isn't easy. When she was mayor of Santa Fe, we could present her as an artsy woman with a long proud history in New Mexico. That sold in Santa Fe. But when Estella is nervous, her voice becomes shrill… cold… like her mother's."

"What did you and Nelson do to help Estella?"

"I hired a voice coach… and then a life coach… but they weren't much help. A couple of weeks ago, Nelson thought a health scare would win voters' sympathy and then admiration if we could show Estella's steeliness enabled her to overcome a health problem." Jules licked his lips. "He must have thought about it a lot. He said it couldn't be a chronic disease, like cancer or heart disease, because voters wanted a healthy, vigorous senator. He thought a broken leg would be the ticket."

The story was so bizarre that Sara gasped. "What did you say?"

"Nothing, I decided I wanted to get away from Estella and Nelson." He smiled sheepishly. "I applied for a position on the governor's re-election campaign staff. I'm being interviewed."

"When?"

"Soon."

"How soon?"

"Tomorrow."

***

An hour later, Sara sat in a small conference room in the FBI building with Barbara listening to Mopsy on the speakerphone. Mopsy spoke rapidly but stopped frequently to cough, noisily swallow, or to check her notes. To break her boredom with Mopsy's report, Sara doodled along the edges of the page in front of her and only occasionally wrote a word or two.

Mopsy, with the help of Curry County health officials, had tracked down the four churchwomen. They still had the fruit cocktail because they planned to serve it at a church supper that evening. Test strips designed to detect botulinum toxin rapidly in food indicated no toxin was present in the fruit. That was no surprise. *Clostridium* bacteria didn't grow in acidic environments like that of canned fruit.

The women also had unopened cans of green beans, cheese sauce, and fruit cocktail, which were purchased at the same time as the food served at the rally. Mopsy had confiscated the cans because she wanted the state lab to examine the contents microscopically for spores of *Clostridium botulinum*. "But I don't think… the canned beans… or the canned queso sauce… caused the botulinum poisoning of attendees at the rally even if the lab finds botulinum spores in the canned products. LuAnn is right. They were cooked long enough… to denature any botulinum toxin. And no one at the senior center got sick."

"And you said there was nothing else to send to the lab because no traces of food were found in the McCarrans' garbage." Barbara waited for Mopsy to reply. When she didn't, Barbara added, "Right?"

"Yes. I also reviewed the food recalls. Everyone who's sick... admitted eating figs. Well, except for Jules. The figs must be our... culprit, but... *Clostridium* rarely grow in even improperly canned fruit. Too acidic."

Sara stopped doodling on and began to write. "Since LuAnn didn't know the woman who brought the home-canned figs with nuts to the rally, did you ask her to describe the woman?"

"No."

"What did Bo say?"

"He... all but refused to talk to me and said preparing food was women's work. He paid no notice to the food... or the cooks."

"Did you believe him? Let me rephrase that question. Do you think he was hiding something?'

"I don't know. He just kept saying Jules found the cooks."

"Wait." Sara suddenly felt alert. "Jules claimed Nelson arranged for the four churchwomen to make the meal for the rally."

Sara could hear Mopsy cursing in the background.

"Mopsy, what exactly did Bo say?" Barbara voice was sharper than her usual smooth low tones. "I thought I told you to record your interviews."

"I'm looking." A slight snorting noise came from the phone. "I recorded LuAnn's comments—the whole, long conversation." More snorts. "But Bo didn't want to be recorded. I had to take notes. He wouldn't sit down. I had to follow him... around his equipment rental store, while I took notes. They're sketchy."

Sara now understood why Barbara had doubted Mopsy's competence. It was unfortunate that Mopsy had not documented key evidence—the apparent contradiction in Jules's and Bo's comments. However, she suspected Bo would be difficult to interview even by police who could force him to sit during an interview.

"Mopsy, relax." Sara tried to sound motherly. "When I'm frantic, I never find anything. Let's change the topic slightly. Did Bo mention Nelson or refer to an argument with anyone?"

"Yes. He said didn't know who was worse... the husband or the manager. He said... I want to get this right." There was a long pause. "Estella would make a poor senator... if her selection of campaign staff reflected her management skills. He called them a 'pair of pretty boys waiting on an aging princess.'"

Barbara seemed to ignore Mopsy and Sara as she concentrated on her phone. When her call ended, she announced, "A Sandoval County Sheriff's deputy found a comatose woman in her home in Corrales after a neighbor alerted police that the woman hadn't answered her phone or left the house during the last day. The deputy called the FBI because he had seen our alerts and saw a jar of home-canned figs and a flier about Estella's rally in Clovis on the woman's kitchen counter."

"Wait. I found the note I wrote… as Bo drove away. It says, 'He knows something important.'" Mopsy whimpered. "Does that help?"

CHAPTER 5: Barbara and Sara Sort Clues

Barbara gritted her teeth as she finished her phone conversation with Mopsy. She might as well admit it. She couldn't depend on Mopsy. Barbara turned to Sara. "I need a crash course in microbiology. Please explain the difference between live *Clostridium* bacteria and their endospores." She noticed Sara's lips quivered in amusement.

"You really don't trust Mopsy's advice, do you? Now remember I'm not a microbiologist either, but I think I can help you formulate questions better. The bacterium *Clostridium botulinum* is an anaerobe. That means oxygen is toxic to it. It is also a spore-forming bacteria. The endospores aren't damaged by oxygen or even boiling water but can be destroyed by cooking in a pressure cooker because the temperature inside a pressure cooker is higher than 212 degrees Fahrenheit. When botulinum spores are in a friendly environment—like the anaerobic conditions inside a can of nonacidic food—they germinate into reproductive, growing cells that produce a toxin. The toxin can be deactivated by boiling the food for a couple of minutes. In an unfriendly acidic environment, like canned tomatoes and other fruits, the spores don't germinate."

"Does that mean that home-canned fruits, like figs, are acidic enough that they can be canned safely in a hot water bath?"

"That's an interesting question. Figs are less acidic than most fruits when ripe. Most recipes suggest adding lemon juice to figs as a safety precaution when canning them to lower their pH."

Barbara felt annoyed. "Please stop the double talk."

Sara looked puzzled for a second and then laughed. "I think I understand your problem. pH is a confusing term because it's the inverse of the amount of acidity. Acidic foods have a low pH—that is a pH below seven. Nonacidic foods have a pH above seven."

"Is there any other lab jargon that I need to know?"

Sara frowned and responded with a non sequitur—something Carbonne had warned Barbara that Sara would do frequently. "I think Mopsy gave you a good lead. Bo's and Jules's comments are inconsistent."

"I know that. I need real help from you now." Barbara banged open a desk drawer and pulled out a sleeve of crackers. "The four cooks need to be interviewed on who hired them, but you do not want to drive to Clovis." She chewed a cracker. "I guess even though the Clovis police do not know the details of the case, they could do it immediately. You struck out with Jules and do not want to drive to Clovis to interview Bo." She chewed another cracker. "I've exhausted the obvious leads for locating Nelson. He's either dead, kidnapped, or in hiding." She smiled. "You can talk to the woman who the sheriff just found. Her name is Beryl Marks, and she is being transported from her home to University Hospital. See if she contributed the figs for the rally and…."

"If she did, I'll question her about her procedures and arrange if necessary for the FBI lab crew to collect jars of figs from her home."

Barbara typed rapidly on her phone. "The lab will be ready for your direction."

As Sara opened the door to leave, she turned. "There is one more confusing scientific detail that the lab might mention. There are—I think—seven strains of *Clostridium botulinum*."

"What can I do with that information?"

"Maybe nothing, but it might be helpful in tracing the source of the poisoning if we ever get useful samples. And another thing—Jules Smith knew more about botulism than I would expect for a nonscientist with no experience in home canning. I should have questioned him more, but I didn't want to admit I was with the FBI and not the health department."

"I'll check his background before I bring him here for an interview."

***

Sara thought about Barbara's grumpiness as she drove to the University Hospital. Barbara had always been a stickler for details and spoken carefully using little jargon but today and yesterday she was easily annoyed and stiff. The responsibilities of being an agent were wearing on her. Perhaps her relationship with Carbonne added to the tension. Carbonne had wisely arranged for Barbara to not report to him directly, but ultimately he was her boss as chief of the field office.

Then again, this case was complicated, and perhaps not worth the effort. No one had died, and Estella wasn't apt to be a successful candidate for the senate seat even if she recovered. Barbara wouldn't gain much praise from her associates if she solved this case.

***

Sara knew one reason FBI agents hated interviewing patients in hospitals as she tried to locate Beryl Marks—the woman with the canned figs in her kitchen. After waiting in the emergency room for fifteen minutes, Sara learned Beryl had been transferred to the ICU. In the ICU, Sara discovered that Beryl had been placed on a ventilator. If Sara had skipped the emergency room and gone directly to the ICU, she might have arrived before Beryl was put into a medically induced coma and intubated.

Sara knew nothing was gained by pouting about the lost opportunity to question Beryl. After talking to a nurse tending Beryl, she texted the sheriff's deputy who had accompanied the ambulance to the hospital. He was already en route to Beryl's home to fetch a jar of the home-canned figs for analysis by the hospital lab for *Clostridium botulinum*. Sara convinced him it would be better if he met an FBI technician at Beryl's home and let the technician retrieve the evidence. Sara called the FBI lab and instructed a technician to retrieve and test jars of canned figs—both in and out of the refrigerator. She instructed him to check the jars for DNA and fingerprints on the outside and to test the contents for botulinum toxin and spores.

Before she left the ICU, Sara held Beryl's hand and listened to the throbbing ventilator. Beryl must have been attractive. Her hair was a pretty copper shade. Her arms and legs suggested she exercised regularly. Her next of kin, a daughter who worked in Santa Fe, had been notified but hadn't arrived yet. Sara felt tears in her eyes as she thought about the grim reality the daughter would face. The physicians had administered the antitoxin for botulism. However, Beryl's vital signs were poor and not improving. The antitoxin could not remedy harm already done, only prevent further damage by the botulinum toxin.

As Sara was leaving the ICU, a young woman ran in screaming. "Where's my mother? Where's Beryl Marks?" Sara knew she shouldn't pounce on her immediately with questions but decided the young woman might be able to answer key questions.

Ten minutes later, Sara showed her FBI badge—actually only an ID card—to the sobbing young woman. "I'm sorry to bother you at this time but I think you might be able to help your mother and another woman fighting for her life."

"What do you mean? The nurse thought Mom probably had botulism. Why is the FBI here?"

"Let's sit in the lounge down the hall and talk. I only have a couple of questions."

"No, I don't want to leave Mom's side."

Sara motioned to a male nurse at the desk, who glided into the cubicle. "Ma'am, you'd help us, too, if you'd answer a few questions for the FBI. We'll take good care of your mother until you return."

The woman kissed her mother's hand and followed Sara out of the ICU to a nearby lounge. Sara thought it felt good to be out of the tension-filled ICU. The only others in the lounge were a couple holding hands and crying.

"Thank you for talking to me." Sara motioned the daughter onto a chair and pulled another one around to face it before she turned on her recorder and sat. "My name's Sara. What's yours?"

"Davita Lopez."

"Davita, does your mother know Estella Garcia Davis, the former mayor of Santa Fe?"

Davita started to stand. "I thought this was going to help Mom."

Sara pulled her down. "It might. Estella has symptoms like your mom's. Did your mom ever mention Estella?"

"Yeah. Mom was all gaga over meeting her at the spa."

"Did your mom ever mention going to rallies or supporting Estella's bid for the senate?"

Davita wrung her hands. "I'd like to get back to the ICU."

Sara doubted anything would change even if Davita was absent from the ICU for hours but knew better than to voice a negative opinion. "Just a few more questions. Did your mom support Estella's bid for the senate?"

"She was wild about knowing a potential senator. Mom held a fundraiser at her home last fall—when Estella was beginning to think about a senate run." Davita stared in the distance. "Oh, and she brought her terrible fig preserves to a rally last week."

"How do you know that?"

"She told me." Davita sighed. "I was glad because it meant she got rid of the crap."

Sara tried to not act excited. "Why don't you like your mom's canned figs?"

"We've always had figs trees. Figs don't usually grow here but they seemed to like our courtyard. Mom thought they were special and always canned the fruit." Davita grimaced. "The preserves were okay on toast occasionally. Then she got a recipe from Estella's husband after he noticed all the fig trees in her courtyard at the original fundraiser. It was bad—no lemony tartness. The chopped nuts and honey added to the figs in this recipe made them grittier and gooier."

"Do you think you could find the recipe?"

"Why?"

"An FBI technician and a Sandoval County Sheriff's deputy are collecting jars of your mom's canned figs for analysis. We…"

"When?"

"Probably now as we speak. The sheriff's deputy saw a jar of the figs on the kitchen counter when he found your mother. He's seen the FBI and Department of Health alerts on potential botulism poisoning of everyone at Estella's rally in Clovis. Public health workers have narrowed the potential sources of the botulinum toxin to a few foods. Home-canned figs are one of the items."

Davita turned pale. "Can Mom be sued?"

Sara hadn't expected that question. "I doubt it, especially if she followed a recipe."

Davita sighed. "Mom was stickler for following recipes exactly, especially when she was canning." Davita leaned forward. "Let me think… where it would be" She stared into space again. "Mom wouldn't have pitched the recipe because Estella had called it her favorite recipe. She was in awe of Estella." She turned to Sara. "Have you met Estella?"

Sara shook her head no.

"You haven't missed anything. She's a real queen but so dumb she doesn't even realize her husband flirts with every woman."

"Including your mother? And you?"

"Mom says he's being friendly. He must not have patted Mom's butt."

Sara decided not to follow-up on Davita's comments about Nelson because the FBI technician was probably already at Beryl's home. "Let's get back to the recipe. Where would your mom put it?"

Davita closed her eyes. "Mom tucks her favorite recipes into her *Betty Crocker Cookbook*. It's on the lowest shelf of the cabinet over the desk in her kitchen. I'm sure I could find it, but if the FBI technician is at the house he might as well collect it."

Sara was glad she'd recorded the conversation. "Thanks for your help. If you don't mind I'm going to text the technician and sheriff's deputy now. I'll look in on you and your mom after I update them and the FBI agent in charge of this case." Sara hugged the young woman.

***

The FBI technician had found an open jar of canned figs in Beryl's refrigerator, an unopened jar on the kitchen counter, and several more with different labels in the cabinet. He had completed swabbing surfaces for DNA and fingerprints when Sara called.

J. L. Greger

As Sara reported Davita's instructions, he quickly found the apparently well-loved cookbook. The front cover was barely attached to the rest of the book. He thumbed through the book looking for loose pages, noting that many pages were stuck together because batters or other cooking sauces had been dripped on them. Finally, he found a typed page labeled "Canned Figs and Nuts" and read the ingredients aloud. "Ripe—or even overripe—figs, honey, ground almonds. That's it."

Sara thought Davita was right. The resulting product would be overly sweet and gritty. "Anything unusual in the instructions?"

The technician replied, "I've never canned. Everything looks unusual to me. The instructions say to rinse the jars with a solution containing baking soda so that they're squeaky clean. The jars are processed in boiling water, not a pressure cooker."

Sara thought it was strange to rinse the jars with baking soda not vinegar. "You'll want to measure the pH of all the canned figs when you check them for botulinum spores and toxin. Rinsing the jars with a solution of baking soda would tend to raise the pH. I think the almonds would, too. It's a strange recipe. Is anything else written on the page?"

"Yes, someone has handwritten 'Estella Garcia Davis's favorite recipe.' It's dated November thirteenth of last year."

"I think you found the recipe. Did you wear gloves so the sheet can be dusted for fingerprints and DNA?"

The technician snorted. "Of course, but there's sticky debris on the page. I bet the lab will find only the cook's DNA."

The sheriff's deputy interrupted, "I'm needed elsewhere. The technician has collected everything in sight—even a toothbrush from the bathroom. He claimed it would be a source of Beryl's DNA."

"Thank you both. I'll talk to the daughter now." Sara emailed a long note to Barbara before she sauntered into the ICU. She figured the only changes possible in Beryl's condition would be bad, but sometimes modern medicine was amazing.

CHAPTER 6: Barbara Stalks Prey on Friday

Barbara convinced a judge to grant her a search warrant for Estella Garcia Davis's home in Santa Fe. She hoped she might find clues to Nelson Davis's whereabouts. Mopsy also wanted all foods in Estella's refrigerator checked for botulinum spores and toxin. In the process, Barbara was surprised to learn Estella had not amended the deed to her house to include Nelson when she married him. She wondered whether that indicated Estella had doubts about her marriage or was a smart businesswoman.

Barbara was pleased the judge had been slow to act because it meant she didn't have time to drive to Santa Fe and prepare for her interview of Jules. Lately she had become nauseated during long drives. Thus, she ordered Sara and a young lab technician to drive to Santa Fe to work with the resident agent there.

***

Jules Smith didn't have a criminal record, but the records of the New Mexico Motor Vehicle Division indicated he was sloppy when parking his car. He had five unpaid tickets in Santa Fe for this month alone. All were for parking in handicapped spots on one small side street in the Canyon Road shopping district of Santa Fe.

Jules's college records were spotty. He'd majored in restaurant, hotel, and institutional management for two years at Texas Tech in Lubbock. Barbara didn't know what that major entailed but noted he'd taken a course called "Food Sanitation." She suspected botulism would have been discussed but surmised he didn't get much out of the course. He'd earned a "D." During the following eight years, he took one or two courses at the University of New Mexico each semester. Most were related to history or political science. Thus, the claim on his resume that he was a few courses short of a degree in history was logical.

The most interesting facts she'd found about Jules involved his family. His father was a successful lawyer for a gas company based in Amarillo and his sister was a practicing dermatologist in nearby Lubbock.

She suspected his family regarded Jules as bit of a black sheep because he had not succeeded in a profession. That was probably the best way to goad him in the interview.

She looked at the monitor in the interview room. The short, blond man passing through the screening process at the entrance of the FBI Building in Albuquerque didn't appear skittish. She was disappointed. Many people tensed as they walked through the monitors and were frisked. Nervous people were usually more talkative. She purposely did not stand when he was escorted into interview room because she hoped to foster his nervousness. "Mr. Smith, I think the botulism poisoning of Estella Garcia Davis was an intentional attempt to kill her..." She paused to make her statement more dramatic. "... or injure her enough to gain publicity for her campaign."

Jules reddened and awkwardly fell into a chair.

She'd succeeded in surprising him. "I have just learned at least one other person at the rally may not survive."

Jules gasped.

"Accordingly, I expect your full cooperation. This is apt to be a murder investigation soon. When did Estella start planning to run for a senate seat?"

Jules twisted a ring on his right hand. Barbara was pleased because Sara had told her Jules seemed to do that behavior when he was nervous.

"We held our first fundraiser last November."

"Where? Can you be more specific on the date?"

Jules pulled his phone from his jacket pocket. "I'll have to check my calendar."

As he fingered the phone for over a minute, Barbara doubted he kept careful records on the campaign.

"November eleventh. Nelson thought it was patriotic to have a fundraiser on Veterans Day." He paused. "Estella was nervous as usual and wanted it held in a friendly location." He shook his head. "We held it at an old, adobe house in Corrales with an enclosed courtyard and a big orchard in the back."

She noted he had answered her question in a friendly manner but had not provided useful details. This man was experienced at answering political questions. "Who was the host? Who attended the event?"

"The hostess invited the members of a yoga class that she and Estella attended and members of arts groups in Santa Fe and Corrales."

"What about Democratic party regulars? Or previous supporters?"

Jules returned his phone to his pocket. "You'll have to get a search warrant for records in our campaign headquarters to get the list of invitees and attendees. Donors often don't want to be identified."

Barbara emailed a message to staff to prepare the warrant. "That will not be a problem. We already have a warrant for Estella's home and will have one for your phone and her campaign headquarters in less than an hour. Now what was the name of the hostess of the event?"

He was silent.

"We know the hostess was Beryl Marks."

She debated whether to add that Beryl was near death in University Hospital but decided that would limit future bluffs. She found the hardest part of her job with the FBI was bluffing because it was counter to her Native American heritage. Bluffing was really lying. She swallowed hard. "We can get the answers from Beryl, but it would be to your advantage to cooperate. Did Beryl share any activities, besides yoga, with Estella or Nelson?"

Jules began tugging at the ring on his right hand again. "I avoid knowing much about Estella's private life."

"That is strange. I thought that you were a professional campaign manager. That usually means you know all of your candidate's activities and problems."

He stared blankly at her.

She decided it was time to hit his weak spot. "But I forgot, you never finished a degree and are not a professional person like your father and sister."

He didn't take the bait. "C'mon. This is. just a matter of sloppy food preparation. You don't want to admit the churchwomen goofed up. I don't want to accuse them either. Too many votes nowadays are along religious lines."

"Did you forget your interview yesterday was recorded?

"Why does that matter?"

"You pretended to have botulism to a healthcare provider and basically admitted yesterday to the interviewer that you lied."

"That's not how I remember it. I was scared and did see double images even with one eye closed."

"Second, you indicated yesterday that you strongly suspected the food was not safe, but you allowed others to eat it. If anyone dies, you could be considered responsible." Barbara thought the last point was unlikely, but she was desperate to get Jules's cooperation.

He looked down at his hands.

Barbara reread the email that Sara had sent from Beryl's home yesterday afternoon. It was long but she took time to read it because she hoped it would increase Jules's nervousness. It did. He twisted the ring on his right hand again.

"I have to instruct an agent about to enter Estella's home. Is there anything you want to tell me before they enter the house?"

"No."

"Fine. You might as well give me your phone. We will have a subpoena for it soon."

He didn't reach into his jacket pocket.

"If you do not give it me now, I will have someone sit in here with you to prevent you from destroying evidence."

He handed her the phone.

She was pleased because it should have his fingerprints and DNA, but to be sure she'd send a can of soda in. "Do you want diet or regular soda?"

"Diet seltzer, please."

***

Barbara outlined the limits of the search warrant to Sara on the phone and diplomatically described Hank Snow, the in-residence FBI agent in Santa Fe. She didn't mention that she had more confidence in Sara's ability to notice potentially useful data than the resident agent's skill. Hank had reiterated on the phone several times that he had more important things to do than "track the work of sloppy cooks." Instead she said, "Hank has been to the address several times. He says you are in for a workout. This old adobe is huge with five bedrooms, four bathrooms, and a kitchen designed for caterers."

Sara whistled. "How does he know so much about the house?"

"It seems Estella invited the Santa Fe police chief, lieutenants, and sergeants along with the resident FBI agents in Santa Fe to a picnic at her home at least once a year while she was the mayor. He also noted Estella called the police several times during the last two years when Nelson threatened her, but the local police 'lost' the records of her calls as a favor to her."

"Wow, are you sure one technician can collect all the necessary samples?"

"No, but the lab chief was short-handed today. Hank asked the housekeeper to not enter the house after I notified him of Estella's poisoning on Wednesday, and he should have done a preliminary check of the house yesterday."

Before Barbara could end the call, Sara said, "Don't forget Jules claimed he had a job interview today with another campaign. It's odd that he's ready to switch his allegiance so quickly."

***

Barbara was smiling when she reentered the interview room, "Jules, when is your job interview today?"

Jules stared at her. "In two hours. I need to leave here soon."

"I only have a couple more questions for now. What do you think of Nelson Davis?"

"He's a good nature photographer and an effective lobbyist for conservation causes."

"You do not seem to like him. Why?"

"He's abusive of Estella."

"Have you witnessed him abuse Estella?"

"He's not a fool, but she seems to fall a lot and walk into doors frequently."

Barbara observed he was again twisting the ring on his finger and giving minimal answers. "You seem to twist the ring on your right hand frequently. You should avoid doing it during your job interview. It makes me—and I expect others—think you are not telling the whole truth."

He twisted the ring again.

"Yesterday you said in an interview that Nelson had mentioned a rather odd way to make voters more sympathetic to Estella. What did you think and do when you heard him?"

"That public health interviewer has a big mouth."

"Remember she taped the interview. Do not dodge the question. What did you think and do?"

"That's why I'm interviewing for a job today."

CHAPTER 7: Sara Explores Santa Fe

Sara's phone rang. "This is Hank Snow. Darn women don't want me to take the campaign records from Mrs. Davis's campaign headquarters. Don't enter her house without me."

Sara tried to be diplomatic because Barbara had warned her he could be testy. "I understand. When do you think you'll get to Estella's house?"

"How do I know? At least an hour." Before he disconnected, Sara heard a woman scream in the background.

Sara turned to Winslow, the young FBI technician who had driven the FBI crime van from Albuquerque to Santa Fe. "Looks like we have an hour to kill. Let's eat after we check out an address Barbara texted me. Seems Jules got several parking tickets at this location."

Winslow looked at the address on Sara's phone and entered it on the van's GPS. "Jules either was too lazy to walk or was delivering or picking up heavy items. It's one of the little side streets off Canyon Road. Both Estella's home and a parking garage are only a few blocks away."

As he followed the GPS instructions, Sara thought about how much she hated driving on Canyon Road. Shoppers were apt to dart into the one-way street without looking as they moved among galleries and shops. However, Winslow seemed unperturbed and in less than five minutes found the last parking spot without a yellow curb along the narrow street.

"Winslow, let's see if anyone knows Jules or Estella in the shops here."

The technician readjusted the leather tie that held his long black hair in a pony tall "I'm game, but I'm a newbie with the FBI and only authorized to collect physical data—not to do interviews."

"Fine. I'll play the confused tourist. You note the addresses and names of shops we visit."

They entered several shops. Each time Sara played a lost tourist looking for her friend Jules Smith. After the fifth shop, Winslow said, "Your line is getting better with practice."

On their way to a sixth shop, Sara looked down a narrow passageway between the buildings. She thought she must be hallucinating. A tall, middle-aged man with brown hair was lolling by the side door of the shop. He looked like a photo of Nelson Davis but without a beard She realized that neither Winslow nor she had the authority to arrest him, but she hurried down the passageway toward the man anyway. "Excuse me, we're lost. We're trying to find…"

The man glanced at Sara, turned, and sprinted down the alley behind the building.

"Sara yelled to Winslow, "Follow that man. I think he's Nelson Davis." She focused her phone on the man as he sped down the alley, took a photo, and emailed it with a note on his location to Barbara and to Hank Snow. She ran back to the side street hoping to surprise the stranger at the point where the alley looped back to the side street.

He wasn't in sight. Then she spied the stranger twenty yards in front of her. She screamed. "Nelson, this is the FBI."

The runner didn't even glance at her.

Tourists on the sidewalk and side street paid no attention to her either. They didn't move from their positions ogling items in store windows. She pushed them aside as she ran forward, but the stranger was more successful at weaving through the crowd. So was Winslow who quickly passed her.

She gasped for breath because she wasn't used to running and Santa Fe's altitude was two thousand more than that of Albuquerque. She checked her phone. Barbara hadn't replied.

Hank's text read:

> *Sent photo to SF police patrolling the area. Won't help much*
> *as man's face is not visible.*
> *I'm tied up for at least an hour more.*

She texted the direction that Winslow was running because she no longer could see the tall stranger. When she looked up, Winslow was walking toward her and shaking his head. "He disappeared in the crowd. I saw Santa Fe police in a cruiser slowly moving down Canyon Road. Maybe they'll spot him." Winslow wiped sweat from his brow. "You're awfully red. Are you okay?"

"I just proved I'm not fit enough to be an agent" She thought for a second. "We might as well visit more shops along this side street. Nelson was at the side door of the next store we were going to visit."

The sixth store sold designer clothes for children. It rapidly became obvious that no man had entered the store in the last hour.

At their seventh stop—the Green Way to Beauty Spa—Sara began her spiel again. "I'm supposed to meet my friend, Jules Smith. I think this is where he said he'd meet me. Do you know him? He's a regular here."

The clerk looked confused.

Sara scanned the shop's deep green walls and shelves full of jars with light green and yellow creams and lotions. She decided to try another approach. "Your products must be good. Jules's complexion is beautiful. No worry lines for him. He suggested I could use the help of this spa. He claimed it did wonders for Estella… you know—Estella Garcia Davis?"

The clerk pouty lips formed a big O when Sara mentioned Estella. "I'm sorry but the manager isn't here now. She had a family emergency in Albuquerque. But our nurse can answer your questions." She pressed a button and rushed past the frosted glass doors that slid open.

Several minutes later, a woman with the look of a deer caught in headlights and wearing a pale green lab coat appeared. Sara wondered what gave her face the perfect but stiff look. It was disturbing and funny at the same time. Sara suspected she'd overused her own products.

"I'm the nurse here. We're always pleased when our regulars refer a new patient to us. She studied Sara's face. You know several of our products, especially Botox, can do wonders, but you can't expect your face to look like Jules's. He's been getting injections for years, and I suspect younger than you."

Sara heard Winslow suck in his breath and then cough loudly. She tried not to laugh and continued the bluff. "Of course not, but maybe you can help me… like you did Estella. Can you tell me about the injections of Botox that Jules and Estella get?" Sara touched her face. "I want to lose my crow's feet like Estella did." She paused. "But nothing too obvious."

"Patient records are confidential, but I can tell you about the type of treatments our physician might recommend for you."

After Winslow agreed to wait in the store, the nurse led Sara to a pale green cubicle behind the frosted glass doors. The nurse ceremoniously peered at Sara's face and gently rubbed spots with her gloved hands. After five minutes of listening to all the work needed on her face, Sara said, "It looks like Jules stood me up. You know he's so busy with Estella's campaign and current problems. Why don't you give me your card and I'll get back to you?"

The nurse placed a business card and a pamphlet on Botox into a pale green envelope and pressed it into Sara's hand. "Our physician is here only twice a month. The sooner you act, the more pleased you'll be with the results."

Sara resisted the urge to run as the nurse led her back to the lobby where Winslow was intently studying a green jar of goo. He grabbed Sara's arm and whispered, "I was beginning to think I needed to call for help to rescue you."

As they cleared the entrance, Winslow whistled. "They do a hard sell in that joint. The clerk tried to convince me at twenty-five I need to start taking better care of my skin before the lines on my face got too deep."

Sara gave him no sympathy. "The nurse called my face a 'desert begging for replenishment.'"

Winslow stopped and pulled Sara around to face him. "Let me check." He studied her face. "You don't have any wrinkles on your forehead and the smile lines around your mouth are normal. The place is a rip-off, but the clerk convinced me I was in the wrong business. They're making a killing selling beauty products that are nothing but cheap hand creams and lotions with a little hemp oil, retinol, vitamins C and E, and green dye added." Sara checked her watch. "I think we missed our early lunch."

"No problem. I enjoyed watching you act like a rich matron with a poker up your… You know what I mean." He chortled. "The old timers in the lab said you were Carbonne's favorite partner until Barbara came along. Now I know why. You and Carbonne are both actors. Barbara and most of the male agents would not have gained half as much info at that place."

***

Ten minutes later, a black SUV pulled up behind the FBI lab van, which Winslow had parked one block away from Estella's home as Hank had ordered. The man who strode from the SUV looked like a TV cowboy—tall and lanky with a lined face that had seen too much sun. Sara couldn't stop herself from saying to Winslow, "The nurse at the Green Way to Beauty Spa would have a field day analyzing *that* face." Both Sara and Winslow were snickering as they greeted Hank.

"There's nothing funny about the two hours I spent at Mrs. Davis's campaign headquarters. The campaign staff were as confused as

                                    J. L. Greger

the candidate always seems in televised interviews. It took me and two Santa Fe officers to wrangle a file cabinet and three computers from those biddies."

"How did you decide what was relevant?"

"I didn't. Barbara Lewis told me to gather all the records on donors, volunteers, and fundraisers for Mrs. Davis's senate campaign. When I objected that included everything but the kitchen sink, Barbara put Carbonne on the line. He sympathized with me but said we couldn't afford to botch this case." Hank looked Sara up and down. "You look too experienced to be as particular."

Winslow chuckled, "You're the second person in the last hour to tell Sara that she looks old."

Hank coughed. "Didn't say you were old, ma'am, just *experienced*."

Sara smiled inwardly. Hank couldn't afford to be too grouchy after that faux pas. "Did Santa Fe police locate the man we saw?"

"No. Probably wasn't Nelson Davis. Mr. Davis is a real dude. The man in the photo looked a bit saddle-worn."

Sara nodded. "We've just learned Estella and her campaign manager, Jules Smith, are big fans of Botox. That means we're looking not only for food with botulinum toxin and spores in the kitchen and campaign records in any offices but also for any strange cosmetics and solutions in the bathrooms and the bedrooms."

Hank lifted his Stetson to scratch his ear. "You mean Botox contains the same toxin as spoiled food with botulism?"

"Basically yes," said Sara.

Winslow grabbed Sara's arm. "I think I can distinguish between them. Botox is always made from the toxin produced by the 'A' strain of the *Clostridium botulinum* bacteria. Food can have several types of botulinum toxin. It…."

Hank interrupted, "I like the lady's answer better. When I knock on the door, you two should stand to the side. I talked to the housekeeper when I picked up her key on Wednesday" He shook his head. "You'd think a house this uppity would have a computer keypad instead of a key."

"I got the impression that Estella was…" Sara paused to think. "…technically challenged and too traditional to use a keypad."

Hank grimaced. "The word is *dumb*. Well, the housekeeper says no one should be home, but surprises are possible because Nelson's whereabouts are unknown." He continued to give instructions for five more minutes.

***

Hank's plan was destroyed almost as soon as he opened the front door to Estella's home. Three piles of red clutter lay on the steps to the second floor and a brown and fuzzy item was draped on the newel post at the bottom of the stairs.

"I think that counts as physical evidence," said Sara. "Surely it wasn't there when the EMTs took Estella to the hospital."

Hank growled, "Tech man, do your thing."

Winslow knelt by his case and snapped on gloves. "My name's Winslow—not 'tech man.' I'll do the basics now and get the details later." He snapped several photos, turned on the recorder hung around his neck. He held up the brown, fuzzy item. "The first item is a woman's fake fur jacket." He picked up one part of the red pile at the foot of stairs. "Red leather women's boots at the foot of the steps."

"Odd. A cheap fake fur jacket with expensive red leather boots," said Sara.

"Nah, see a lot of that in Santa Fe lately. The ladies don't want to kill a mean vermin like mink for a coat and forget leather comes from a cow, which is a lot nicer than a mink." Hank scratched his ear. "I talked to the housekeeper and picked up a key Wednesday night after Barbara ordered me to inspect the house. The housekeeper told me that she had the day off because Mrs. Davis liked to sleep late after her rallies. I told her not to enter this house until I had time to inspect it. She complained." He snorted again. "But she complied. She's too proper to let stuff like that lay on the stairs."

Winslow climbed two stairs. He snapped photos before he picked up the second red item with a gloved hand. "Red leather skirt. A mini skirt."

"The woman wasn't here for business."

Hank snickered, "Oh, I was thinking this looks like the gear of a pro. Not a cheap one."

Winslow climbed three stairs and held up the last item—a red, lacy piece of lingerie. "I don't usually find teddys on stairs."

Hank snorted. "Too small to be Estella's or the housekeeper's."

Sara thought Hank's lackadaisical attitude on the scene was problematic. The house had been left unattended from when the EMTs had taken Estella to the hospital on Wednesday afternoon until now on Friday afternoon. Nagging would not help the situation. "Can we assume someone entered the house since Wednesday afternoon? They might be here now." Maybe a little nagging wouldn't hurt. "Do you need backup?"

Hank growled. "No. The other agent in Santa Fe is busy today. Every available state trooper is at a big event at the governor's mansion. I

J. L. Greger

already got help from Santa Fe police this morning. We're on our own. Guess I'd better announce our presence again."

There was no response.

Hank pointed to Winslow. "You stay here." He pointed at the bottom of the stairs and then turned to Sara. "You follow me up the stairs." He pulled his gun and walked slowly up the stairs announcing his presence again.

At the top of the stairs, he motioned for Sara to remain on the last step as he walked to an open doorway on their left. She could hear his footsteps along the wood floor of the hallway but not once he entered the room. Sara guessed it was the master bedroom and carpeted. She heard him open and close several doors and heard his steps again. She guessed there was an attached bathroom. He called, "All clear."

When he walked past her, he said, "Stay here but be ready to call for help if I'm in any of the next rooms for more than a minute without calling 'all clear.'"

Sara didn't respond because she'd already texted Barbara that Hank was too cavalier and needed police backup. She had also texted Winslow to contact the Santa Fe police and explain the situation.

There were three closed doors along the hallway on the right of the stairs. Sara assumed two were bedrooms and one was a bath.

Hank opened the door to a room almost across from the stairs. Sara strained to look past him. The room appeared to be used as an office because she spied a desk and bookcases. She thought it must be a large room as she listened to the sound of Hank's shoes on the wood floor. Hank slammed a door, probably of a closet, and finally called, "All clear."

Sara felt sweat running down her back and desperately wanted Hank to wait for the police but didn't want anyone in the remaining two rooms to know how easy it might be to escape. As Hank emerged from the room, she hissed, "psst," and motioned him to the stairwell. "Hank, this is crazy. Wait until the police backup arrives. They should be here in a minute or two."

"I don't want them to snicker at me for needing their help twice in one day." He entered a room on the right of the hallway.

Sara strained but couldn't peer into the room. She surmised the room was carpeted because she couldn't hear Hank's footsteps. Sara heard a noise below her. Winslow was talking to a Santa Fe police officer. She motioned to them to hurry because she'd heard two doors slam in the room on the right of the hallway but nothing from Hank.

The two officers with their guns out rushed up the steps. Sara pointed to the room on the right. "Hank's in there. Better announce your presence because he's armed and ready to shoot. Don't know what's in the room at the end of the hall." She pointed to the last room.

The officers nodded and the older one yelled, "Hank, we're here to back you up."

There was no reply.

The officers cautiously entered the room. Silence, then whispers. Then one yelled, "All clear," as they raced to the last room. They yanked open the door. Sara looked past to them and saw a large, claw-foot bathtub on a white tile floor. Almost immediately, one officer yelled, "All clear," and ran down the stairs.

The other police officer ushered Sara toward the third room where Hank had remained. "My partner has called for an ambulance and the medical examiner. He also will send the lab technician up here, but you might as well see if you can help Hank while we check the rest of the house."

Sara stomach muscles tightened as she peered into the room. Hank was leaning across a body and blocked Sara's view of the woman's torso. Sara was aghast at the staged position of the body. A long, tanned leg and a bare foot with red toe nail polish was tied with a black net stocking to one bed post. The other leg awkwardly dangled while the woman's arms were stretched above her head on the blue carpet. Her long red nails were also polished red, and her wrists were tied together with another black net stocking. Hank's awkward stance suggested he had placed his feet to avoid stepping on bloody spots on the carpet.

Hank didn't look toward the doorway where Sara stood. "Sara? I can't find a pulse. Someone appears to have stabbed her in the chest and left her to bleed out." He straightened and stepped back.

Sara suppressed a scream.

Hank motioned to green fabric around her neck. "She might have been strangled with the scarf. Doubt that was the cause of death. Too much blood from the wound."

Sara gulped. "What do you want me to do?"

"Tell the medical examiner the timetable when he arrives. I've got to help the officers check the rest of the house, garage, and grounds." He turned to leave. "Tell Winslow not to touch anything until the examiner gives the okay—just take photos. Record the time anyone enters or leaves the room. Start with my initial entrance. Estimate the time..." He looked at his watch. "...as fifteen minutes after one. It's twenty-three minutes

                                                                J. L. Greger

after one now by my watch. Oh, and call Barbara and tell her to get her ass up here. We need help."

Winslow entered the room at twenty-four after one, glanced at Sara, and began to snap photos immediately. "Is this the first time you've seen a murder scene?"

"Hardly, but it always shocks me."

Winslow stopped clicking his camera. "I pretend it doesn't bother me, but I always see the scenes at night as I try to fall asleep. I'm all right when I'm working."

He took a shot of the woman's feet and the black net stocking holding her one foot to the bed post. "Looks like the red teddy was hers. It matches the nail polish." He peered but didn't touch the green fabric around her neck. "The scarf doesn't match the rest of her costume."

A bald, stout man panting from running raced into the room. He knelt by the body and checked it vitals. He shook his head and pointed at Sara. "You the record keeper?"

She nodded yes.

"Record the time and note the medical examiner confirmed the woman was dead. I'll determine the cause of the death when she's in the morgue." He pointed at Winslow. "Are you the FBI lab technician?"

Winslow nodded.

"You through with the initial photos?"

"Yep."

The medical examiner checked the body temperature of the already stiff corpse. "She's probably been dead about twelve hours."

CHAPTER 8: Barbara Ponders Problems

"The attending physician has pronounced Beryl Marks as brain dead." The phone line was silent for a few seconds before the nurse in the ICU at University Hospital said, "Her daughter, Davita Lopez, has requested a second opinion and wants to talk to the nice agent she spoke to yesterday before she decides whether to turn off the ventilator."

Barbara assumed the *nice* agent was Sara. "Sara is in Santa Fe and will not return to Albuquerque until late this afternoon. Is the daughter comfortable with not deciding until tomorrow morning? If the food poisoning that sickened Beryl Marks was intentional, the medical examiner will have to pronounce the cause of death as homicide. We may not have a definite decision for several days."

"That's why the daughter asked me to call you. She wants all the facts before she acts."

Barbara felt her funk deepen. Now there was little hope of learning who—Nelson, Bo, or Jules—had encouraged Beryl to can figs by the strange recipe and bring them to the rally.

Hank or Sara should have reported their progress in Santa Fe by now. All she knew was Santa Fe police had not been able to locate the man Sara spotted. She doubted the man was Nelson Davis. Others would have recognized him if he was that close to his home.

Barbara wanted to complain to her immediate supervisor about Hank's lack of response to her emails, but she knew she was being unfair. There were only two agents in residence in Santa Fe. Usually that was enough because the Albuquerque field office supplied laboratory and staff backups for Santa Fe. It wasn't today. Moreover, if she told her supervisor that she needed more help on this case, he would say this case wasn't a real FBI case. Worse still, he'd ask Carbonne to hire more staff. She didn't want to hear Carbonne grumble again tonight that he was short-staffed. Then she'd never get him to concentrate on their real problem.

Her phone rang. Sara began without greeting her. "We—Hank, Winslow, and I—found a woman's body in Estella's home. She probably died of a stab wound to the chest, but it could be due to strangulation. It occurred about twelve hours ago. There's a sexual overtone to this murder."

Barbara felt her muscles in her shoulders and neck tighten. She and Carbonne had worked late the last two days because they wanted to have a leisurely dinner at Pappadeaux Seafood Kitchen tonight. She'd been practicing for the last week how she wanted to approach the discussion of their problem. Now she feared she'd have to drive to Santa Fe and work late again.

Her thoughts were interrupted when Sara said, "Please, send a computer expert up here to help me sort through all the records Hank seized at Estella's campaign headquarters. He claimed the women couldn't identify files that would list Estella's donors and volunteers or even a list of her past and future fundraising events. So, he took a file cabinet and all the computers from Estella's campaign headquarters. I thought that was overkill, but he claimed the women weren't doing anything anyway because they were waiting to see whether Estella survived—actually he said, 'kicked the bucket.'"

Barbara's mood flagged more. "Oh, Hank must be pouting."

"Don't worry. He's interested now that we have a more traditional victim. However, I think he wanted to teach the women at the campaign headquarters a lesson for being uncooperative." She paused for an uncomfortably long time. "I think the campaign staff will be more cooperative in the future if we can return their computers to them today or tomorrow. I'll do a preliminary sort of the paper files and decide what we can release quickly while the computer technician downloads the computer records, including any deleted files."

Sara paused as if she expected Barbara to agree. Finally, she said, "The women at the campaign headquarters are apt to know ways to reach Nelson or at least a few of his secrets. You need their cooperation."

"I guess I have no choice. I will send a computer technician to help you immediately even though the lab director will complain. I hope you do not expect me to send another lab technician, too."

"No. Two technicians from the Santa Fe Forensic Lab have already arrived. We have enough lab technicians. That leads me to a potential problem."

Barbara sighed. She suspected Sara was about to suggest that Barbara must drive to Santa Fe. "Do we need to worry about a *potential* problem when we have so many urgent ones?"

"The Santa Fe police, like Hank, aren't interested in the botulism cases but are eager to investigate the unknown woman's death."

"What are you trying to say?"

"A turf war might erupt here. I doubt I can influence Hanks's actions, but I think I can convince Winslow to be more interested in gathering data related to food and *cosmetic* sources of botulinum toxin and let the Santa Fe Forensic Lab take care of the blood and prints due to the murder here."

"What do you mean by 'cosmetic sources' of botulinum toxin?"

"Remember my email an hour ago about the Green Way to Beauty Spa? They were really pushing Botox."

"That is injectable botulinum toxin, not a cosmetic cream containing the toxin."

"Perhaps it doesn't matter. Won't the fact that Estella's house is a murder site give us the right to search carte blanche?"

Barbara knew Carbonne would tell Sara to follow her nose. "Remember you are investigating a homicide and two attempted homicides, not fraudulent business practices." She sighed because she knew what Sara had been suggesting. "I should be in Santa Fe in an hour."

***

Barbara tried to think positive thoughts as she drove toward Santa Fe. At least the other agents would have to consider this case a real one now. There was a traditional murder to be investigated.

None of her colleagues, except Sara, would argue with her if she labeled Beryl's imminent death and Estella's maiming as the results of unfortunate accidents. But it didn't seem right to not give the two women the respect they deserved. Moreover, if the poisonings weren't investigated as potential murder cases the poisoner might strike again.

Nelson was one logical suspect for both murders. Barbara allowed her mind to fantasize. She hoped that Nelson's DNA would be found on the corpse in Santa Fe because that would mean Nelson was alive twelve hours ago. Live individuals were easier to find than corpses, especially in New Mexico with all its barren desert areas. She didn't even seriously consider Sara's sighting of a tall man as a useful clue.

A more obvious suspect was Jules. Barbara had seen him probably seven hours after the murder in Santa Fe. Yes, he was nervous, but not that nervous. If he was the poisoner, he would be difficult to trap.

Central to her confusion were the conflicting statements by Bo and Jules as to who had hired the churchwomen at the last minute to prepare the food for the rally. Bo's recalcitrance when answering simple

J. L. Greger

questions had made Barbara suspect he could be involved in the poisoning. Mopsy's ineptness had increased her confusion.

Carbonne had reminded Barbara before she left the FBI building that she was lucky to have Sara's help on this case. "Odd details and science are up Sara's alley." However, Barbara was not sure that was true. Sara would get the credit if the case was solved, but Barbara knew she would be blamed if it remained unsolved. Barbara thought it was a no-win situation for herself.

She thought about asking the resident FBI agent in Las Cruces to interview Bo McCarran, but Las Cruces was farther away from Clovis than Albuquerque. Neither Mopsy nor local public health workers had gotten civil answers from Bo, but Mopsy thought he knew key information. That meant Barbara needed to drive to Clovis to interview Bo. Barbara felt like crying.

She was going to miss a romantic dinner with Carbonne tonight and lose her chance to discuss their problem. He kept saying that Sanders and Sara worked together successfully and were a happy couple without marriage. Why couldn't they be?

She thought Carbonne had ignored key points. Sanders had a daughter about to graduate from law school. Sara and Sanders were older than her and Carbonne and they didn't want children together. Barbara still wanted at least one child and hopefully two. Her mother often spoke of Acoma traditions, which actually was a way of reminding Barbara that she wanted to become a grandmother and teach Barbara's children about the Acoma pueblo.

Barbara was unsure how Carbonne felt about children. She knew he disliked interviewing children as an FBI agent. She had asked Sara once about how Carbonne interacted with children under the guise of knowing how to handle her own interviews. Sara had given a lengthy answer which ended with, "I suspect Carbonne likes children, but he's afraid of them because they represent a need for committed attention. Then he feels guilty because he can't make that commitment." Sara had smiled, "But I think you could change his mind over time."

Barbara concluded that Sara had not been fooled by Barbara's question and had warned her that Carbonne didn't know his own potential as a father and husband. Obviously, this discussion with Carbonne was not one to be approached over a quick meal. It needed to be developed slowly, and her biological clock was ticking.

As she turned onto Old Pecos Trail Road heading into Santa Fe, Barbara decided she'd better focus on the current case now. Thoughts of

Carbonne and their relationship would have to wait. She called the medical examiner for an update.

He had only preliminary information. "I'm hypothesizing an attacker strangled the victim because her hyoid bone was broken. Then the victim must have indicated that she was not dead. The original or a second assaulter then used a knife. The wound suggests the knife had a serrated edge and was probably fairly small. The woman also sustained extensive bruising on her arms, shoulders, chest, and pelvis." He sighed. "I won't have the official autopsy report ready until tomorrow, but the technicians and your aide, Sara, can supply you with more details."

CHAPTER 9: Barbara in Santa Fe

A Santa Fe policewoman was hunched over a portable table nearly blocking passage to the front stairs of Estella's house. She was reviewing footage from security cameras and grunted when Barbara flashed her badge. "We expected you an hour ago when the FBI computer technician—I think he called himself Pete—arrived. He's upstairs working on the computers in the owners' office."

The shrillness of the officer's voice suggested her—and probably Hank's—annoyance. Hank, Winslow, and apparently a technician from Santa Fe Forensic Laboratory were arguing as they examined the railing on the stairs a few yards from the front door. None of them acknowledged Barbara's presence.

Sara had been right. Estella's house had become the scene of a turf war and she needed to take charge. She gulped and decided to start slowly with the policewoman. "I assume you're documenting all entries into the house because it's an active crime scene?"

The woman didn't look up from her computer screen which was filled with views of three doorways. "I've entered you on the log."

"Where were the cameras located?"

"Obvious spots. The front door, a side door to the garage, and the patio door in back."

"How long does the footage go back?' Is there anything interesting or surprising?

"Not really." The technician finally looked up. "Well, one thing is surprising. Someone deleted all camera footage before three days ago. Usually, people let the tape record until they run out of storage space. Then they let the new footage overwrite the old footage. That's usually about a week. I transferred all the recorded footage to my computer and have bookmarked any action that I found."

"What was the first thing on the tape?"

The policewoman located the section of tape as she spoke. "Estella opens the front door for a short man with blond hair on Tuesday around ten. He enters and a minute later carries out a box."

Barbara glanced at the tape. The man's shoulders were bent forward as if the box was heavy. "That is Jules Smith."

The policewoman nodded. "A couple of minutes later Estella backs out of the door with a rolling suitcase. Then nothing happens for about thirty minutes on any of the recordings. Then a tall man with a neatly cropped beard leaves through the garage door. He looks like the picture of Nelson Davis."

Barbara noted that Nelson was carrying a suitcase and a tote. "What is next?"

"Nothing, until Estella staggers in the front door around one on Wednesday morning." She played a short footage in which Jules helped Estella stagger through the front doorway, left two minutes later, carried a box in, rolled a suitcase in, and left."

Barbara wondered whether Estella was sick already, but decided Estella was just drunk.

"Nothing more until two-thirty in the afternoon when the EMTs arrive. Then lots of standard action." The policewoman became absorbed in pressing buttons on her computer. "I've spotted nothing on the tape for the next twelve hours. That's as far as I'd gotten when you interrupted me."

"Thank you for the update. When you are done with this task, please check with Pete. He may want to copy your file."

"Yeah." The officer tinkered again with her computer. "Now, that's strange. There's only fourteen more hours on the tape left. Someone must have turned off the security cameras around five on Thursday afternoon."

Hank had finally noticed her and was ambling down the stairs. Barbara quickly said to the policewoman, "The next fourteen hours should be more interesting because someone had to enter the house to turn off the security cameras."

"Doubt it. The cameras are programmable remotely." She returned to her hunched position as she viewed the frames of the three entrances simultaneously. "This is the deadest footage I've ever scanned."

Barbara decided to take the offensive with Hank. "What the problem on the stairs?" She pointed to the two technicians who were still squatting on the steps and looking intently at the polished wooden banister.

"A lot of smudged prints. The tech from the Santa Fe Forensic Lab says it's hopeless. Winslow says there a new technique for determining the age of prints, especially those that are fewer than two or three days old. He wants to use that technique to identify the most recent prints. Hopefully those of the murdered woman and the murderer."

"It might be a good idea. I will speak to them and the Santa Fe police officer in charge of this case."

"The sergeant is in an upstairs bathroom with Sara."

Winslow stood as Barbara began to climb the stairs. "With a TOF-SIMS technique I can ionize the chemicals on the top surface of the smudges. The fatty acids, particularly the palmitic acid, in fingerprints migrate with time—at least the first three days. Thus, I can distinguish three-day-old prints from day-old ones."

The other technician stood, too. "You're looking for a way to use new equipment in the FBI lab. You can't be sure whether…."

Barbara held up her hand between the two men. "Please tell me what TOF-SIMS is."

"Time-of-flight secondary ion mass spectrometry."

Barbara was sorry that she had asked the question. All she knew was there were mass spectrometers in the FBI laboratory. "Have data from this type of mass spectrometer been accepted in courts as a reliable source of evidence?"

Winslow shrugged. "In a few cases."

The other technician smiled. "But not in New Mexico. And if he tries this technique, he'll destroy the samples for further DNA analyses."

"But as we wait, the fingerprints are aging." Winslow smiled almost triumphantly. "And the prints on this banister are useless for standard techniques now. The DNA probably is too. It's worth a try."

"Go ahead and process…" Barbara pointed at the banister. "…appropriate areas for this new type of mass spectrometry and other areas for DNA analyses."

When Barbara reached the top of the stairs, Hank whispered in her ear, "We have a disagreement in the bathroom, too." He announced loudly as they walked into the bathroom attached to the master bedroom, "We think that's the murder weapon."

Sara, who was apparently inventorying items in an under-the-counter refrigerator, looked up and pointed to a small serrated paring knife sitting on a cutting board with a browned, quartered apple. "The medical examiner upon his quick analyses of the body thought the fatal wound was caused by a small, serrated knife. I left the knife where I found it. I think the lab will be able to determine whether this knife is consistent with the wound, but I doubt we'll find blood or DNA. Winslow thinks this knife was thoroughly scrubbed and rinsed with bleach. I searched the four bathrooms and the kitchen in the house and found bleach only in this bathroom. However, there was bottle of bleach in the laundry room. That suggests the killer was familiar with the house and knew bleach was stored in this bathroom."

A Santa Fe police sergeant entered the room. "The killer may have left the bottle here after he found it elsewhere in the house."

Sara didn't wait for him to finish. "I think the bleach was stored here. There are several pale rings the size of the bleach bottle on the wood underneath the sink here in this master bath, but I found no such rings under the sinks or in closets of the other bathrooms or the kitchen." She crawled to open the door under the sink. "You'll note the rings are in various tones. That suggests bleach had dripped from this bottle or other bottles several times."

The sergeant squatted and looked at the rings. "Okay, it's likely the bleach was stored here, and the murderer was either lucky or knew the layout of the house." He responded to a text on his phone and murmured, "It would be nice if the FBI could locate Nelson. I expect he knew the layout of his own home and he's rumored to be a ladies' man."

Sara looked up. "It would have been nice if the Santa Fe police had located the man I spotted this morning. He looked a lot like Nelson Davis."

Barbara thought it best to ignore the comments. "Sara, did you find anything else useful in the master bath?"

The sergeant looked up from his phone and interrupted, "My tech in the garage says she's almost through sorting the garbage. She found and syringes but didn't see much else of potential interest. Are we sure neither Estella nor Nelson were diabetics?"

"That's a good question." Barbara turned to Sara.

"I checked with the hospital. Estella is not a diabetic. I put through a request to subpoena Nelson's medical records."

Barbara suddenly realized that she had not obtained Jules' medical records either. There was no reason to admit that now and give the sergeant further reasons to degrade her work. "What have you found in the master bath and bedroom?"

"Nothing that was worth my time. I don't have a fat budget like yours at the FBI," said the sergeant as he left the bathroom. "I'll tell my technicians to stop wasting time on the stairs and garbage. They'll bag the knife and finish processing the bedroom where the murder occurred. The officer at the front door should be through with the security tapes soon. She can help me canvas the neighborhood. I doubt the neighbors saw anything because the murder occurred last night after everyone around here had gone to bed. Then we're out of here."

"After our initial observations, Winslow and I left examination of the bedroom where the body was found to the Santa Fe police and techs. We focused on the master bedroom and bath." Sara waited until the sergeant's footsteps echoed on the stairs before she whispered, "That is until Winslow became convinced the tech inspecting the hallway wasn't up to the task."

"I resolved that issue. Have you...."

"We found a bag of unused syringes in the second drawer of the chest by the bed but no syringes or drug paraphernalia in the wastebaskets upstairs. Winslow wants to claim jurisdiction for the syringes the other tech found in the garbage because he thinks the Santa Fe police and lab will look for only insulin and street drugs."

"What do you two expect to find in the syringes?"

"We found dozens of light green jars of concoctions from the Green Way to Beauty Spa on surfaces in the master bedroom and bathroom and in the bathroom closet. I already emailed you those tallies."

Barbara felt impatient and wished Sara would skip the long-winded explanations and answer questions quickly. "All they prove is that Estella and Nelson were obsessed with looking young."

Sara flashed a grin. The one she'd beamed at the Santa Fe police sergeant before she convinced him that the killer was familiar with the house. "Winslow and I found several multi-injection storage vials in this refrigerator. They were unlabeled. That suggests they're not prescriptions from a physician. We're both betting they come from the Green Way to Beauty Spa and will contain botulinum toxin."

Barbara snorted. "That is a big assumption. I read your email after you left the spa. Although I agree with you that the spa seemed overly aggressive in promoting Botox as an anti-aging treatment, Botox can only be injected by physicians and nurses in a clinical setting."

While Barbara spoke, Sara tapped keys on her laptop. She shoved the laptop in front of Barbara. "This information from the FDA may interest you. It is recommended that botulinum toxin be injected by physicians or nurses in a clinic, but Botox parties do occur. It seems all botulinum toxin products, including Botox, are shipped in a concentrated form that must be diluted before they are injected. At these parties there is no wastage of diluted Botox so it can be offered at a cheaper price than in clinics."

"Is it legal?'

"Yes, in New Mexico if it is administered by a nurse or physician, not an esthetician." Sara rolled her eyes. "I'll never get used to the term *esthetician*. To me, they're just fancy makeup saleswomen."

Barbara glanced at the screen. This is all interesting, but how does it relate to the current murder or the food poisoning of Beryl and Estella?"

"The medical examiner plans to look for injection sites on the woman's face in locations logical for Botox or keratin injections. He thought he saw two small hematomas near her eyes before he had her body moved to the morgue."

"Hematomas usually do not appear immediately."

"The woman might have gotten Botox injections before and wanted more."

"I will repeat my question—how does finding syringes and perhaps vials of Botox relate to these cases?"

"I don't know. But until you find Nelson, we have to consider all evidence as potentially useful clues."

J. L. Greger

CHAPTER 10: Sara Compromises

Pete found little of interest on Estella's home computer. He told Sara and Barbara, "Estella's emails to Jules and her husband are short and pathetic. She accepts their commands and whimpers a bit. There's nothing unexpected in the deleted documents or messages. Others can study the download back at our building in Albuquerque, but it's not worth much time."

Barbara snorted. Sara recognized Pete's appearance was less than professional with his thinning short hair and gut bulging over his belt but she knew he was arguably the most experienced computer technician at the FBI in Albuquerque. "So, could we say Jules had Svengali-like control of Estella?"

"I doubt it, but Nelson is another case. My wife would divorce me if I tried to control her like Nelson does Estella." He pointed to Nelson's computer in the office. "The crew in Albuquerque are going to have a field day examining the content I downloaded from this computer. I think you'll find the deletions, especially messages to Bo McCarran and Beryl Marks, interesting."

Barbara flushed with annoyance. "Why did you take time to look for those names in emails and documents?"

Pete looked back and forth between Sara and Barbara. "Sara gave me those names as a way to guess which files might be useful. Was that a mistake?"

Sara wondered whether Barbara was feeling threatened and wanted to dispel the uncomfortable situation. "Barbara is surprised that we may have finally found something useful."

Barbara seemed to regain her composure. "Yes, add Clovis and San Diego to your search list. I'd like to learn about Bo's plans for the day of the rally and the time since then."

"Okay, but I think you should look at three of Nelson's emails to Bo and Beryl right away. Sara summarized the case for me when I arrived and noted several unanswered questions. I think these emails provide answers." A short email appeared on the screen. It was dated the twelfth of November in the previous year:

> *Beryl,*
> *Thanks for hosting the fundraiser at your home yesterday.*
> *Estella and I appreciate your generosity.*
>
> *Estella's favorite recipe for canned figs and nuts is attached.*
> *Could you use the figs from your beautiful trees to make these*
> *preserves? Your trees show small things can grow and survive*
> *in hard situation if given a little shelter. They should be the*
> *signature treat at Estella's rallies.*
>
> *Thanks in advance for putting Estella in the U.S. Senate.*
> *Nelson*

"Well, we know now who gave the questionable recipe to Beryl. Nelson is certainly political." Sara looked at Barbara. "He may have plotted poisoning Estella for a long time."

"Pete, please show me the other emails you bookmarked."

Another short email appeared on the screen. This one was dated three days prior to the rally in Clovis:

> *Bo,*
> *Please forward the name of the caterer for the rally. I'm sure*
> *I can convince her to serve Beryl Marks's canned figs and*
> *nuts.*
> *Nelson*

"I thought Jules had lied and was implicating Nelson as the villain. Maybe not. What do you think, Barbara?"

"I want to see the last email before I comment."

A third short email appeared on the screen. It was dated the day prior to the rally in Clovis.

> *Bo,*
> *Jules hired an alternate caterer. They'll be ready to set up at*
> *eleven at the VFW. Have the building unlocked.*
>
> *I've not told Estella about the problem with the caterers.*
> *Don't distress her by bothering her with that detail.*

"Sara, you were too optimistic. It appears Jules lies selectively. He told me that Nelson had found the caterers. These emails also reveal a lot about Nelson. He's charming when necessary and always controlling." Barbara scanned a message on her phone. "Suddenly we have too many viable leads. Mopsy insists that I talk to Bo immediately."

"Barbara, why don't you drive to Clovis? You're the only one who may be able to get info from Bo because you have the authority to arrest him for withholding evidence if he refuses to cooperate with you."

"That is easier said than done. I am afraid to go because Hank is apt to let the Santa Fe police take short cuts here."

"Look, you can trust Pete, Winslow, and me. We'll collect everything needed here."

Sara turned to Pete. "If you're done here, we should process the stuff that Hank confiscated at Estella's campaign headquarters. I think Hank technically had the Santa Fe police claim the computers and files at Estella's campaign office this morning and then leave them in a rental storage unit by his office. He told me that involving the Santa Fe police with the collection of materials at the campaign office wasted time this morning but would save him days of frustration while dealing with the Justice Department. It seems the local police have done him this favor before. Basically, they agreed to be too busy to check items from the storage unit into their evidence room until tomorrow. Hank thought by then one of us from the FBI office in Albuquerque would have done the necessary sorting and he'd only have to claim the essentials."

Barbara, who had been texting, jerked her head up, "You must have misunderstood Hank. The situation you describes breaks all the chain of custody rules."

"I heard fine." Sara didn't add that Hank had smugly noted, "I may have created work for you, but this will teach Barbara and the biddies at the campaign office to be more cooperative in the future and not waste my time." Instead, Sara said, "Barbara, Hank's no fool. He knows those records may be important." Sara pointed to the Pete. "If the two of us hurry, we can download everything on the computers and do a rough sort of the files. Then while we return the computers and files that were *mistakenly* collected to Estella's campaign headquarters, Hank can officially claim the needed materials."

Barbara murmured. "I do not like this."

Sara winked at Barbara. "I think Hank gave you another reason for leaving soon for Clovis. You can claim honestly you don't know what Hank did with any evidence found at the campaign headquarters."

***

The storage unit was only a block from Hank's office. Hank had placed the computers and files inside a cabinet with special locks inside the padlocked storage locker. Sara suspected the files had been safer than in most police evidence rooms. She also wouldn't be surprised if Hank had tacit approval of this storage unit from a key Justice Department official because there was no storage space in his small office.

Sara quickly discovered the file cabinet served primarily as warehouse for hundreds of copies of fliers, publicity shots, and position papers on various issues. Hank hadn't needed to confiscate all these materials because the campaign workers would have given copies of these to anyone. Sara photographed each of the thirty handouts just in case.

There was one drawer in the file cabinet that contained potentially useful material. One file contained a list of all major donors to Estella's campaign for mayor and dated back nine years. Background material on these donors made the file almost three inches thick. A similar files contained data on all volunteers for Estella's mayoral campaign and was equally thick. A third file— only a half-inch thick—contained lists of all those Estella had appointed to various unpaid committees while mayor. A note at the front of the file noted resumes of each individual could be found in the archived records of the mayor's office. An even thinner fourth file contained a list of all those Estella had appointed to paid positions while mayor.

Sara didn't know the values of these files but thought the FBI could claim these files would provide useful contacts for locating Nelson. She guessed that was a stretch but thought it would be deemed by the Justice Department, if investigated, to be logical.

The fifth file was much more interesting. It was labeled *Opponents—Mayor* and contained statements—mainly in the form

                                                              J. L. Greger

of newspaper clippings—against Estella while mayor. There were a few letters in the file, too.

The next two files paralleled the first two and contained data on donors and volunteers for Estella's bid for the senate. Only, these support files were thinner—at most an inch thick—than the mayoral files. The last file—an *Opponents-Senate* file—was almost an inch thick and Sara guessed the most important for the current investigation.

After Pete had downloaded all the files from the three computers, he'd thumbed through the paper files while Sara sorted through the last file. "My job was easy. All three computers were purchased in the last six months. There were no records pertaining to Estella's mayoral campaign. The computer files on her senate campaign are more extensive than these paper ones. Looks like someone is modernizing Estella's senate campaign."

***

Hank and Sara negotiated a compromise after he announced, "I'm not giving those hens a second chance at me." Hank helped Pete load the file cabinet and computers into the van and then unload them at Estella's campaign headquarters, but Hank didn't help Pete wheel them into the building. Sara was left to appease the women in Estella's campaign headquarters.

"I'm sorry that Hank Snow of the FBI and the local police disrupted your operation this morning but the officers were investigating a murder in Estella Garcia Davis's home."

All three women gasped. The office manager spoke, "We heard on the radio that police were investigating a death in the Canyon Road area but no details were given. Who was killed?"

"I'm not allowed to release the name, but you can see why Hank Snow wanted to secure any relevant data immediately." Sara realized she'd stretched the truth. Hank and the police had confiscated of the records at the campaign headquarters prior to the discovery of the murder, but she doubted that the women would ever learn that detail. They seemed to accept her explanation as logical.

"We knew you needed your computers and records, so we rushed to sort through your files. We're now returning your three computers and all but eight of your paper files. Here is a list of those files. If you need copies of the materials in these files, let me know." She pointed to Peter who now stood behind her. "He also downloaded a copy of your computer files for FBI use. None of your data will be released to the press or political interest groups. The data will only be used in ongoing police and FBI investigations."

The manager sniffed. "Why did the FBI involve the Santa Fe police in the investigation? The Santa Fe police talk too much."

Sara knew she needed to be careful how she answered this question because it would be best if the details of Hank's deal with the Santa Fe police, or at least one sergeant in the Santa Fe Police Department, never became known. "The FBI often works with local police in complicated cases."

Sara's phone beeped. "Excuse me—I need to take this message." Winslow had texted:

> *No print match in IAFIS.*
> *No DNA match in NDIS.*
> *Help. Here's the best photo of the victim.*

Sara had to think to understand all the abbreviations. IAFIS was the Integrated Automated Fingerprint Identification System, and NDIS was the National DNA Index System. Sara figured the women were more apt to answer a question from her than from Hank. The photo that Winslow had sent was scary but not horrifying. The woman's long black curls hid most of the bruises on her neck, and the blood from the chest wound wasn't obvious. "Do you recognize this woman?"

The manager's hand shook as she stared at the photo. "She's not a local woman and hasn't done volunteer work for this campaign, at least not from this office. I think she's associated with the Green Way to Beauty Spa."

The second women gasped. "She works at the Albuquerque shop."

The third woman stared at the ceiling. "I always thought Estella should dump Nelson."

"Ladies, spit it out. What do you know?"

"Rumor has it this is Nelson's girlfriend, Catalina Herrera." The manager shook her head. "We don't mention her name here because no one wants to upset Estella."

Sara's phone pinged. "Just a minute, I need to take several messages." Sara walked a bit away and turned her back on the women after she noted Pete was engaging them in light banter.

J. L. Greger

Sara knew Hank wouldn't like her message so she spoke quickly and gave him no chance to speak. "I know we agreed you could stay in the van, but the three women here agree our corpse is Catalina Herrera, a so-called girlfriend of Nelson Davis and an employee of the Green Way to Beauty Spa in Albuquerque. You'd better take their statements now. I'll inform Barbara."

She disconnected when she heard Hank say, "damn," and then counted to twenty to allow him time to leave his car and enter the building. She smiled as she turned to the women, "Agent Hank Snow will take your statements individually."

The manager straightened.

Before she could object, Sara said, "I assume you'd rather be interviewed here than at the Santa Fe police station. He'll be quick because we know your time is valuable."

Hank must have heard Sara's comment because he pointed at the manager as he strode by her. "You're first. Let talk in your office." She led the way to a small side office.

The other two women looked nervous, and Sara figured they'd talk more to Hank if calm. She whispered to Pete, "I'll get the conversation started but then I've got to respond to a text."

She motioned for the women to be seated on a settee at the front of the headquarters and pulled up a chair. "Pete and I noted that Estella's senatorial campaign seems more sophisticated than her mayoral campaign. Who modernized the office routine?"

The women stared at her. One gulped. "Nelson forced a lot of changes on Estella. It wasn't fair to Jules or those of us who have backed Estella for years."

Pete pulled up a chair. "I can sympathize with you, but a statewide senatorial campaign is different than a mayoral campaign. Do you know the name of the computer consultant Nelson hired?"

As the women bickered, Sara whispered, "You'd better record this. I doubt you'll have any problem keeping them talking while I make my calls." She walked behind the counter to a desk near the back of the large room.

She reread the text from Sanders:

> *Did you send a present to my secretary yet?*
> *Sanders*

She called Sanders in Brazil. A man informed Sara that she had the wrong number. Sara ignored him. Sanders, if he was conscious, was never far from this satellite phone. "Tell Sanders not to give me excuses. I'm his girlfriend."

The man gasped. "Please wait."

While she waited, she prayed the man would hand the phone to Sanders.

"Sara, I was worried about you. Are you okay?" Sanders's voice was higher pitched than usual. The word *worried* was his code for indicating that the call was being monitored.

She decided the truth was her best cover as she notified him that she couldn't get to a secure communication route in Albuquerque for an hour. "We found a body in the Santa Fe home of Estella Garcia Davis. Sorta ruined my timetable for today."

Sanders coughed.

"So, I haven't shopped for a present for your secretary? What would she like?"

"I'll send a photo to give you an idea. She'll be disappointed if she and her sister in Boca don't get real good luck charms before Carnival begins. Got to go." The line went dead.

Sara had scratched down his words on a piece of paper on the desk as he spoke. She knew that was bad form, but she liked to work crosswords and Sudoku puzzles on paper not on the computer, too. She shoved the two pages under the note into a shredder after she had emailed a memo to Carbonne.

She walked into the office Hank was using and interrupted his conversation with one of the women. "I've got to get back to the Albuquerque FBI office right away."

"No way. We've got several hours of work to do here and at Mrs. Davis's house."

Hank's phone beeped. He read the text. "Carbonne says he must see Pete and you immediately." He squinted at Sara. "Doesn't make sense. Pete transferred all the computer records electronically already. There's nothing gained by talking directly to you two."

"You can finish this up here without us. Winslow can help you secure the house. Please?"

He eyed Sara. "I'm not being told the whole story. That Barbara has Carbonne tied around her little finger."

Sara hated to leave Hank with the impression that Barbara had anything to do with her request, but she had no choice. "Thanks. We should have some lab results for you tomorrow."

Pete already had pulled the van to the front door of the headquarters by the time Sara emerged. "Carbonne texted me. I won't ask you any questions but don't think that you and Carbonne fooled me. I know it's above my pay grade."

CHAPTER 11: Barbara Learns about Herself on Friday and Saturday

As Barbara pulled into Clovis, she looked at her car's clock. There was no need to stop by the McCarran's equipment rental store. It was past five-thirty. Mopsy had told her the store closed at five when she told Barbara that she was leaving Clovis at three-thirty. Mopsy had insisted she had to get back to Albuquerque for supper with her son and wheezed in her usual way. "He counts on… starting the weekend with me. It's one of our traditions." Barbara had been annoyed because she also was missing an important dinner and maybe her last chance to start family traditions of her own.

LuAnn greeted Barbara at the door her home. "Bo's just got home. He's changin' because we're got reservations at the House of Joy at six. You know it's the best restaurant in town."

"I drove from Santa Fe to talk to him." Barbara flashed her badge.

LuAnn fluttered her Barbie-like eyelashes. "Can't you talk to him tomorrow. House of Joy doesn't hold reservations long."

"No. This is not a public health request now. It is FBI business."

"Mebbe, you can join us?"

A balding, lanky man smelling of Old Spice cologne appeared. "LuAnn, why'd you have to do that? You don't have to be friendly to her."

LuAnn put an arm around his waist. "Bein' nice is always good. She drove all the way from Santa Fe."

He scowled.

"It's not every day we get to talk to a real FBI agent. She showed me her badge. There's no way we can talk now and keep our reservation."

Bo scowled again and then kissed the top of LuAnn's head. "Can't say no to my lady." He glanced at Barbara. "You can follow us in your car."

Barbara wanted to say no, but she realized Bo was more apt to be cooperative if she acquiesced. She doubted he would be hostile in front of his wife, and Barbara was hungry.

***

Barbara looked at the menu and choked. House of Joy might be the best restaurant in Clovis, but it was a glorified hamburger joint. She listened as the McCarrans described and then ordered Dragon Lady and Calamity Jane burgers, but she selected the Leticia burger for herself. She waited until the waitress disappeared. "Bo, this is now a murder investigation."

LuAnn's eyes grew big. "Who died?"

"I would like to hear Bo's answers first." She shifted in her chair slightly so she was looking directly at Bo and hoped the subtle move would quiet LuAnn. It worked.

Bo explained how he had talked with Nelson and Jules after a political event. "It was odd. Usually they seem like best pals—two sneaky vermin livin' off a good woman. You know Estella was a good mayor. That's why LuAnn and I agreed to host the rally. Oil and gas are good, but those movie crews brin' real money to our business when they come to Clovis." He shook his head. "That day Jules and Nelson were in a fightin' mood."

"What do you mean?"

Bo cocked his head and appeared to think. "Jules kept sayin' things, like 'Estella'll crack if she doesn't get her sweets. Be her defender for a change.'"

"I was told Nelson didn't argue with Jules, but with you."

Bo shook his head. "All I did was tell Nelson the truth. The caterer would quit if homemade food not prepared in a certified kitchen was served at the event. She claimed she could lose her food service license, but Nelson went crazy."

As Barbara questioned Bo more, he admitted he might have confused Mopsy with his previous comments. Nelson had fired the original caterer and identified the four churchwomen as potential caterers for the rally. However, Jules had hired the alternate caterers—the four churchwomen.

"Funny thing. Those four usually are not bad cooks."

LuAnn shook her head, but remained silent after Bo said, "Not now." He looked back at Barbara. "They said Jules was payin' so little that they had to cut corners. Another funny thing—Nelson had promised the original caterer more money. I can't figure why Jules was so cheap."

"Let's change the topic slightly. Do you know why Nelson didn't come to the rally?'

"Shor'—he couldn't face me after makin' a donkey of himself."

As Bo guffawed at his own joke, LuAnn squeezed her husband's arm. "No need to talk like that."

He gulped his beer. "Estella claimed Nelson had an important book deal that would advance her campaign. Jules… he claimed poor Estella hadn't been told the truth."

When he finished answering Barbara's questions, LuAnn beamed. "I'll vote for Estella if she survives. It's easy to be a nice when your life is happy, but it takes a real lady to be nice when nothin' in your life is right. Estella is such a lady."

Barbara decided her trip to Clovis had not been a waste of her time. She'd eliminated Bo as a co-conspirator in the poisoning and learned a bit about the troubled relationships among Nelson, Jules, and Estella. It was time for her to be a nice lady and enjoy a meal with two nice people.

***

"The lab results have begun to roll in," was the way Carbonne began his call.

"Does that mean I made a mistake in coming to Clovis and not returning to Albuquerque?" Barbara hoped that Carbonne would say yes and tell her that he missed her or that she had gotten an important call.

"No, you made the right decision because now you have the data to force constructive discussions with Bo and the churchwomen who prepped the food for the rally."

"Oh." Barbara felt like crying but figured it was wise to not act needy. "I've already talked to Bo. He's convinced me that he played no part in causing the botulinum poisoning at the rally but Nelson or Jules—individually or working together—might have."

"That could be consistent with the lab data," said Carbonne. "The blood tests on Estella, Jules, the patients around Clovis, and Beryl confirmed the clinical observations. All, but Jules, had botulism. The lab found no botulinum toxin or spores in the unopened cans Mopsy confiscated from the churchwomen."

"That means either the women were unlucky and selected to use the wrong cans or the food they prepared was not the source of the botulinum toxin."

"The latter is more likely because the canned figs are another story. The jars of figs that Winslow found in Beryl's kitchen were all dated, presumably with the date they were canned. Figs canned before November eleventh had a pH below five—the lab crew say that's good—

                                        J. L. Greger

and contained no botulinum spores. The unopened jars dated later in November and labeled as "Estella's Favorite" had a pH above six. The lab director thinks the microbiologist was not thorough because the microbiologist reported no botulinum spores in any of those jars either. The open jar of figs in the refrigerator contained botulinum toxin but no spores."

Barbara thought for a moment. "I see why the lab director is concerned. The unopened jars with the higher pH should contain spores, especially since the spores in the opened jar had apparently germinated and produced toxin."

"That's why the lab director will have the preserves reexamined for spores."

"In any case, I think we can conclude Beryl did not intentionally poison anyone because she ate the canned figs, too."

"Agreed. The other good news is that Pete took another look at the contents of Nelson's computer and decided to work tomorrow and take Monday off instead. It seems he learned Nelson had an appointment with a book publisher in San Diego last Tuesday—the day of the rally."

As Carbonne talked, Barbara had scrolled through her emails. "Why do I have a note from Hank? He says he and Winslow are leaving Estella's home at eight because Sara and Pete left before four. He claims that he is too tired to send me any of the data until tomorrow."

"Sara had no choice but to leave him holding the bag. She had to get back to Albuquerque."

"She promised me."

"Don't worry. She's talking to Beryl's daughter, Davita, at the hospital as we speak. And Winslow is convinced he bringing every scrap of useful evidence from Santa Fe to the FBI lab."

"Why did she leave early?"

Carbonne seemed to stall. "I don't want to discuss this on the phone." He paused. "Didn't it strike you as odd that the FBI allowed Sara to be listed as an active employee during the last several months?"

"I thought it was a way you found to reduce paperwork because you knew you would use her as a consultant again."

"Partially true, but I was doing a favor for Sanders because I knew Sara might need access to our facilities at times with no questions asked. Remember I used to work for him when he was chief of security for the Cuban embassy."

"You took a big risk for an old friend."

"No, it was cleared at a high level." He seemed to sigh. "We've got a lot to talk about." He paused. "Umm… umm…Sara told me to stop trying to be the perfect boss and to listen to what you tell me that you need."

Barbara was curious and almost enjoyed his discomfort.

"I made a reservation for dinner at Pappadeaux for Sunday afternoon. That way, you can finish up in Clovis tomorrow, and we can have a relaxed, private conversation on Sunday morning before dinner. Love 'ya."

The phone went dead before she could reply, but Barbara was not unhappy. She didn't have to worry about gingerly approaching touchy topics on Sunday. It appeared Sara had set the stage.

***

Barbara questioned the four churchwomen individually and then talked to them as group on Saturday morning. Their comments were consistent. Jules had apologized when he hired them for the "extremely lean" budget that Nelson had given him. Two of them had met Nelson previously and thought he probably limited the budget because he wanted to keep Estella from eating too much and gaining more weight.

The four were all delighted to learn that their food was not the source of the botulinum toxin. All commented on how much they liked Mopsy. One said, "She never accused us of doing anything wrong even when all the county health personnel treated us like criminals." Another said, "She took the time to answer all our questions even though she had a sick son at home." A third bowed her head and added, "We've all prayed her son's cancer and her asthma would go into remission. It can't be easy when she's sick herself to care for him alone." The last woman cried as she listened to the others. "We've done a lot of praying this week for Estella and those at the rally. This has been a terrible week for us."

As Barbara drove home, she thought about Mopsy. Maybe she should get to know Mopsy better. A friend in the Department of Health would be good for her career. Then she thought about LuAnn and Sara, too. Maybe this trip had been worthwhile on a personal level. She needed women friends if she was going to survive in the men's world of law enforcement.

CHAPTER 12: Sara Is Stumped

Sara sat alone in a private office at the FBI building in Albuquerque. The room was equipped to receive and send encrypted messages whether by email, phone, or fax. Carbonne had rushed her to the room as soon as Pete dropped her at the front door. Then Carbonne had quickly briefed her on how to use the equipment but had asked no questions. He had winked at her when he left the room. "Tell Sanders that he doesn't appreciate you."

All the way from Santa Fe, she had thought about Sanders's message. First, she had tried to put it in context. At six this morning, Sanders had called—as he did most days at that time—and said, "I made the captain move our boat to the middle of the river so my satellite phone was clear of the jungle's canopy and could transmit this call. The captain resisted because he didn't want river pirates, illegal gold miners, and drug smugglers to notice our presence." Sanders had laughed. "I'm sure they've noticed us already." He had not mentioned these potential menaces on the three previous days of his jungle river trip.

She had thought Sanders's trip was suspicious when he announced a week ago that he would accompany several biologists studying amphibians in the upper reaches of the Amazon. Sanders wasn't interested in saving frogs from extinction. However, she had accepted his statement that as the chargé d'affaires of the U.S. embassy in Brasilia, he had to demonstrate the U.S. government's support of conservation efforts in the Amazon. She also knew despite Sanders's present title of chargé d'affaires, he was at heart a security officer, or as he preferred to be called, "an information specialist."

She had begun to analyze his words in their short conversation this afternoon as he spoke. He had used the words "worried" and "safe" almost immediately. It was their agreed upon codes to indicate the call was being monitored and his important message must remain secure, but he was not in danger. His reference to a "good luck charm" for his "secretary" probably meant several things. The words "luck" and "secretary" definitely meant Sara needed to go to the FBI building on Luecking Place in Albuquerque and transmit the message to his boss—an undersecretary in the State Department.

She was less sure about the rest of the message and hoped it would be clearer when she saw the fax he'd sent. She pressed the buttons as Carbonne had instructed. Slowly the printer on the fax churned out a picture of a yellow frog in dense green foliage.

Sara stared. *What was that supposed to mean?* She decided she didn't need to understand the whole message, but she needed to interpret any clues with her scientific knowledge and personal understanding of Sanders so that security experts at the State Department could decode the message. Mainly, she wished Sanders hadn't set up this elaborate scheme for transmitting secret information to his boss.

She thought this yellow frog might be a golden poison dart frog. Natives in the jungles of South America had used the poison in the skin of these rare frogs to poison hunting darts for hundreds of years. The poison was infamous among toxicologists because except for botulinum, it might be the most toxic natural compound known.

She consulted Wikipedia for key terms, as Sanders knew she always did at the start of her investigations. She'd been right. The frog in the faxed picture was the golden poison dart frog—*Phyllobates terribilis*. She was surprised to learn the frog was found in the Pacific jungles of Columbia, not in the Amazon jungle of Brazil. She doubted that Sanders and members of his group had wandered into Columbia. Perhaps Sanders had spied the movement of drugs from Columbia to Brazil.

The frog on the fax looked suspiciously similar to a frog pictured in Wikipedia. The only differences that Sara could see between the two pictures was the frog in the faxed picture had more black spots than the frog pictured in the Wikipedia entry for the golden poison dart frog. *Could Sanders have added the black spots to a copy of the Wikipedia photo?* She enlarged the spots on the faxed picture. One was too perfectly square and could be a QR code. She scanned the dark green and black background for QR codes, too. She faxed Sanders's picture to the undersecretary with a note:

> *Look for QR codes, especially in the black spots on the skin of this*
> *golden poison dart frog. The frog is found in the Pacific jungles of*
> *Columbia, not in the Amazon jungles of Brazil. The batrachotoxins*
> *in its skin are extremely potent.*
> *I'll think a bit and send more information and guesses later.*

Sara doubted embedded QR codes were the only messages in the photo. Sanders had sent *her* this message because she was a biologist and might catch clues that computer experts would miss. *What could they be?*

As she scanned research articles on the batrachotoxins, she remembered a silly discussion—one in which they played a brain-teasing game—that she'd had with Sanders before he went to Brazil. She had pointed out that lab situations couldn't always duplicate what occurred in a disease state or in the wild. She gave as an example the golden poison dart frogs. When scientists raised these frogs in the lab, their skins were not toxic to the touch as they were in the wild. It had taken scientists a while to learn the toxins in the frog's skin in the wild were derived from toxins in insects, that the frogs ate. Sanders had asked, "Does that mean the skin of these frogs could be made more toxic if they were fed more toxic beetles?"

She had answered, "I don't know, but I guess it's possible. However, if the beetles were more toxic, they might overpower the frog's protective systems and kill the frogs. It would take a lot of fancy chemistry to get an answer to your pretty esoteric question."

That had been one of those times when she realized their conversations weren't normal, but now wasn't the time to analyze Sanders's and her personal problems. It was time to focus on his clues. She decided Sanders wasn't into chemistry and delving further into the chemistry of the toxin was a waste of time. Perhaps she was overthinking the science in general. Golden might be the operative word. Perhaps Sanders had spotted gold miners along the river? Gold mining along the Amazon was banned, but reporting that illegal activity didn't require secure communications to his boss.

He'd use the word "gift." *Did that word have significance?* She googled Etsy. She couldn't believe that frogs made of gold were widely available as good luck charms. She doubted Sanders knew about these charms, but the breadth of his knowledge often surprised her.

Finally, she thought about the words "Carnival" and "sister in Boca." She guessed the fact that Carnival celebrations began today in Rio was significant. She doubted the undersecretary had a sister in Boca. She emailed the undersecretary:

I'm guessing something related to gold or drugs is going to happen in Boca Raton today or at least before Ash Wednesday, which is next Wednesday. That's Carnival time in Rio.

I'm sorry but I can't figure out the scientific significance of the golden frog. If it does have importance, it's related to the batrachotoxins in its skin. The toxins in their skin are derived from compounds in the beetles they eat. Sanders once asked me if the toxins in their skin could be made more toxic by making the beetles they eat more toxic. I don't know.

She left the secure room and found Carbonne. "I think Sanders overestimated my ability to decipher his clues this time. Don't repeat his mistake. Make your thoughts clear to Barbara this weekend. I sense she's overwhelmed by this case and needs your support—not as a boss but as a… husband."

Carbonne winced.

Sara didn't give him a chance to answer. "I'm too tired to be diplomatic. Do you realize how tough the mid-thirties are for a career woman who dreams of a family? You've got to listen to her now."

"Gotcha."

She smiled. "I'll take one problem off Barbara's shoulders and visit with Davita at her mother's bedside in the hospital before I go home to Bug."

"See 'ya at ten tomorrow."

***

Davita's red nose and eyes told her story well. "I think I'll scream if I have to listen much longer to the hisses from the ventilator as Mom lies here motionless."

"What did the doctors say?"

"There's no hope. Mom's brain dead, but I didn't want to turn off the ventilator until I talked to you." Davita sniffed. "Does the FBI think Mom is responsible for the poisoning of the thirty or more people who got sick?" Davita bowed her head. "Could those people sue her or her estate?"

Sara tried not to show her surprise at the last question. "I doubt it." She thought a second and decided it was unwise to share info with Davita. She was here to comfort Davita and to collect data. "Did your mom complain of feeling sick this week?'

"Mom's a hypochondriac. No cap—she complains of aches and pains daily."

"Did she complain more on Wednesday after the rally?"

Davita shrugged. "I didn't talk to her on Wednesday. After work, I was too busy helping my older daughter with her math homework and making cookies for my younger daughter to take to school for her birthday. I was supposed to pick up a birthday cake for my daughter after work on Thursday. Then my boss called a special meeting at our spa in Santa Fe at five. I had to leave that meeting when I got a call from the hospital."

Sara had a terrible thought. She tried to not show any emotions as she asked, "What's the name of your spa?"

"Green Way to Beauty Spa." Davita didn't take a breath before she continued with her story. "My sitter had to take over and celebrate my daughter's birthday with her on Thursday night because I was here at the hospital. An hour ago, the sitter quit."

Sara hated to ask the next question. "Did anyone from the spa contact you today?"

"No. Well, I ignored a call from the nurse at the spa that came in less than five minutes before you arrived. I couldn't face a new problem. I wanted to clear Mom's name before I turned off the ventilator."

Sara gulped. "I need to make a call."

Sara stepped away so that Davita couldn't hear her conversation. "Carbonne, I know I should call Barbara but she's not here. I'm with Davita at the hospital. Turns out, she's the manager of the Green Way to Beauty Spa in Santa Fe."

"What? Does she know…"

"She hasn't talked to anyone from the spa. I think we should question her about what happened at the meeting on Thursday before her answers are tainted by recent discoveries, but I'm not up to it alone. Barbara won't be back until tomorrow."

"Gotcha. I'll be at the intensive care unit in fifteen minutes."

"We may be in the waiting room outside the unit."

"Oh, before I forget. Your friend in Washington called. Your messages were helpful and filled several gaps."

"Why did she call you?"

"She didn't want to wake you because she assumed you were in bed, exhausted from your day. She agrees with me that Sanders doesn't appreciate you."

CHAPTER 13: Carbonne Starts a Weekend

Carbonne hated visiting intensive care units. The clicking noises and pulsating waves on screens in darkened cubicles reminded him of horror movies. A nurse pulled back the curtain to one bay to reveal a thirtyish, dark-haired woman stroking the ashen hand of a woman covered by equipment and a white sheet.

Sara reached over and touched the standing woman. "Davita, special agent Carbonne is in charge of the Albuquerque FBI office and can answer your questions better than I could."

Davita gave him a tired glance without letting go of her mother's hand. "Well?"

"Neither the FBI or local police will charge your mother with a crime." He thought of adding *even if she was alive* but decided the addition would be insensitive. "But our decision doesn't prevent lawsuits in civil courts."

Davita's head jerked.

"However, I think those are unlikely in this case."

Davita nodded.

Sara murmured, "I need to ask you a few more questions before you decide what to do. Did your mom mention any visitors during the last few days? Maybe a day or two before the rally?"

"Mom and I had a low-key relationship," Davita snapped. "Sometimes she ghosted me for days. I always figured we'd have time together after my girls were grown. Now I'm shook because that won't happen."

Carbonne stepped out of the cubicle and returned with a chair, which he shoved near Davita. "For you." He whispered into Sara's ear. "The nurses don't like three in an alcove but stopped complaining when I explained this was urgent FBI business. Make it quick."

"Odd, they never complained about Bug once I explained I was with the FBI."

"Bug's cuter than me. Get the show on the road."

Sara repeated her question to Davita. "Did your mom have any visitors in the last week?"

Davita sat down but kept stroking her mother's hand. "I'm tired. It's hard to remember anything, but she emailed me Tuesday that Nelson had stopped by to see her Monday afternoon. I guess he planned to take the preserves to the rally on Tuesday."

Carbonne felt suddenly alert. "We thought your mother attended the rally and brought the fig preserves."

Beryl's fingers twitched. Carbonne had been told this could occur in brain-dead individuals, but he still found it unnerving. He noticed the movement almost pleased Davita.

"I like to think she's trying to answer you." Davita smiled. "She said in her email that Nelson had made such a fuss over the preserves and tasting them that she'd changed her mind and was going to deliver them herself. I figured she wanted to *flex*."

Sara winked at Carbonne. He knew she was about to start a new series of questions.

"Has your boss been understanding? I imagine the spa in Santa Fe doesn't run itself when you're here with your mom."

"No cap."

Carbonne suspected Sara was finding Davita's slang hard to follow, but Sara was smart enough to not interrupt the flow of the conversation. She knew others would listen to the tape of this discussion.

"What's your boss's name? We could contact him or her to explain. Sometimes people behave better when they know they're speaking to the FBI."

"Dr. Abigail Fix Smith."

Carbonne choked back a chortle. "Fix is an odd name for a physician."

"She's weird enough to like it. I was told her dad was a fan of Jules Verne. Abigail Fix is a character in *Around the World in Eighty Days*. I guess that's why he named her brother Jules, after the author."

"So, is Jules around the spa a lot?"

"He's the GOAT. He softens his sister's commands."

"So, did Jules attend the meeting at the spa on Thursday?" When Davita didn't respond, Sara added. "The one Abigail called with you and Catalina?"

"Abigail said he was busy." Davita looked at Sara with tears in her eyes. "I think it's time. Mom's not coming back. My kids needs me. She doesn't anymore."

Sara gulped. "One more silly question. What did Catalina wear to the meeting?"

"Nothing dope. She wears mainly greens to match the décor of the spa… all the time."

"Do you want me to notify the nurses that you're ready to say goodbye? Your mom may die quickly after they turn off the ventilator or she may linger for hours."

"No cap. I just want to kiss her cheek before she goes."

***

Davita decided she wanted to be alone with her mother at the end. When Carbonne returned from the food court with colas, Sara said, "I stopped by Estella's alcove in the ICU. The doctor decided to bring her out of the induced coma and remove her from the ventilator this morning. So far, she's made no attempt to talk or communicate, but her brain appears to be functioning. Well, at least the monitors still show blips of activity in her brain."

Carbonne handed her a lidded plastic glass with a straw already inserted. "It isn't fair to question Davita more tonight."

"Agreed, but I think we have to tell Davita of Catalina's death. She'll lose her trust in us if she hears of the murder from others or on the news."

"Mmm. I guess I can talk to her as I drive her home to Corrales. Then you can get home to Bug."

***

Sara looked tired when she plodded into Carbonne's office with Bug on Saturday morning. "Sanders didn't have much to say when he called."

"Did he mention his message of yesterday afternoon?"

"No. He was still on the boat in the Amazon, and I suspect his communications are still being monitored. Would you mind if I update his boss using one of your secure computers?" Sara only stopped moving when she reached the door to the secure room behind Carbonne's office. "Will Barbara be joining us by phone?"

"No, she's interviewing the churchwomen and public health officials in Clovis. I don't want her distracted when she's driving."

"Coward."

"No, I didn't see any reason to upset her this morning."

"Or yourself." Sara closed the door behind her.

***

Fewer than five minutes later, Sara emerged. "I've been thinking. There is one weird way to explain the flukes in the lab results. What if

J. L. Greger

Beryl was lucky and there were no botulinum spores in her later batches of canned figs? So, no toxin was produced even though the pH was probably high enough to allow any spores present to germinate and grow?"

"But the jar in the refrigerator…"

Sara held up a hand. "I admit this is weird. What if Nelson, when he stopped by Beryl's house on Monday, added botulinum toxin to the opened jar before he returned it to Beryl's refrigerator? He had a source of the toxin. We found vials of botulinum toxin leftover from Botox parties in his house."

"That seems like an awfully complicated way to kill someone."

Sara arranged Bug's bed on the floor by the small table in Carbonne's office, turned on her laptop, and pulled out a pen and notepad. "I agree, but the technicians in your lab are seldom wrong."

"What did he have against Beryl?'

"Probably nothing. She was just collateral damage as he built the case that her canned figs were the source of the botulinum toxin."

"That's cold and will be hard to prove." Carbonne handed her a can of diet cola and popped the tab on his own can. "Let's get back to facts, not wild theories. I checked on Green Way to Beauty Spas, Inc. It's a family-held corporation with the others members of the board of directors being Abigail's brother, Jules, and father Verne, a lawyer in Abilene. The corporation has spas in Abilene, Lubbock, Santa Fe, and Albuquerque."

"Well, the good news is the corporation is involved in interstate commerce and that is firmly in the realm of the FBI." She stopped taking notes. "As you probably guessed, I had trouble understanding a few of Davita's comments last night. What is a GOAT?"

Carbonne laughed. He couldn't decide what was funnier—the way Sara's mind flipped between subjects or the way she still took notes with a pen and paper. She always had a laptop with her and was a real whiz at mining data with a computer.

"Greatest of All Time." He gulped his soda. "Davita's comments last night were surprising. For example, you found the clothes of a hooker at the murder scene in Santa Fe, but she described Catalina's clothes as…"

"I think a lot of women don—or maybe shed is a better word— colorful gear to turn on their boyfriends or husbands. However, you're right the clothes we found certainly were not green and sedate. I just had a weird thought. We haven't proven Catalina wore those clothes."

"I already thought of that and left a note for Winslow to look for Catalina's DNA on the clothes found on the staircase. Another long shot." Carbonne retrieved a laptop from his desk. "Pete suggested we look at the last five minutes of the security camera footage at the house."

Three images appeared on Carbonne's computer screen. Two showed no movement. A person, not as tall as Nelson at six-three and dressed all in black with a black knit stocking cap and mask entered Estella's house from the garage on the third screen. Less than two minutes later the tape ended.

"The police officer reviewing the tapes told me that the cameras could be controlled remotely. So, Nelson could have turned off the cameras without entering the house. That suggests it wasn't him."

Carbonne replayed the short segment of tape. "You're jumping to a conclusion. Anyone who knew the code could control the cameras remotely. Did you notice the individual swayed like a woman in high heels?"

"Not until you pointed it out. Perhaps the individual wore heels or elevator shoes to frame Nelson."

Carbonne shrugged. "Pete needs to analyze the tape more." He closed the screen. "We should interview Davita."

"She's probably busy with funeral arrangements."

"No, when I drove her home last night I convinced her to leave Beryl's body in the morgue until our investigations were closed. I was surprised how quickly she agreed."

"Perhaps she knows more than she admitted last night."

"That's why I arranged for us to be at her house at eleven." Carbonne stared at Bug. "He might as well come, too. He makes our questions seem friendlier."

"Shouldn't we let Barbara question her?"

"No, Barbara and I are taking tomorrow as a vacation day. We need it. And the longer Davita thinks, the less she'll be willing to say."

"You caught what I did. Davita doesn't trust her co-workers at the spa even though she tried to pretend they were best buds."

CHAPTER 14: Sara Tracks Suspects

Corrales is a rural village with a split personality along the Rio Grande River within the Albuquerque metropolitan area. The one downtown street is flanked by artists' galleries, trendy restaurants, and a feed store.

The homes fall mainly into two categories—modern million-dollar mansions on fairly small lots and old adobes often on old Spanish land grants. The latter often include orchards, vineyards, and pens for animals—donkeys, horses, goats, llamas, sheep, pigs, and chickens. There are no codes to prevent keeping livestock on residential properties in Corrales. The adobes from the outside are in various stages of decay. Many like Beryl's have been modernized while retaining a historic air on the exterior. Others might be described kindly as "cozy" with bathrooms and kitchens reflecting the 1950s or earlier. Davita's home fell into the last category.

Sara tried not to cringe when she stepped on the old brown tile floor. She watched her feet, so as to not trip, as Davita led Carbonne and her through the living room and kitchen to the long wooden table in the dining room. The floors in the rooms were at slightly different levels and all seemed to roll a bit. The house reeked even though it appeared clean. Bug must have noticed the smell too because he seemed to pull on the leash and tried to explore corners.

"We know this is a hard time for you and appreciate that you agreed to answer a few more questions." Carbonne pulled a chair at the head of the table for Davita.

Davita hesitated and then fluttered her eyelids as she sat.

"Although we still think your mother's death was an accident due to improperly canned food, we think if we better understand the characters involved in preparing for the rally in Clovis that we may gain clues for the murder of Catalina Herrera in Santa Fe. Thus, Sara and I may ask you seemingly strange questions. Please be patient. We both sympathize with you for your loss." He nodded to Sara.

Sara was glad Carbonne made the introductory remarks because it gave her time to settle Bug on the chair next to her. She was afraid what he might find if he explored this musty house. She had also noted Davita had made no attempt to pet or greet him. So much for idea that Bug might relax Davita. Sara decided to get down to business immediately. "We'd like to learn about the Botox parties your spa ran. Who came up with the idea for these parties?"

As Davita shifted in her chair and peered past Sara, it creaked. "We don't have Botox parties. We conduct beauty workshops in homes of clients. It's a straight fire way to offer our customers quality products at a reduced cost because there's no wastage of supplies. Clients compete to have the workshops at their homes because we offer several products at reduced cost to the host or hostess." She frowned. "I guess Jules first mentioned the idea of doing demos in homes after he participated in an event in California, but we've all contributed suggestions to improve them."

Carbonne shoved his laptop toward Sara. Her perception that Davita was delivering a memorized statement was confirmed when she looked at the mission statement on the Green Way to Beauty Spa's website. "How long have you been doing these workshops?"

"I guess for a year, or so. Each store can only manage two a month." Davita again appeared to peer past Sara.

"Where and when was the last event?"

"At Jules's condo in Albuquerque a couple of days before the rally. It was smaller than most of our events in Santa Fe, perhaps because only men were invited. Ten attended. Then too, I've developed our clientele more in Santa Fe than Catalina has… I mean *had*." She wiped a tissue across her eyes even though Sara had not noticed tears. "We were supposed to hold one at Estella's house next week." She twisted her mouth. "That'll have to be cancelled now. Too bad, it would have been well attended."

Sara thought the loss of business bothered Davita more that the loss of her co-worker or illness of a client. She made a mental note to explore that later. "I think I can see these events are great ways to flex your products." She hoped she'd use the word *flex* properly. "Why did Abigail call a meeting at your spa in Santa Fe at five on Thursday?"

Before she replied, Davita again stared at something past Sara. This time Sara turned to see what was distracting Davita. A wooden kitchen clock was mounted above the entrance to a short, empty hallway.

"When Abigail comes to town from Lubbock, she expects us to be ready to meet with her. Usually, we meet at eight on Wednesday

　　　　　　　　　　　　　　　　　　　J. L. Greger

morning in Albuquerque before her clinic appointments there, but we couldn't because Catalina had booked a business trip to San Diego on Tuesday and Wednesday." Her voice became higher, and she spoke more rapidly. "We're thinking about putting our super new face cream in a hot new green jar. We saw ones that looked like urns online, but we wanted them decorated with a little silver or gold. Abigail wanted to see examples of the new jars that Catalina brought back from San Diego as well as to check on the new herbs Catalina had purchased at Chinese markets there."

Sara noticed that Carbonne looked like he'd explode in laughter. She hoped Davita didn't notice. "Did you like the jars that Catalina found?'

"The pictures of the jars were better than the real thing. That's why the meeting dragged on. None of us were satisfied. I got the call from the hospital about Mom at six and left. I don't know when Abigail and Catalina locked up the spa and left."

"Is it likely Abigail and Catalina went to dinner afterwards?"

"Doubt it. Abigail doesn't socialize much with us employees. She usually stays at her bro's condo in Albuquerque and pals with him." She contorted her mouth again. "At least that's what she tells me."

"Do you feel Abigail treated Catalina better than you?"

"No, I wouldn't say that… but I might think it."

"Do you know why? You said more clients attended spa events in Santa Fe than in Albuquerque."

Davita sighed, "I have two kids. I don't have time to party with male clients."

"What do you mean?'

"Are you about done? I have to pick up my younger daughter from soccer."

Carbonne leaned forward. "Here's my card. Sara and I both think you know or suspect problems in the Green Way to Beauty Spa organization. It could be dangerous for you to wait too long to tell us all you know."

***

Carbonne put the car in gear as soon as Sara had locked Bug into his carrier in the back seat. The car was moving down the short driveway before Sara fastened her seat belt. "What's your hurry?" When he didn't respond, Sara said, "There's something odd about the Green Way to Beauty Spas. Both Winslow and I felt pressured in the Santa Fe spa. I could feel tension in Davita's answers. With enough time I could have gotten more information."

"Doubt it. After she made several suspicious comments last night when I drove her home, I asked Pete to snoop in her bank accounts."

"Is she broke?"

"Quite the contrary. I think she's found other sources of funds besides her job. She has deposited large amounts of cash—a thousand or two dollars at a time—into her accounts two or three times a month during the last year."

"Cash, not checks?"

"Yes. Last night, I had the feeling she expected to be getting a lot more money than just her inheritance from her mother soon. She spoke of buying a franchise of the Green Way to Beauty Spa."

"What?"

"If she hasn't already, she's going to approach someone for money."

"She certainly was watching the clock this morning. I don't think most parents are that tense about picking up their children from soccer games on time."

"Agreed. We're going to park a block away and wait a while. Trouble is I'm too short of agents to put a tail on her."

Sara bit her lip. She'd up to now thought of Davita as a victim. However, she'd noticed Davita's voice sounded sharper—more determined—this morning than it had last night. Sara had assumed Davita was over the shock of her mother's death and had thought of the implications for her family. As she watched Carbonne staring down the road at Davita's lane, she realized Carbonne might be right.

"Hell, I'll assign my rookie to watch her for the next two hours. That's all I can do."

***

"I'm glad I decided to work today. No one was here to bother me." Pete didn't look up as Sara and Carbonne entered the computer workroom. "I know Sara likes printouts better than staring at a screen. Look at the ones on the table as I check the phone records."

"We brought you a Big Mac." Sara handed the sandwich to Pete and then applied catsup to her own sandwich. She carefully pulled off several pieces of meat and gave them to Bug before she began to eat.

By then, Carbonne was almost through with his burger and was texting rapidly. He glanced at Bug as he sniffed the pieces of meat. "Wouldn't Bug like the meat better without catsup?"

J. L. Greger

"No, he's a connoisseur and likes catsup or mayonnaise, not mustard, on his meat." Sara pulled a two-page section of printout to study as she ate.

Pete whistled. "That's the quietest I've ever seen you two." He printed a few pages and joined them at the table. "I'm ready when you are."

"Start with anything that might help us to understand Nelson and locate him." Carbonne scowled. "We would have heard from kidnappers by now if they wanted a ransom. That means he's either dead or really doesn't want to be found."

"I think he doesn't want to be found." Sara shook her head. "I know everyone thinks I hallucinated yesterday, but the tall stranger that Winslow and I saw looked like Nelson."

"Winslow was sure too, but he's still a kid dreaming of adventure. Perhaps what I found on Nelson's home computer will help. He had an appointment at one on Tuesday with a publisher in San Diego. I found a copy of a manuscript entitled *The Past Meets the Future in New Mexico* on his computer." Pete tinkered with a laptop and turned the screen for Carbonne and Sara to see. "I like to play with photography but Nelson is a real pro. In the preface to the book, Nelson claimed all the black and white shots of modern scenes are his, but he staged them to be reminiscent of Ansel Adams's famous photos. For example, he starts a section called 'Rags to Riches' with the famous Ansel Adams's photo *Moonrise over Hernandez, New Mexico*." It's followed by pictures showing ramshackle adobe stores and homes in nearby Española and photos of austere modern buildings at Los Alamos National Lab. The most amazing shot is called *Moonrise over Walmart in Española*."

Sara perused a table of statistics comparing Los Alamos and Española. There were facts and figures about the poverty and poor schools in Española and the wealth and award-winning schools in nearby Los Alamos. "I can't believe this is the work of the shallow womanizer described by others." She read sections of the text aloud. "This man is a crusader for political change."

"Wait until you see the chapter on 'Arts in New Mexico' with old and modern shots of Native Americans throwing pots and weaving rugs. He advertises Estella and her galleries a bit in this section."

Carbonne nodded. "Nelson appears to be a smart businessman and lobbyist, as well as a skilled photographer. This manuscript would be great publicity for Estella's businesses and political ambitions. I also see now why Barbara considered Estella to be a friend to the pueblos and their people."

"I saved the best for last. The chapter entitled 'Honoring and Degrading Nature' starts with copies of a couple of Georgia O'Keefe's paintings and goes on to shots of uranium mines and fracking operations in New Mexico."

Sara stared in amazement as she examined a technical diagram explaining fracking next to an artistic photo of an oil drilling rig against a purple and rose sky at sunset. "Surely, the editor was eager to publish this manuscript."

Pete smiled. "I found an email from the editor after the meeting. The addendum was a signed contract. The editor promised to put the book on a fast track with publication before the November elections."

"I had the impression that Nelson was jealous of Estella and wanted a political career of his own. Yet, he featured her in at least one section of the manuscript. Did you find any correspondence between them?" Sara pulled Bug onto her lap to cuddle.

"Not on his computer, but I haven't perused his computer trash files much yet. On Estella's computer, I found an email from Nelson at four on Tuesday." Pete fiddled with his computer and then read from the screen:

> *Dear Estella.*
> *The book will be published in October and should bolster*
> *your senatorial campaign if we get through the primaries.*
> *Good luck tonight.*
> *Nelson*

"The note might not be lovey-dovey, but he seems supportive of her."

"You've convinced me that Nelson is a much more complicated individual than Jules and Davita suggested." Sara cleared the table of debris from lunch.

"Agreed." Carbonne didn't look up as he scanned his phone. "Barbara got an update from the police in San Diego. It seems a clerk at the desk of the hotel where Catalina Herrera stayed recognized a photo of Nelson Davis. He was with Catalina on Wednesday morning. The clerk remembered because Catalina was a frequent visitor at the hotel and the hotel keeps records on their frequent visitors. Seems Catalina usually paid with a credit card issued to the Green Way to Beauty Spa, was always alone, always asked for only one key to her room, and usually ordered room service for dinner. Her room service order for last Tuesday at seven p.m. was enough to feed two."

"Well, we know Nelson was still alive on Wednesday morning and may have eaten dinner with Catalina the night before." Sara frowned. "But why didn't he bother to check out of his hotel?"

Barbara got a couple of emails this morning that might give us insights," said Carbonne. "Catalina picked up a car at the San Diego airport at seven on Wednesday. Hertz staff at the Albuquerque airport found it at six when they opened on Thursday. That's distance of about 770 miles but the odometer indicated she'd driven the car 910 miles." Carbonne stood. "I've got administrative paperwork to handle. The rest is up to you."

***

After Carbonne was out of earshot Sara said, "He's certainly growing into the role of being the boss. He's much more authoritarian now."

"Some of the agents have given him a hard time but the lab crew and analysts love him because he's forcing agents to give us more respect." Then he grabbed the pages that Carbonne had studied. "These are the printouts on Catalina's credit cards. Look at the last four entries. She bought gas in Phoenix at one on Wednesday afternoon, in Gallup at eight on Wednesday evening, and in Albuquerque at five on Thursday morning."

Sara began to scribble calculations on a page. "That means she— actually I'll assume Nelson was with her—drove straight from San Diego to Phoenix with minimal stops. The distance from San Diego to Phoenix is longer than the distance from Phoenix to Gallup, but their gas bill was higher for the second leg of their trip. She appears to have bought enough gas in Albuquerque to be able to return the rental car with a full tank. The bill is less than half the previous bills."

"You're thinking they added 140 miles to their trip between Phoenix and Gallup?"

"Actually, I think they went somewhere within sixty-five miles of Gallup on a side trip."

"Why?"

"Just a hunch because so many of the pictures in Nelson's book appear to have been taken in Gallup and on Native American lands. And his book is on New Mexico, not Arizona." Sara picked up another page of printout from the table. "I know you printed this out to please me, but it makes no sense to me without headings."

"It's a record of where calls from Catalina's and Nelson's phones were received and sent—or at least the nearest tower to where they were received and sent—during the last week. Catalina didn't use her cell phones on Wednesday. She initiated two calls from Albuquerque to the Gallup area around five and seven on Thursday morning. Both of them were to the same number, but it's not the number for Nelson's cell phone. Appears to be to a burner phone. The towers routing the call were near her apartment and near the Hampton Motel in Gallup."

"Does that suggest a third party was involved? Is it possible Catalina was involved in kidnapping Nelson?"

Pete shrugged. "Nelson's cell phone was turned off on Wednesday morning in San Diego and hasn't been turned on since. He or someone didn't want his activities monitored." He pointed to the sheet again. "Note Catalina called one number three times later on Thursday in Albuquerque by the courthouse but made no other calls on her phone."

"Maybe that was her co-conspirator?"

Pete shrugged. "Could be. He or she will be hard to identify if the phone was a burner."

Sara nodded. "I need a break from numbers. Bug and I are going to visit Estella next. The doctors took her off the ventilator yesterday. So in theory, she should be able to communicate, but last night she just lay there with her eyes open and her face like a mask. Eerie." Sara trembled slightly. "The doctors say that's to be expected because the botulinum toxin had paralyzed the muscles in her tongue and face. I thought she moved her hands slightly when I massaged them, but she made no noises. I expected her to grunt because the doctors do not think the botulinum affected the muscles in her throat and torso. At least she swallows and breathes normally."

"Sounds ugly."

"I'm hoping she'll respond to Bug today. These cases would be a lot easier to solve if we had her input."

CHAPTER 15: Carbonne Is Challenged

Barbara stood flanked by the doorway. Her long black hair was loose. Her rose knit top and black leggings nicely showed her assets. Carbonne was surprised she wasn't in her work uniform of a black suit with her hair braided and piled on her head. He studied her. The worry lines on her forehead weren't apparent and she seemed relaxed as she cocked one hip.

"Did you enjoy your trip? Was it more successful than your call last night indicated?"

Barbara smiled, closed the door, and sashayed toward him. She put her arms around his neck and began to nibble at his lips.

He wasn't going to miss this opportunity and nibbled only briefly at her lips before he thrust his tongue into her mouth and pulled her closer. His desk had only a few pages on it. Sara had left for the hospital already, and no one in the late Saturday afternoon skeleton crew on duty, except Pete, was apt to want to talk to him. They were too busy.

He lifted her and laid her on his desk and began to pull her leggings down. Instead of resisting as she usually did when he tried to be amorous at work, she sighed deeply, and lifted her hips. He pulled her leggings off. Darn things looked great but were hard to remove. He unzipped and was ready to act.

A knock on the door.

"Damn," he whispered. Barbara had pushed herself off the desk before he yelled, "Just a minute."

He readjusted his clothes. Barbara crawled holding her leggings in her teeth to the adjoining secretary's office. He straightened his desk as he yelled, "Come in."

Pete looked around the office and must have spied Barbara in the secretary's office and gave a broad grin. "I think Barbara will find my new stuff interesting…" He winked at Barbara as she chose a seat at the large table in Carbonne's office. "…but not as much fun as what you were sharing with her."

Carbonne saw an attractive pink glow appear on Barbara's cheeks and decided to get Pete to focus on him and not Barbara for a moment. "Why don't you pull up a chair to my desk?"

"Barbara emailed me from Clovis three hours ago and asked me to locate all the properties that Estella and/or Nelson owned." He slid a printout across the desk to Carbonne. "Estella's quite a rich lady and she doesn't share any of it—at least the real estate—with Nelson. I circled a property that caught my eye. After you noted that Catalina drove an extra 140 miles, Sara and I figured they must have gone somewhere fewer than sixty-five miles from Gallup."

"How?'"

"Sara's calculations and intuition. Doesn't matter. Estella owns a duplex in Crownpoint. She rents one side out. Sara made a call from the hospital."

"What! Is she ill?"

"No. She was holding Estella's hand and thought she might as well call the renters. Anyway, the renters said Estella used the other side of the duplex when she came to monthly rug auctions in Crownpoint and Nelson occasionally used it as a base when he was doing photo shoots"

Carbonne groaned. "Remind me why she made the call."

"The round trip from Gallup to that duplex is about 130 miles. The only problem with our theory is the renter didn't admit to seeing Nelson or anyone at the duplex last Wednesday or Thursday. Sara would like you to request the resident agent in Farmington to check the duplex tonight or tomorrow morning. She thought the renters were beholden to Estella and doubted they would disclose anything bad about Estella or Nelson unless facing a stern-looking agent."

Carbonne stared at Barbara. "Why did you think to have Estella's property holdings checked?"

"Over dinner at the House of Joy last night, Bo McCarran relaxed and added to one of the stories LuAnn was telling me about Estella. It seems, his parents and Estella's mother had neighboring cabins in Chama." Barbara pulled her chair from the table to the desk. "I wondered whether Estella might own other properties and asked Pete to check."

"Oh, you didn't mention that last night on the phone." He decided to tease Barbara a bit. Maybe she'd get that rosy glow again. "Do you mind if I call the agents in Farmington, or do you want to check out the duplex near Crownpoint yourself?"

He placed the call as Barbara glared at him. "You are not funny."

After the quick call, Carbonne asked, "Do either of you have any other surprises for me?"

                                    J. L. Greger

Pete eyed Barbara. "I couldn't act on your other request."

"And?" Carbonne looked between Barbara and Pete. "I don't know about you two, but I'd like to call it a day. I'm not up to guessing games."

Barbara smiled. "Again, my casual conversations in Clovis proved useful. The churchwomen agreed to cater food for Estella's rally because they respected Estella. They felt they might not agree with all her political positions, but they never doubted that she worked for the good of small businesses like theirs. Then too, Nelson had called them and promised to take their photos at the rally. They evidently thought it would be fun to be photographed by a famous photographer."

"Are you going somewhere with this?"

Barbara flushed. "The women said that they couldn't say no to Jules because he was so charming."

"What does that mean? Would you call me charming?"

Barbara winced. "They noted Jules always gave each of them a compliment on their appearance. For example, 'Your pink blouse gives your face a rosy glow.'"

"Dumb stuff."

"We women like little, thoughtful comments."

Carbonne winked. "You mean like, 'Your hair looks sexy now because it's not combed.'"

Barbara's jaw tightened. "One of the woman ran to catch up with me as I was leaving. She started her comments by saying, 'We were all raised to believe if you can't say something nice, don't say anything. And that's easy when it comes to Estella, but I think it might not be honest when it comes to Jules.'"

Carbonne sighed, "I think I'll like this."

Barbara frowned. "She heard Jules tell Estella before the rally, 'Do not eat like a pig. I'm tired of Nelson yelling when you gain weight.' She remembered his words because she was shocked."

"Is that it?"

"As they were cleaning up after the rally, she overheard Jules say on the phone, 'I did my part. Now do yours.' She said Jules scowled when he saw her and walked away rapidly."

"I'd like to know who he was talking to." Carbonne looked at Pete. "Maybe you can check on that?"

"Barbara already ordered me to check all of Jules's calls during the last week, but I didn't get it done." Pete winked at Barbara. "You know she's the one officially in charge of this case." He stood. "I think I'll leave before you give me more instructions. Remember I won't be in on Monday."

***

After Pete left, Barbara remained seated. "Now it is my time to ask questions. Why did you take a risk for Sanders yesterday?"

Carbonne had stood and was organizing papers on his desk. "What do you mean? I told you it was cleared at a high level."

"Yes, but I also know you idolize him."

"I wouldn't say that, but I respect him. I also know he can be ruthless when cornered or angry."

Barbara frowned. "Do not give me your pat answer that you worked for him in Cuba. I know that. This is more complex."

"Give me a break. If we're going to argue, give me your specific gripes. "

"You only use your last name. I think you are imitating him. I do not know his first name, but yours is a perfectly acceptable one—Paul."

"Hmm. I guess that's true. But you don't understand. Sanders's security clearance is off the charts."

"But he is a chargé d'affaires now, not a security officer."

"A leopard doesn't change his spots. I don't know—and I don't want to know—what he's looking for in Brazil. I don't think Sara even wants to know the details, and she's no slouch when it comes to risky behavior."

"Are you sure about Sara?"

"Yes. It's not like her to leave early. She did today because she was stressed."

"I thought she went to see Estella."

"Sara's vigils at the bedsides of the dying are morbid, but I guess it's her way of taking time to think."

Barbara stood and walked toward the door. "That is a pretty cavalier way to speak about her. Would you say that about a male agent? Sitting alone with an unresponsive patient is never pleasant."

He followed her and laid his hand on her shoulder. "I'm sorry for all the wrong things I've said and done. Sara and Pete have both reminded me today that I shouldn't butt into your cases. It's hard. Not because I doubt your abilities but because I hate to see you struggle if I can prevent it. I don't want you to be like me or Sara. We've both fought too many battles without adequate backup, and it shows. We've lost our ability…."

Barbara turned and kissed him on the cheek. "I think Sara would say that you are still a young man in your thirties and should do what young men do—raise a family."

  J. L. Greger

He pushed her away. "Is that what you want most from me? Kids?"

"Not exactly." She bit her lip. "I want to create a loving family with you now and not wait until it's too late."

CHAPTER 16: Sara Believes Too Much on Monday

Sara and Bug breezed into the ICU on Monday at seven-thirty. She waved at the aide at the desk. "I figure Estella deserves at least one visitor daily."

The young woman shook her head. "Actually, she gets two visitors most days. A tall man in surgical scrubs usually stops by around two."

Sara was stunned. She wanted to yell, *Why didn't you mention this mystery man before?* Instead, she went into Estella's alcove and grabbed her hand. She had no one to be annoyed with but herself. The staff in the ICU had not been asked to specifically monitor Estella's visitors. She hadn't signed the roster in the ICU when she visited and suspected no one in scrubs would have been asked to sign in.

After a couple of minutes, Sara felt calm enough to approach the aide. "Can you describe the man in scrubs who visits Estella?"

The aide shrugged. "Tall, brown hair, clean shaven, middle aged."

Sara flashed a photo of Nelson Davis on her phone. "Could this be the man if he shaved?"

"I'm not sure."

"May I speak to your supervisor?"

***

About ten, Barbara strolled into Sara's office. "I need a Bug break. I feel calmer when I pet him."

"That's why I keep him with me whenever possible. We comfort each other." She watched Barbara. "I don't want to know details, but did you have the talk with Carbonne? And was the dinner afterwards romantic?"

"Partially and yes."

Sara nodded. "Good. What's gone wrong today?"

"I was embarrassed to learn while I searched the whole Southwest for Nelson Davis, he was only a couple of miles from my office at University Hospital. Do you realize the jokes that must be circulating in this building?"

"Nonsense. The only thing that's important now is to catch Estella's visitor today."

"I guess."

"But don't get your hopes too high. It might not be Nelson. Remember I thought I spotted him in Santa Fe last Friday. And as we found out, lots of people like Estella. I know Carbonne thinks my visits to victims and suspects in the hospital are silly and morbid."

"How did you know that?"

His face gives him away. He looks like a scared jackrabbit when he enters a hospital room. But he's wrong on two counts. I'm not the only person who visits hospital patients. And he's not spent enough sick time in a hospital bed to appreciate the loneliness. That's one of the limits of most healthy young men."

"I guess." Barbara didn't even look up from petting Bug.

Sara decided to focus Barbara on the positive. "I talked to FDA officials. The FDA has received several complaints about the Green Way to Beauty Spa's Botox parties." Sara stopped. "I know you think that's my slang term but that's the jargon the FDA official used. Evidently, two women claimed they'd been cheated because their lips lost their plumpness one day after the injection." Sara shook her head. "I must say I never thought big pouting lips were attractive on anyone but Brigitte Bardot and nymphets under twenty."

Sara decided Barbara must be depressed. She didn't laugh at the joke. "Maybe this will brighten your day. My FDA contact hinted he'd be willing to audit the Green Way to Beauty Spas in Albuquerque and Santa Fe. He'd crosscheck their inventory of botulinum products against their filed reports if we made an official request. So, I filed a request. Carbonne signed off because you were at a meeting with Mopsy." Sara didn't take a breath. "How did that go?"

Barbara looked up. "I was wrong about her. Her son's cancer is incurable. Her asthma is getting worse." She petted Bug. "I never would have made so many demands on her if I knew."

"Did she complain?"

"No. She thanked me for my patience."

"Stop thinking *if only I knew*. That's what makes research—scientific and criminal—interesting. The ground rules change daily as you gain more info."

Sara's phone rang. After listening for a minute, she said, "Barbara is in my office now. Let's do a video conference." She pressed several buttons and waited. When images of a man and a woman in a small room appeared on the screen of her computer, Sara introduced Barbara to Ezra Benson, the FBI agent in residence in Lubbock, and Abigail Fix Smith.

Ezra Benson, a fortyish Texan, spoke first. "Dr. Smith has never been questioned by the police before. She's a little shy, but she wants to be helpful."

Sara scratched a note on paper and slid it to Barbara, who nodded.

"Dr. Smith, first we want to learn about your meeting with Davita and Catalina last Thursday at five in Santa Fe. Davita intimated on Saturday to Special Agent Carbonne and me that it focused on little green jars for a new beauty cream."

Abigail a pale, thin woman with her hair pulled severely back from her face snorted. "No way. We discussed the jars but the real reason for the meeting was I wanted to know how we lost a shipment of Botox. I suspected that either Davita and/or Catalina with my brother's encouragement had conducted more home beauty workshops than they admitted. That's a problem. If the FDA discovered that anyone but me, as a physician, or the nurses at our spas injected the botulinum products into patients, I could lose my license. Neither nurse has claimed overtime pay during the last month. We arrange their schedules so that they each do only two home events per month."

"Let me be sure I understand. Are you suggesting your and the nurses' time is the limiting factor for how many home events the spas can conduct?"

"Yes to a certain extent. I also think these home events are… tawdry. Sara, Agent Benson indicated you were a scientist. You understand Botox is not a toy. It can give huge relief to patients with a variety of painful spasms in the neck and mouth. Many patients suffering from frequent migraines swear it reduces their number of unproductive days. Those injections are medical treatments and are my highest priority. My brother convinced my father that making injections through the Green Way to Beauty Spas would appeal to those patients because we could provide treatments at convenient times in the early evenings and on weekends."

Sara had noticed two things as the physician spoke. Abigail's voice became enthusiastic as she spoke of the medical benefits of botulinum products, like Botox. Sara guessed Abigail enjoyed being a physician. Second, it appeared Abigail had taken her own medical advice seriously. Her complexion was smooth and pale probably because she rarely sought a tan. Her chin line was taut and her bare arms appeared to be toned when she took off her navy suit jacket. In general, Abigail appeared to be the opposite of her brother. She was thin and disciplined; he was prone to paunchiness. Sara guessed their personalities were as dissimilar as their looks. "Did you have other objections to the home events?"

"My brother is always desperate for money. He fritters it away on clothes, beauty routines, and God knows what else. I think it's his way of compensating for being short. My parents always excused his bad behavior as teen because they felt guilty that they hadn't taken him to a pediatric endocrinologist until he was twelve. By then, there were limits to what could be done to increase his height."

"Why is your brother's need for cash to maintain his lifestyle important?"

Abigail snorted. "I don't think you understand the amount of money that can be made at a single home event. We charge several hundred dollars for a single treatment of Botox in the clinic. It costs us about one-third less to deliver the same treatment at a home event. Thus, we charge less for procedures at these home events than at the clinic, but most women decide to get two or three different treatments at the events. They fix the crow's feet around their eyes and the laugh lines around their mouths as well as the worry lines on their foreheads. Many decide to plump their lips."

"What causes them to suddenly decide their faces need so many fixes?"

Abigail snorted. "You don't realize how clever my brother is as a salesman. He makes sure there's plenty of rich savories and desserts at the events. He tells the women that the Botox is available at a sale price. They'll regret missing this opportunity for savings. And he has trained Catalina and Davita in his sales techniques."

"Have you attended many of these events?"

"Only two. It's disgusting to see the feeding frenzy among the women."

"Then why do you allow these events?'

"You don't understand. The Green Way to Beauty Spa is a family corporation with three people on the board. My father and brother often outvote me. Moreover, the income from these events is significant. The average woman at one of our home events spends seven hundred dollars.

We don't run a party for fewer than ten participants. Our costs are reduced because there's no wastage of unused, diluted Botox. A home event in four hours usually nets more profit than two days of clinic procedures because of the clinics' high overheads."

Sara wanted to explore Jules's motivation, other than greed, for potentially stealing a case of Botox. "Is it possible that Jules gave the missing Botox to someone who threatened him?"

Abigail jaw dropped. "I don't understand your question, and you don't understand my brother. He's a scam artist at heart. If the spas fail, he'll move on." She sniffed. "But I could lose my medical license as well as my investment in the spas. Jules has nothing to lose."

Sara guessed the siblings didn't like each other and felt sure that Abigail's statement was biased. "So, who actually runs the spas? Technically as president of the Board, you are responsible."

"I know it looks bad for me, but Jules runs the spas. And… now I'm stuck." She announced forcefully, "I'm tired of being stuck. I'll cooperate with the FBI in their investigations as long as you guarantee I won't lose my medical licenses. So far, I know nothing but I am suspicious."

Sara whispered to Barbara, "Her request is reasonable, but we can't speak for the FDA or state medical boards."

Barbara stopped scanning items on her phone. "We have already requested the participation of the FDA in this case and will forward the tapes of this conversation to them. I see no reason why they and state medical board will not accept the explanations you provide, but we all will expect your full cooperation."

"That's what I expected. I should have contacted the police after my meeting last Thursday but didn't know where to start." Abigail sniffed and wiped tears from her eyes.

Sara understand Abigail's predicament. "I personally can't blame you for not immediately reporting your suspicions to police. It's taken me four days to get to you. So, let's gather a few more facts about the meeting last Thursday."

Abigail spoke in a monotone for at least fifteen minutes. Her comments could be summed up simply. Catalina was scared by Abigail's accusations that a case of Botox was missing. Davita was hostile. After Davita left in response to the call from University Hospital, Catalina quickly agreed to check the inventory at the Albuquerque spa herself.

After Abigail had wound down, Barbara asked, "What did you and Catalina do after the meeting?"

　　　　　　　　　　　　　　　　　　　　J. L. Greger

"We had a light supper. I don't know what Catalina did, but I drove to my brother's condo in Albuquerque. He wasn't home and I went to bed. I also don't know when he got in, but he was asleep the next morning when I went to the Albuquerque clinic."

"Did you know Davita's mother, Beryl Marks?'

"I gave her Botox injections for the lines around her eyes. She seemed pleasant enough and was a real fan of Estella Garcia Davis. That's all she ever talked about."

Barbara pointed to the time on Sara's computer. "I think that's all for now. Please do not mention this conversation to anyone including your family and employees. If anyone makes a comment or suggests knowledge of this discussion, call us immediately no matter the hour. Thank you."

Agent Benson called from his car about five minutes after the video conference ended. "Physicians often react negatively to being questioned by the FBI. They think their authority is being challenged. Colleagues had warned me that Abigail was competent, almost too conscientious, and reserved to the point of being taciturn. I was ready for the worst, but I think she liked being interviewed by a scientist. I think her ex-husband's comment sums up her situation. 'She hates her overbearing father and loser brother but doesn't have the guts to sever ties with them.'"

***

"No good news." Barbara scrutinized her phone. "I've been waiting for a call or letter from an FBI office in Washington, but it has not come. Worse still, no visitors have stopped by Estella's cubicle in the ICU this morning."

"We've got to be patient."

"Tell that to Hank. He thinks I have not told him all the details of the case. Winslow wants to explain his new lab results to me." She smiled at Sara. "You can give Winslow better feedback than I can. Then I will have time to discover whether the rookie who tailed Davita for two hours on Saturday learned anything. His report was pretty skimpy." Barbara sighed. "It sure looks like another dead-end."

"Maybe not, if we put a bit of pressure on Davita."

"How?'"

"We'll forget about being nice ladies and bluff like swaggering male agents." Sara dialed the work number Davita had given her on Saturday. "Davita, I hate to bother you as you grieve your mother's death, but the FDA is sending an audit team to the Santa Fe spa tomorrow. Have your books ready for inspection by noon.”

“They can’t come tomorrow.”

“You don’t have a choice.” Sara hung up.

Barbara stared at Sara. “You were awfully aggressive. She might try to destroy records”

“I’m hoping she does attempt to doctor the books because that would be an admission of guilt. I know Pete can find anything deleted from the spa’s computers.”

CHAPTER 17: Sara Scores in the ICU

"I was eager to get to work today because this case—or maybe I should say *cases*—is so weird." Winslow motioned Sara to a small table in the lab with two stools. "These results blew my mind." He adjusted his laptop screen to show a summary. "There is none of Catalina's DNA on the coat, skirt, boots, or teddy." He stared at Sara. "Think about it. I could see how the skirt and coat might have so many different DNA samples that we couldn't locate Catalina's snippets, but the underwear, no way."

"Are you sure?"

"I made the tech repeat her analyses. The amount of DNA on the teddy suggested it had never been worn by anyone." He shook his head. "Such a waste."

Sara thought it best not to let Winslow expand the discussion of his fantasies. "That might not be weird. At least two people have told me that Catalina dressed conservatively. The clothes we found on the stairs were not conservative, but I figured she was trying to excite her lover. Maybe I was wrong, and…."

"The scene on the stairs was staged. That means her murder was premeditated, and…."

"That suggests the murderer wanted to keep Catalina quiet."

Winslow nodded as he fiddled with his laptop. "On to the next topic. I ordered the microbiologist on Friday to send samples of the fig preserves from Beryl's house to the Department of Health's lab. They do more food analyses than we do, and our results were weird. The lab boss also had the microbiologist re-examine the samples under a microscope. Both labs agree—there were no botulinum spores in the figs, even though the open jar of figs in the refrigerator had botulinum toxin."

"Can you do phenotype analyses of the toxin in the opened jar?"

Winslow winked at her. "You're like a dog with a bone. You really think the toxin was added later to the open jar, don't you?"

Sara shrugged. "This is a weird case and the spas have botulinum products."

"We already did the analyses. All the toxin is the type A phenotype. Cosmetic botulinum products, including Botox, are all the type A phenotype."

"So, my theory is possible, but botulinum toxin found in food under other circumstances may also be the type A phenotype."

He screwed up his mouth as he stared at Sara. "If you keep going, you may replace Carbonne as my favorite person in the building. You both enjoy exploring the lab data with the lab crew. Most of the agents see it as a necessary evil."

"They're preoccupied. Poor Barbara is now apologizing to Hank again for Pete and me leaving you two in the lurch on Friday."

"Hank was pissed, but I liked that Hank didn't have time to second guess me. Besides, Pete, as an old-timer here, explained."

"Really?"

"He said it was above my pay grade."

Sara couldn't think of an appropriate response and changed the topic. "Have the fingerprint analyses provided any new info?"

Winslow winked at her. "When anyone asks you about your boyfriend's activities, you close up like a clam. I assume he was the cause of your speedy exit. Pete explained that when the mysterious Sanders flits in and out of Albuquerque, our old boss—and now Carbonne—takes notice."

"You were saying the fingerprints were useful?"

"Yep, like a clam." Winslow snickered. "I wish they were. Hank did his part and provided me with examples of the housekeeper's fingerprints and DNA. We got Jules's prints and DNA off the can of diet soda which Barbara gave him when she interviewed him here. Estella's and Catalina's samples were easy to collect. Nelson's were a bit more of a challenge. Thank the gods for toothbrushes and the revulsion most people feel for even touching other people's toothbrushes."

"So?"

"Only the expected fingerprints were found in Estella's bedroom. The last person who touched the knobs at the sink and opened the door under the sink wore gloves and smudged all earlier prints."

"I guess we can assume Catalina's killer was careful and thorough. That seems like a better description of Nelson than of Jules." Sara stood as if to go.

"Wait, I got more. It took me all morning to catalog all the medications and anti-aging gunk in the master bedroom and bath. The only interesting items were the rubber-topped, multi-injection bottles you

                                    J. L. Greger

found in the refrigerator. All of them contained botulinum toxin. All had been diluted but the toxin hadn't degraded."

"It's odd that Nelson and Estella tried to save money by using diluted botulinum toxin presumably leftover from the Green Way to Beauty Spa. How about the drawerful of syringes in the bedroom?"

"All were unused. The Santa Fe police found lots of syringes in the garbage. All had traces of botulinum toxin but no other drugs. Most fingerprints were smudged but several had Estella's or Nelson's prints."

"That kills Hank's theory that one of the main characters was a diabetic or into street drugs. We can conclude that drugs, other than botulinum toxin, were not involved in this murder. We can also assume that Estella and Nelson were self-injecting the botulinum toxin. Now what did you find in the bedroom where the murder occurred?"

"Zippo. Someone had cleaned, not merely wiped, the door knob and all surfaces with bleach. We didn't even find Catalina's DNA, except in the blood on the carpet.

"Okay, I hope you saved the best for last. What about the fingerprints on the stair rail? Did your new technique using mass spectrometry work?"

"Yep. The new TOF-SIMS technique—you got to admit the name 'time-of-flight secondary ion mass spec' is cool—is time sensitive. I convinced another tech to do the initial analyses on Friday night when the last fingerprints should have been less than a day old. Here are her pictures. They can't be improved because oils in the fingerprints have stopped migrating by now."

Sara saw brownish fingerprints on top of a mass of greenish prints. "So now the prints would all be greenish?"

"Yep." Winslow fiddled with his computer keyboard. A picture of a mass of greenish smudged prints appeared. "This was the image we got this morning."

"Could you identify the brownish prints?"

"Yep—definitely Catalina's, but they're wonky."

Sara stared at Winslow who was grinning from ear to ear. "Explain."

"The handrail was to the right of the steps. When you use a handrail while going up stairs, you use your right hand." He demonstrated by grabbing a ruler. "See my thumb print and forefinger prints should be at ten and two positions and pointing upward."

"Okay?"

"The prints on the rail match the fingers on her *left* hand."

Sara frowned. "She would have used her left hand when descending the stairs."

"Yep, but then the prints would be pointing downward. They're not. The prints are of her thumb and fingers and pointing sideways."

Sara twisted her hand. "That is almost impossible to do."

"Like I said—it's wonky."

Sara frowned. "You think they're staged, don't you?"

"Yep."

"How was it done?"

"I think someone held Catalina's hand and pressed her fingers on the banister."

"So, the prints were staged like the clothes on the stairs. But if someone took the time to think that much why did they make a mistake and use the left hand?"

"Wonky. It makes no sense." Winslow stared at the image on the screen. "Unless… unless she was attacked on the stairs and grabbed the rail to keep from falling. You'll remember there was none of Catalina's DNA, except in the blood, in the bedroom where we found her." He typed rapidly and looked at a page of calculations. "Actually, there is one other strange findings. There wasn't enough blood at the supposed murder site."

"Could she have been killed on the stairs? If so, there should be blood there."

"Yep. And the staging of the clothes was designed to distract us." He paused. "I didn't look for blood on the stairs. If she was killed there, then the fingerprints aren't wonky. Catalina was grabbing the rail to keep from falling as she was being stabbed."

"So, are you going back to Santa Fe or asking the local techs to look for traces of blood on the stairs?"

Winslow winked. "Don't be silly. Of course, I'm going back. The crew up there would only notice obvious blood on the stairs. I bet the killer used bleach to scrub the stairs, but in crevices I should find Catalina's blood."

"Remember how thoroughly the handle of the wooden knife was cleaned? You didn't find any traces of blood on it. Even though it's blade fit the pattern of the fatal wound."

Winslow winked again. "I'll be lucky this time. Although it would have been easier if the stairs had a carpet runner."

Sara's phone pinged. She exhaled a sigh as she read the text. "I've got to go now."

***

                                          J. L. Greger

Sara carried Bug as she rushed into University Hospital because he liked to saunter down the hallways. He seemed to think every child in the hospital wanted to pet him. Today she didn't have the time and carried the squirming dog from the parking garage, past the food court, to the elevators in the lobby. When the elevator doors opened, she and Bug strolled to the ICU. Bug was confused by her sudden change in pace and sniffed the floor more than usual. There was no way to explain to Bug that she was trying not to alarm the mystery man if he spied her. Bug was used to her irrational acts and trotted willingly beside her after thirty seconds.

As instructed, Sara and Bug didn't enter the ICU but stood near the door. She knew an agent had spotted a tall man in green scrubs enter the ICU ten minutes before. There were women and men outside the ICU, but she recognized none as an agent. However, she was sure at least one in the crowd was a law enforcement officer because Barbara had noted she didn't want a scuffle in the ICU and had posted police and agents at the front and emergency exits to the ICU.

Sara looked down the hall into the ICU, and thought she saw a tall man in scrubs approaching. She picked up Bug and stepped back as she tried to casually position a cane in front of the exit. The cane had been Barbara's idea. Sara had never intentionally tried to trip anyone before. If she wasn't lucky, she'd break the leg of a busy attending physician. She guessed the FBI would cover her legal bills if he sued her.

The man in scrubs pushed the button to open the doors. Sara edged the cane forward slightly. The man started to step through the doorway as Sara said, "Nelson, I'm glad you visited your wife."

The man glanced toward Sara without looking at his feet. He stumbled over the outstretched cane.

Two men from the crowd rushed forward and grabbed the arms of the stumbling man. A woman suddenly pulled Sara backward.

Sara gulped and Bug trembled a bit. "Nelson, you might as well admit your identity. The FBI needs to talk to you. You can't get away."

As the male agent slipped hand cuffs on Nelson and read him his rights, the man in scrubs looked at Sara. "You've got the wrong man, again."

CHAPTER 18: Sara Meets Her Match

"Are you sure?" Sara looked through the one-way mirror at a man in green scrubs sitting in the small conference room. His brown hair and height matched the pictures of Nelson Davis, but his hair was disheveled, his glances darted about the room randomly, and his right eye blinked spasmodically. He didn't look like the handsome, dignified man in photos around Estella Garcia Davis's home.

Barbara nodded. "His fingerprints and DNA match those on Nelson's toothbrush in the home he shares with his wife Estella. He has refused to answer my questions but said he would talk to the woman with the dog who visited his wife daily."

Sara led Bug into the room and placed Bug on a chair out of Nelson's reach because she feared what he might do. "Mr. Davis, your wife needs your help. I may be silly, but I think she'd benefit if you could be with her for more than just a few stolen minutes a day. And I think you agree. So, why were you hiding from the police and the FBI?"

"They'll kill me like they did Catalina."

"Who are they?"

"Not sure." The speed at which his right eyes convulsed increased. "Jules." He appeared to stare at one corner of the small room. "Maybe his sister, Abigail." His stare shifted to another corner. "His father, Verne." He sighed as he gazed at the ceiling.

"What about Davita and Beryl Marks?"

The tic in his right eye was so violent when he looked at her that Sara felt her eyes blinking. It was hard to believe this man had written and illustrated the beautiful manuscript she'd admired. She doubted he was capable of answering questions. She texted Barbara who she assumed was viewing the scene through the mirror:

> *Are you sure a psychiatrist shouldn't evaluate him before we question him?*

Nelson clenched his right fist and stood.

Sara reached for Bug. She'd never seen the trained pet therapy dog shrink from a patient in the hospital, but now Bug leaped into her arms. She didn't want to move too rapidly because she feared it would provoke Nelson more. She wrapped her arms around Bug, stood, and took one step backward toward the door. *Barbara should be in here by now. Carbonne would be.*

The door opened. A male agent with his arms extended with a stun gun inched into the room. "Mister, I don't want to stun you, but I will if you move."

Nelson gave a low moan, lowered his head, and seemed to shuffle his feet. Sara thought he looked like a bull ready to charge.

"Nelson, it's a stun gun not a real one," Sara squeaked. She gained control of her voice. "Nelson, sit down. We want to protect you from bad people, but you've got to stay calm… and answer our questions."

A tremor seemed to move from Nelson's head to his shoulder to his legs. Then he dropped onto a chair. "You tried… to trick me. Beryl's dead." He convulsed again. "Not stupid. I heard whispers in the ICU."

Barbara and another man with a bow tie had now entered the room. It seemed crowded to Sara with five people and a dog. She guessed it must seem stifling to Nelson. Sara waved to the agent with the stun gun to move back and returned to her chair but kept Bug tightly wrapped in her arms. "You're right. Beryl died, but you could have thought of her as a threat."

Barbara remained at the open door. The man with the bow tie sat at the far end of the table while the agent with the stun gun disappeared.

Nelson cocked his head. "No." He thumped his fist on the table. "Beryl loved Estella. Not hurt her."

"That's what I thought, but what about Davita?"

He shook his head. "They argue… a lot." He frowned. "Not hurt her mother… Don't think."

"That's what we concluded, but someone did poison Beryl."

Nelson stared at Sara. "No." He shook his head. "She ate the bad figs."

"How do you know she ate the bad figs?"

Nelson cocked his head. "I hear… It was in paper about…" His tic accentuated. "…about botulism."

Sara decided to gamble and talk to Nelson as if his mind was still functioning normally. Even though, his tic and behavior suggested otherwise. Moreover, she thought the man with the bow tie was the new psychiatrist that the FBI put on retainer. Any responses she elicited from Nelson might help the psychiatrist evaluate Nelson. "We—the people in the lab and I—think the botulinum toxin in the figs that Beryl ate wasn't there because of a canning mistake."

Nelson leaned toward her.

She spoke slowly. "The toxin was added intentionally." Since her conversation with Davita on Saturday, Sara had suspected Nelson had sprinkled the toxin on the preserves in the jar after he tasted them. If that was true, Sara expected Nelson would react violently to her comment because she doubted he was capable of acting now.

Nelson's tic slowed. "I wondered... I didn't get sick from eating her canned figs."

Sara remained silent hoping Nelson would say more.

"How? How would anyone get this botulism toxin?"

That wasn't a logical question for a man who had at least a dozen half-empty bottles of Botox in his bathroom refrigerator. She debated how to tease answers from him. "What do you think is in the Botox solutions you inject in your face?"

The tic on his right eye went wild. Nelson sighed. "No. Can't be." Tears appeared in his eyes. "I didn't do it." After he stopped sniffling, he said, "They made me look guilty. I don't know who to trust."

Sara decided it was time to raise the questions she and Barbara had discussed before this session. She put Bug on the chair next to her, leaned toward Nelson, and gently put her hand on his shoulder. "We at the FBI don't know who to trust either. Let's see if we can figure it out. We'll start with several simple questions. Don't overthink your answers. We just want to check a few statements by others. Do you remember visiting Beryl in the last week—before the rally in Clovis?"

He nodded.

"When? And why?"

He frowned as his eye muscle spasmed. "She... Beryl called me on Monday... I think. Wanted to know if I could take the fig preserves to Clovis." He shook his head and closed his eyes as he spoke haltingly. "Couldn't. Going to San Diego. But Estella said it was rude to ignore Beryl." He pounded the table and spoke more rapidly. "That's it. I went to see a lawyer in Albuquerque Monday afternoon. I wanted advice on what I should insist on when I negotiated with my editor in San Diego on Tuesday."

Sara waited until he paused. She decided not to question the discrepancies between his and Davita's statements, but to focus on things that could be verified. "Which lawyer?"

"His name will be on my computer in the *Book/Legal* file."

Sara noticed Barbara was rapidly typing an email now. "Thank you. We'll check with the lawyer. Did you see anyone else in Albuquerque?"

Nelson swallowed several times as if his mouth was dry.

"Would you like water, coffee, or soda?"

He nodded. "A diet cola."

While Barbara typed rapidly, Sara asked again. "What else did you do in Albuquerque?"

"Stopped by the spa to see Catalina. I know I shouldn't… but she and I had become friends."

"What kind of friends?"

A woman bustled into the conference room with several diet colas and water. Sara poured water into a bowl for Bug and popped a can and drank directly from the can. She had stopped using glasses at home years ago in an effort to generate fewer dishes to be washed and had come to think a cola's flavor was sharper and fresher from the can. She noticed everyone else—Nelson, Barbara, and the presumed psychiatrist—had poured their water or cola into the glasses of ice provided. She missed Carbonne. He never used a glass either. She forced herself to again focus on Nelson. "You were telling me about your friendship with Catalina."

"It's not what you think. We both were confused by Jules's recent bossy behavior. He had ordered Catalina on Monday to fly to San Diego on Tuesday. He was worried about some stupid jars and claimed they were short of herbs. It wasn't that urgent."

Sara continued to ignore the differences between Nelson's and others' statements and focus on *his* story. "How was Jules bossy with you?"

"Jules kept complaining to me that the caterer for the event in Clovis had a bad reputation. He said I had to speak to Bo because he was Estella's friend. I was busy with my book. Finally, I did." Nelson shook his head. "I don't know why I yelled at Bo. I guess I was frustrated. I really wanted to yell at Jules but… I knew he'd get even by poking fun of Estella more."

"Why didn't you or Estella fire him?"

"We talked about it, but Estella was afraid. She thought he was her good luck charm." He snorted. "I thought he was more like Rasputin but didn't want to argue with Estella. If the book deal was good, we wouldn't need him. My credentials as her advisor would be solid."

"What did you and Catalina talk about?"

"I was only at the spa about five minutes because she was afraid Jules might drop in to check on her. We agreed to meet in San Diego."

Barbara was typing rapidly. Sara hoped Barbara's notes included a reminder to check whether anyone saw Nelson at the spa on the previous Monday. "Then what?"

"I stopped by Beryl's house in Corrales on the way back to Santa Fe. She insisted I have a dish of ice cream with fig and nut preserves."

"And?"

"When she learned I wouldn't be at the rally, she decided Estella needed her for moral support and she would deliver the figs to the rally herself."

"Did she like Jules? Did she mention Davita's opinion of Jules?"

Nelson's tic flared again. "She gave her usual lines. 'Estella outgrew Jules years ago. And I don't know why Davita likes him.'" Nelson rubbed his forehead. "Mainly I showed her my book. I even left a copy of the draft with her."

Sara was sure Winslow hadn't found a copy of the book at Beryl's house but let Nelson continue to weave fiction with facts. "Did you give the figs and nuts recipe to Beryl last November?"

Nelson twitched. "Yes."

"Why?"

"Jules gave Estella a couple of jars of fig preserves in October. When Estella had raved about them, he claimed that he'd made them. I challenged him because I didn't think Jules did anything more difficult in the kitchen than warming foods in the microwave. He handed me the recipe the next day."

"Why did you give the recipe to Beryl?"

"She always wanted to help Estella's campaign but didn't have a lot of cash. The enclosed courtyard in back of her house had several fig trees." His tic stopped. "Curious. Figs usually don't grow here—too cold in winter—but her patio enclosed with thick adobe walls seems to protect them."

"On last Tuesday, when did you leave for the airport?"

Nelson twitched. "Don't know. Two… no, three hours before my flight."

Sara wanted to see whether Nelson's answer matched the security camera footage, but she didn't want to give him unnecessary clues. "What did Estella say?"

Nelson's tic pulsated. "Is that a trick question? Estella had left with Jules for the rally before I left."

She thought Nelson was much more alert than he had pretended. "Nelson, you've clarified several points. Now Agent Barbara Lewis will ask you questions. She's more familiar with the next details than I am."

Nelson bit his lip.

"Would you like to pet Bug before she begins?"

He nodded.

Sara picked up Bug and stood next to Nelson. Bug sniffed Nelson's right sleeve and then withdrew into Sara's arms.

"Estella told me about Bug. She's not really sleeping all the time. She talks sometimes."

***

As soon as they exited the conference room, Barbara introduced the man with the bow tie as psychiatrist Jim Jung. "Sara, I am sorry I was not at the window when Nelson flared. I had asked another agent to monitor you while I determined why Dr. Jung was late."

Jim reddened. "Traffic on I-25 was blocked by an accident." He coughed. "I was convinced after you calmed Nelson that he was rational. However, his statement that Estella talked to him about Bug suggests he may be delusional."

Sara cuddled Bug. "Nelson is an enigma. He scared me—no, I was annoyed with myself—when he claimed Estella talked to him because it suggested I'd wasted everyone's time interviewing him. Then I got thinking. All the medical staff think Estella should be able to grunt or make hand signals in response to questions because only the muscles in her face are paralyzed. However, a physical therapist and I were unable to get Estella to respond to simple questions by tapping her fingers. Is it possible, she made sounds to Nelson?

CHAPTER 19: Psychiatrist Jim Jung Discovers Secrets

After he had interviewed Nelson Davis for a half-hour, Dr. Jim Jung was at a loss to diagnose Nelson's mental state. Whoever had devised the poisoning of Estella and the murders of Catalina Herrera and Beryl Marks was smart, careful about details, and ruthless. The endangerment of everyone at the rally in order to attack his target, presumably Estella, suggested the perpetrator was a psychopath. It was logical for Nelson to fear him or her. On the other hand, Nelson could be that psychopath and a good actor, besides.

Unfortunately, Jim was also unsure about the investigators. Barbara was nervous and more hesitant than most successful FBI agents. Her account of why she hadn't been at the observation window when Nelson threatened Sara wasn't totally accurate. Yes, he was late, but only by five minutes. Barbara hadn't needed to wait for him by the front door because he knew his way to the interview room, and she knew it. It was also curious that she hadn't rushed to the interview room after the agent at the window had sounded an alarm. He suspected she was more afraid or physical violence than most agents.

Then there was Sara. She was analytical, even calculating, but tried to hide it by being folksy. He suspected her routine with Bug relaxed most suspects and victims but annoyed or scared insecure agents like Barbara. He decided now was not the time to analyze his colleagues further. "I think we should go on a field trip to the hospital. I'll call the ICU and ask them to move Estella to a private room outside the ICU where Sara, Nelson, and I will attempt to induce her to communicate. Barbara, you'll have to attend to security." He pulled out his phone. "It might be wise to videotape our session as Estella's communication methods won't all be verbal."

Sara responded immediately. "Great idea. I hadn't thought about it before but Beryl's presence—and more importantly Davita's presence—in the ICU may have made Estella and Nelson nervous." She paused. "But Davita wasn't around the ICU after Saturday. Then again, most patients find the ICU scary."

***

The room was prepped with the camera in place. Sara was in her hyper-chatty mode as she walked with a nurse and an aide pushing Estella's bed into the room where Jim and Nelson waited. Barbara and another agent remained in the hallway because they didn't want the room to seem crowded.

Jim was impressed how quickly Sara had gotten the trust of the staff in the ICU. She and Bug had been visiting children in the pediatric ICU for years, but the adult ICU had held firm to its policy of no therapy dogs until Carbonne and Sara convinced them to make an exception for Bug on this FBI case. Today the nurse and aide were friendlier to Bug and Sara than they were to him. He'd consulted in the ICU for years.

Jim was also surprised by Bug's intuition. As soon as Sara had positioned Bug on a small rug by Estella's left side, the little dog had placed first a paw on Estella's arm and then his head. In contrast, Bug had not seemed to trust Nelson.

Perhaps the most amazing transformation was in Nelson. His tic disappeared as his eyes focused on his wife. When Nelson said, "Estella," she moved her right hand as if to reach in the direction of his voice.

This made Jim feel more confident in his plan. He pushed Nelson forward and whispered, "Tell her she's safe and with friends."

As rehearsed, Nelson told his wife that only Bug, Sara, and a friendly doctor associated with the FBI were in the room with them. "We can talk freely. They want to learn who did this to you and get them locked up."

Estella's face remained blank in a cruel mask created by the botulism, but she grunted. Her lips didn't move and the grunt sounded like "Ggg."

Nelson smiled. "She said, 'Good.'"

Jim thought that was a stretch but guessed Nelson was correct. He nodded to Sara.

"We know it's frustrating not being able to speak so we want to see if you can talk with your hands. Now an expert on sign language could teach you several ways to communicate, but you're stuck with me and Bug for now." He was surprised when Sara moved Nelson's hand from Estella's right shoulder. "We want you to answer questions by raising your right hand if the answer to a question is 'yes.' Let's see if you can raise your right hand again like you did when you heard Nelson's voice."

Estella didn't move.

Nelson murmured. "It's all right, Estella. Please, do as she asks. Lift your right hand."

Estella raised her hand. Nelson kissed it. Jim decided that Sara had tried to keep Nelson from signaling Estella with his hand and now Estella had to respond to oral questions directly. That suggested Sara didn't trust Nelson completely although she hadn't voiced any concerns.

"Do you feel safer in this room with us that in the ICU?"

Estella raised her hand slightly and then dropped it.

Jim thought Estella might tire quickly and hoped Sara wouldn't waste time with idle questions.

"If the answer to a question is no, can you make a 'no' sound?"

"Uu," Estella grunted.

"Fine. Would you feel safe if Davita entered the room?"

"Uu."

"Would you feel safe if Jules entered the room?"

"Uu." Jim thought that grunt was louder but didn't want to attach any meaning to the volume of the grunts yet.

"Would you feel safe if your housekeeper entered the room?"

Estella raised her hand. Nelson kissed it.

Sara nodded to the camera. "Now we begin real questions." She faced Estella. "Did Davita visit you in the hospital?"

Estella raised her hand.

When Jim saw Sara was struggling with the next question, he asked, "Did Davita give you an order or suggest what you should do?"

Estella raised her hand.

Sara quickly asked, "Is that why you didn't answer the nurses or me before today?"

Estella raised her hand and grunted "Uu."

Sara turned to Nelson. "How would you interpret that answer of both yes and no?"

His right eye began to blink rapidly. "I'd say it's partially true. I think she feared someone on staff here at the hospital."

"Okay, I'll bite. Who do you think she feared?"

"I've tried to find out for several days. It's a woman in a white coat."

"Although anyone can don a white coat, theoretically only physicians and physicians-in-training are allowed to wear white coats in

                                        J. L. Greger

this hospital." Sara frowned and then smiled. "Let's see whether Barbara can get photos of all the attendings and residents in the ICU."

After Sara left, Jim studied Estella for thirty seconds. "Yes and no questions are slow. Try to answer me with hand signs." He swallowed hard. "Why do you like Sara?"

Estella patted Bug.

Nelson interpreted, "Estella likes Bug."

"'Why do you think that?"

Nelson shrugged. "Estella and I also figured Sara had FBI connections."

Jim thought Nelson didn't seem to realize Estella might not have the same thoughts as he did. He decided to humor Nelson anyway. "Why?'

"The older nurses knew Sara. When an aide stopped Sara from entering the ICU with Bug, I heard a nurse say 'special' and 'FBI.' I decided then that Sara was a way to… get help."

Estella raised her hand and said, "Ggg."

Jim blinked this time. He still doubted Nelson's reasoning, but he was sure Estella had a story to tell."

Sara returned with Barbara. They proceeded to show Estella pictures of physicians who frequented the ICU. They asked Estella for each one—"Have you seen this person?" and "Do you fear this person?"

It was a slow, non-productive process. Estella recognized those physicians who had examined her but feared none of those pictured. In contrast, Nelson seemed jumpy. Finally, Sara winked at Barbara, who immediately insisted that she needed to speak to Nelson privately in the hall. Jim decided he'd underestimated the ability of the two women to work together.

Once Nelson was gone, Sara rapidly determined through a series of questions that the woman Estella feared had long blonde or light brown hair and was older than most medical students or residents. Then she held an image before Estella. "Do you fear her?"

Estella uttered, "Ggg" and raised her hand.

"Has she visited you in the hospital?"

"Ggg."

"Why do you fear her?"

Estella moved her hand sideways toward her neck.

"I don't understand."

Estella began to hit her neck with her hand.

"Did she threaten to hurt you?"

"Ggg." Estella raised her hands into a praying position.

"I think I understand. You want our help."

"Ggg."

***

As they exited Estella's room, Sara announced, "I think Nelson needs to relax in the food court. Perhaps the other agent and Nelson can bring us sodas, while we three take care of procedural issues." Sara then literally pushed Nelson and the other agent toward the elevator.

Barbara whispered, "Thank you."

Jim looked back and forth between the two women. "What happened here?"

Barbara smiled for the first time today. "Estella identified Abigail Fix Smith, Jules's sister, as the woman who threatened her. She is a physician and owner of the spas which Davita and Catalina managed."

"I think a good speech therapist can pull more info Estella than I can. *But* no one can pull useful info from Estella if she doesn't feel safe *and* I think that means keeping Nelson away from her."

Barbara nodded.

Jim felt confused. "Why?"

Sara frowned. "I don't trust Nelson. Too many of his comments today were inconsistent with those of others. Pete's discoveries on the computers suggest Nelson is smart, organized, and often tries to intimidate others, especially Estella. Then too, I'm not sure how much of what Estella communicated were her ideas and not thoughts that Nelson had planted in her mind." She shrugged. "But I don't know if you should trust my intuition. I read Abigail completely wrong. I bought her story about being a sister bedeviled by a lazy, and perhaps evil, brother."

Jim Jung whistled. "I'm easily going to be able to bill the FBI for forty hours of work this week. Nelson is a real puzzle."

Barbara pursed her lips. "I appreciate your ideas, but I have another concern. One or two staff members in the ICU may be naively or intentionally reporting on Estella to Nelson, Abigail, or an unknown stalker. Thus, I do not think we should contact a speech therapist or tell anyone what we have learned today. Estella will be safer if she threatens no one by communicating."

Sara bit her lip. "Are you sure? I think Estella needs to exercise her throat muscles. Delays allow her muscles to atrophy more."

Jim felt sorry for Barbara. Sara would be a challenge for anyone to control. "Maybe I could work with Estella in this room again."

Barbara looked as if she was ready to cry. "Get real you two. Estella is a fragile patient. She belongs in the ICU, but it is a beehive of gossip. You both need to complain bitterly that this experiment was a bust to everyone in the ICU. That will make Estella less of a threat to anyone. I will have guards at all entrances of the hospital be on the alert for Abigail."

Sara hung her head. "I guess you're right, but I think Bug and I should do a short visit tomorrow."

"Okay." Barbara frowned. "My main problem now is placing Nelson in a safe house until I have the evidence to arrest Abigail *or* more proof that Nelson is lying. In any case, the agents in the safe house will keep him away from Estella." She pointed at Jim. "The first step is for you to psychologically profile him."

CHAPTER 20: Sara Thinks

Sara looked at Bug. He lay with his head on the edge of his car seat even as they entered the McDonald's parking lot. The aroma wafting from a fast-food hamburger restaurant usually caused him to sit at attention at least a block away. Sara wasn't sure if his sense of smell was that good or if he recognized landmarks nearby. His apathy today suggested he was worn out.

Sara had declined to participate as Barbara and Jim continued to interview Nelson. She had claimed Bug needed her attention, but that was only half of the story. She had noticed a short article on the third page of today's *Albuquerque Journal*. It had troubled her.

She pulled the article from her purse and reread it after she and Bug had finished sharing a hamburger and fries. It was their usual arrangement. He got half the burger. She got the bun, pickle, and the rest of the burger. He got a half-inch from every fry longer than three inches that she ate.

The newspaper article claimed a major leader in a Columbian drug cartel had been arrested with ten grams of drugs in Boca Raton, Florida, on Saturday afternoon. She wondered why such a tiny amount of drugs was mentioned. Major drug arrests from South America generally involved hundreds of kilos of cocaine. She hypothesized the drug seized could be the toxin extracted from the skins of the golden poison dart frogs. She did a quick calculation. Ten grams of that poison could theoretically kill twenty thousand people. Still, it didn't make sense. *Who was the target audience for this story? Other drug kingpins?*

She thought about her interactions with Sanders since his message last Friday. He had called Sunday at six in the morning from the U.S. embassy in Brasilia. He had been airlifted by a helicopter from the research vessel on Saturday afternoon. His only comment relevant to his urgent message on Friday was: "I was relieved to escape the boredom of listening to scientists talking about frogs and recalling a colleague who disappeared in the Amazon about a year ago."

She had known better than to ask any questions and had replied. "Oh, I don't know. I like to listen to scientists reminiscing about old colleagues." She made a mental note to check past issues of *Science*. She'd seen an article about the dangers of doing research in the Amazon sometime during the last year. The article had mentioned the mysterious disappearance of a toxicologist in the Amazon.

Sanders had quickly changed the topic. "Why don't you meet me next Friday in Boca Raton, Florida? We both should improve our golf game."

She thought that was a hint because he knew she had never played a round of golf, and he hated the game. His urgent message had mentioned Boca. She tried to provoke more clues. "Yes, I should practice miniature golf more."

"Small things can be important. I'll email you my flight schedules to Miami. Then we can drive together to Boca."

She was sure today's newspaper article was related to Sanders's urgent message on Friday. She also suspected Sanders planned to use his *relaxed* weekend with her as a cover for updating himself or others on the case. That meant she would have a lot of free time in Boca Raton, and she didn't enjoy sunbathing, swimming, or playing tennis or golf. Of course, neither did Sanders, and that reinforced her guess that he planned to work in Boca.

This morning at six, she and Sanders had finalized their plans for Friday through Sunday without further mention of his urgent message on the previous Friday or the article in today's paper. She had tried to put all thoughts of Sanders out of her mind as she worked today, but she hadn't succeeded. She was worried. Sanders *more cautious* than usual in his comments.

Sara decided it was time to get back to work and scanned her emails. Winslow had hit gold. He wrote:

> *Sara,*
> *I've nailed it. I found enough blood in the crevices on the steps to convince Hank that the stairs were the murder site. I'll let you know when the lab completes the DNA analyses on the intact blood cells not destroyed by bleach.*
>
> *What's more, Hank re-questioned several of Estella's neighbors. One old woman finally admitted she saw two women enter Estella's house around eight that Thursday*

evening. Hank guessed the women walked to the house because none of the neighbors saw a car parked in the drive or in front of the house on Thursday night. The old woman claimed she'd seen one of the women leave the house around six in the morning. Unfortunately, the only things the woman is sure of are that the women were of similar height, wore similar olive-green trench coats, and must have worn skirts because she could see their legs.

The medical examiner came through. He found traces of Rohypnol in Catalina's blood. That means she might not have been able to fight off her murderer.
Winslow

Sara typed back:

Does that mean a small man or even a woman could have murdered Catalina? Previously, we assumed Nelson at six-three was more likely to have overpowered the athletic Catalina at five-seven than Jules at five-five. By the way, Jules's sister is probably about five-eight and looks athletic.
Sara

Sara forwarded the email exchange to Barbara and hoped this added data might give Barbara an excuse to interview Abigail Fix Smith again. She pitied Barbara. She was in a no-win situation. The session with Estella had convinced both Barbara and Sara that Abigail was involved in Catalina's murder or at least in trying to confuse the investigation, but the tape of their session with Estella alone would be insufficient to get a judge's warrant to wiretap Abigail's phones.

Sara also knew from her experiences doing pet therapy with Bug that Barbara's promise to prevent Abigail from entering University Hospital was an idle one. Sara was sure with minimal disguises she could pass through the hospital security checks without being identified—that is, if she wasn't with Bug.

As Sara was driving home on I-25 she thought about the Smiths. Abigail might still be untouchable with only Nelson's comments to counter hers, but Jules was not. Albuquerque police had searched his condo last Saturday but found nothing

                                                    J. L. Greger

suspicious. Perhaps they hadn't considered the right items suspicious. Sara pulled off the highway and texted Barbara.

As soon as she got home, she worked on her laptop for thirty minutes before she emailed Carbonne.

CHAPTER 21: Carbonne Loses Patience

It was almost seven and Carbonne was ready to go home, although he knew he should complete another hour's worth of paperwork before he quit for the day. He wandered to Barbara's office with a can of diet soda. She wasn't there. Another agent told him she was in a conference room with Nelson Davis. Carbonne decided he'd watch a bit of the interview through the one-way mirror in the observation room as he drank his soda. It would be more engaging than what was left on his desk, especially since Sara's email two hours ago had cast a new light on the investigation.

Jim Jung, the local psychiatrist on call, was the only individual in the observation room. "Barbara can't break Nelson. I think he might even want to cooperate, but he can't stop dithering. After I examined him, I warned Barbara that he was so scared and exhausted that he might be unable to cooperate." Jim Jung shook his head. "If he doesn't, she doesn't have enough evidence to arrest Jules or Abigail. In the long run, Nelson may actually make it possible for them to never be charged for trying to kill his wife."

"Are we sure that's not his intent?" As he played with his phone, Carbonne heard Barbara say, "Did you go with Catalina to pick up the rental car at the airport in San Diego?"

"No. Well, maybe." Nelson began to massage his head.

"What does that mean?"

"We took separate taxis to the airport."

"Why?"

"We didn't want to be seen together. We thought we might be watched."

"By whom?"

"We didn't know who Jules had watching us. He's smarter than he looks."

Carbonne noted Nelson was still massaging his head and thought Nelson was a lousy actor. His motions were too contrived.

"Did you both go to the car rental area?"

"Catalina did."

"What did you do?"

"I went to the United flight area."

Carbonne stopped texting long enough stare at Barbara. He knew she was much more patient than he'd ever be or wanted to be.

"What was your plan for meeting her?"

"I took the free shuttle to the rental car area." Nelson's jaw hung slack, but his hand now covered his mouth.

Carbonne had seen that look many times. It was the look that witnesses often gave when they were purposefully being difficult.

"Weren't you afraid you were being watched?"

Nelson seemed surprised and straightened. "No, why would you think that?"

Carbonne was concerned. Barbara looked pale and had dark circles under her eyes. She had also closed her eyes and seemed to wince before she spoke. "Then why did you take separate taxis to the airport?"

"Did I say that?"

Carbonne had been texting almost constantly as he listened to the interview. Now he tossed his empty soda can into the recycle bin, slammed the door as he left the observation room, and strode into the interview room.

He didn't wait for the door to the interview room to close before he said, "Stop auditioning for a role in a play. You're not in Tucson fifteen years ago. You're not confused or frightened, except of being caught. You're willfully obstructing this investigation." He paused as he walked around the room to stand behind Nelson's chair. "You're smart, no doubt, but I've seen other acts like yours." He waited until Nelson had turned to look at him. "Here's the deal. Stop playing games or we'll arrest you for obstruction." One side of Carbonne's lips curled upward. "Or better yet, we'll let the local police arrest you and put you in one of their central holding cells. You know those cells are often overcrowded because the local courts detain so many on a busy night. You're lucky that this is a Monday night, not a Friday or a Saturday night."

"They can't. This is a federal case."

"The FBI and the Albuquerque Police Department often work together on cases. The APD searched Jules's condo on Friday. When Sara and I realized the significance of what they found, I got a judge to issue another search warrant for Jules's condo a couple of hours ago. Wow—you should have heard what Jules had to say."

"I want a lawyer."

"Okay by me. I don't want to waste any more of time on you now."

Barbara murmured. "I will try harder. His wife needs protection."

Carbonne glared at Nelson. "You're wasting our time so we don't have adequate protection for his wife in place. Right?

"I love my wife. I proved it this afternoon. It's your fault if she's killed in the hospital."

Carbonne winked at Barbara. "He's proven he's not confused."

Carbonne's phone pinged. After he texted, he turned to Barbara. "We're through. I've contacted the public defender. Let's go."

"No, I have a lawyer and want *him*."

"Name?"

"Verne Smith."

Barbara looked startled. "Is that Jules's and Abigail's father? He is based in Abilene and cannot get here for hours."

Nelson rubbed his hands together. "Maybe I should use the public defender."

Carbonne snorted as he pulled Barbara to the door. "He's on his way. And by the way, your wife was moved out of the ICU before you started your latest routine."

***

As soon as the door to the observation room closed, Barbara said, "I think you were a bit rash. I had made progress. Now it is all lost."

Jim nodded in agreement.

"You two didn't read Sara's latest emails." He put his hand on Barbara's shoulder. "Remember I told you that Sara is a great resource, *but* she has a few quirks.? The previous head of the FBI operation in Albuquerque and I both learned—the hard way—Sara does her best work when she's off duty. It's annoying but we both learned to read her emails as soon as we notice them."

Barbara leaned against the wall. "We were in the middle of an intense interview with Nelson. I could not take a break because it would mean starting over. You saw him. His power of concentration is that of a child."

Carbonne snorted, "Or that of a skilled actor. Sara requested the college transcripts and past employment records of all the suspects in the case."

"I know that. She found nothing of interest."

"Not quite. Staff found nothing. On the way home, Sara had a brain storm and reviewed the files herself."

Barbara looked annoyed. "I am waiting."

"Seems Nelson was an assistant stage manager and served as an understudy for roles in *Hamlet* in a community theater in Tucson while he took graduate courses in art at the University of Arizona about fifteen years ago."

"I see where you're going. He must have studied how to act mentally ill for the play."

"Don't know. Could have." Carbonne showed her an image on his phone. "According to this playbill, Amelia Fix Smith played Ophelia. Nelson and Abigail have known each other for…."

Jim Jung interrupted, "What made Sara look for these details?"

"It bugged her that she'd read Abigail wrong. Sara's a real fiend when she gets a bee in her bonnet."

Barbara shook her head. "This information can be the basis of further investigation, but it is not sufficient to arrest Abigail, Jules, or Nelson before they act again."

Carbonne laughed. "I assume you didn't intend to make a pun."

Barbara bit her lip. "I hope you were bluffing about the Albuquerque police or FBI arresting Jules? Lying that you were sick is not sufficient to be thrown into a holding cell."

Carbonne shrugged. "A slight overstatement. We probably could have arrested him for obstructing justice but I wanted Jules panicked and free to act after he overheard Winslow tell an APD officer that Estella had been moved from the ICU."

Barbara dropped into a chair in the observation room. "I am too tired to play games. How did Sara and you convince a judge to issue a second search warrant? And why the hurry to act?"

"APD officers searched Jules's condo on Friday—after you talked to him. Sara remembered that they found several pieces of women's clothing in his spare bedroom."

"That is not surprising. Jules claimed his sister left them there. We all, including Sara, accepted his statement."

"Sara remembered the police had noted the sizes weren't consistent. Most were labeled as large or size fourteen. A few were labeled as small or size eight. Sara guesses his sister wears size eight."

Jim frowned. "Being a cross-dresser isn't a crime."

"No, but Winslow and two other techs from our lab went along with an agent to Jules's condo after Sara emailed me an hour ago. He found two olive-green women's trench coats. One—the large one—had had Jules's DNA on the inside of the sleeve at the wrist. The other—the small one—had Catalina's, not Abigail's, DNA on the inside of the sleeves. Winslow used rapid DNA tests and will do a more thorough analyses of DNA on all the surfaces of the coats tomorrow in the lab. He looked in the closet but couldn't find any matching green skirts and tops like Catalina wore to work but the other techs found them in a trash bag in the garbage bin in back of the condo." Carbonne's lip curled again. "We rushed because the garbage is picked up early on Tuesdays at Jules's condo."

Barbara brought her hand to her mouth as she gagged slightly. "What else did he find?"

Carbonne scanned his phone messages. "Winslow was especially proud that he found what he called 'come-hither gear'—a teddy, a leather miniskirt, and high vinyl boots—in a large size." Carbonne shook his head. "Winslow was sure that the brands were the same as for the ones on the stairs at Estella's house. He's is still young and gullible enough to be turned on by that type of garb."

Barbara said quietly, "Are you really going to build a case on clothes?"

"I've seen weaker cases. We have a witness now who saw two people wearing olive-green trench coats when they entered Estella's house on the night Catalina was murdered and one person wearing an olive-green trench coat leaving the house around six in the morning."

Barbara looked up from the table. "Jules wasn't one of the individuals entering the house in Santa Fe around eight in the evening. I questioned him here in Albuquerque until after seven."

Carbonne's lip curled again. "The witness could have easily missed Abigail leaving the house and Jules entering the house between eight in the evening and six in the morning."

"I guess that is true."

Carbonne turned to Jim. "Doctor, do you still think Nelson is having a nervous breakdown?"

Jim straightened. "It doesn't matter. Everything I've seen and heard indicates that Nelson is capable of distinguishing right from wrong. He can be charged and stand trial. However, he's also capable of confusing any investigator or juror. Barbara has done a superb job with him, considering his mental state—or acting skills."

Carbonne grinned. "Barbara is one of the finest interviewers I've seen. I also know from personal experience that she's more dogged than I am. Tomorrow, armed with a few more facts, she'll get Nelson to talk or get his lawyer ready to make a plea agreement. He'll get cocky if we put him in a safe house tonight because he'll think he's off the hook. Then

                                    J. L. Greger

he'll be sloppy." He poked Barbara's shoulder. "You can thank me later for softening him up."

Barbara eyed Carbonne suspiciously. "Do not overestimate yourself. I still think you are sleeping on the couch tonight. By the way, do you know where Jules is now?"

"With the additional preliminary information gained at his condo, I got the judge's approval to wiretap his phone. He made a call to his sister and several to a phone in the ICU. So far, he's hung up as soon as someone answered the call in the ICU. He also tried to call Nelson's phone, which was turned off." Carbonne patted Barbara's shoulder. "I counted on you to have insisted on that."

"That is standard procedure."

"I know, but most agents are sloppy. Now we wait. Agents are ready to tail Jules, but he hasn't left his condo yet."

Barbara brought her hand to her mouth and appeared to gag again. "My stomach is upset. I need to eat soon." She stood. "You said you had Estella moved. Are you sure she is safe? Abigail, Jules, or Nelson, when he is released, are apt to act rashly. Are you prepared?"

"I hope so to both questions." He opened the door. "Do you want me to make sandwiches or do you want to stop for a burger?"

Barbara choked. "Are you kidding? Your idea of making a sandwich is to slap a slice of bologna on a slice of bread. First, close the door and tell me where Estella is."

"She's still in the ICU. The attending physician insisted she shouldn't be moved from the ICU again and forced me to hire a private nurse for her."

Barbara face twisted into a smirk. "Private nurses are not allowed anymore in ICUs because hospitals already have a ratio of one or two nurses or aides per patient."

"Okay, the attending physician is an old friend and accepted my offer. The so-called private nurse is one of our techs." Carbonne added quickly. "He's an RN but several years ago decided working in our lab paid better and was less stressful."

"That is not enough."

"I agree." He winked. "It seems that Estella's cousins just flew in from Arizona and insisted on seeing her tonight."

"I assume those cousins are agents. You know you made a mistake. Estella does not have any close relatives."

"I know. That's why they're cousins. Best I could do."

Jim Jung had listened intently to the whole conversation. "How did you act so quickly?"

Barbara opened the door to leave. "He will do anything to avoid his administrative paperwork."

Carbonne turned off the light in the observation room. "Barbara was more..." He grinned. "...respectful of me before we moved in together."

CHAPTER 22: Barbara Gets Tough

Barbara had taken only two bites of her fish sandwich when Carbonne's phone buzzed. He said "yeah" twice and waved to the waitress. "Please bring us carry-out boxes and the check."

Barbara kept on eating because she feared she might not get another chance for hours, until he said, "We'll be right there." Then she packed their meals while Carbonne paid the cashier.

After he started the car, he handed her his phone. "Put this on speaker mode."

A woman's voice blared from Carbonne's phone. "ICU. Carol speaking."

"Finally got you." Barbara recognized Jules's breathy voice. "I'm worried. Has Estella been moved out of the ICU?"

"I don't think so, but I'll check."

A recording of "Cielito Lindo" played softly for over a minute. Carol sounded nervous when she returned to the phone. "She was moved to room 458."

"Are you okay?"

"Just unusually busy."

"Thanks." Jules disconnected.

Barbara gasped. "You said you did not move Estella."

Carbonne glanced over at her. "I didn't. The technician doing the wiretap alerted one of the agents posing as Estella's cousin every time Jules placed a call to the ICU. This was Jules's seventh call, but the first time he spoke. The so-called cousin knew this aide must be Jules's informant and intercepted her before she returned to the phone. I guess the aide became helpful after he explained the penalties for abetting murder. Maybe he did too good a job. She was nervous enough that Jules noticed."

"What do you plan to…"

Carbonne's car phone rang. A voice blared, "Jules's called a burner phone. He gave the room number of Estella's *new* room. The person receiving the call said only 'mmm' and hung up. We think the pitch suggests the receiver was a woman, but we're not sure. We also couldn't locate the phone because the call was too short, but we know it was transmitted to a tower near the University Hospital. We're braced around room 458 and the ICU."

"Good. Barbara and I will be at the hospital in fewer than ten minutes. Will go to the hospital security office because if the receiver was Abigail, she would recognize Barbara."

Barbara sat quietly for a several seconds before she asked, "What did the agents do with this aide, Carol? It would look suspicious if she left the ICU immediately, but she could signal to others if she stayed. You know Jules could have had several informants."

"Thought about that. One agent posing as a cousin watched Carol closely until hospital security could whisk Carol to their interview room in the basement of the old part of the hospital. A fake patient named E. G. Davis was moved into room 458 fifteen minutes ago. I thought Abigail or whoever received the call might check the directory before he or she went to the room."

"You should have interrupted my interview of Nelson sooner."

"Took me a while to set up the trap. Besides, you proved Nelson was sane and did what was necessary to trap him."

"You should have texted me."

"Would only have slowed me down. Besides, you don't read texts or emails when you're interviewing major suspects."

***

"Why did you break hospital protocol and tell a non-relative about Estella's location?"

Carol blinked back tears as she lifted her head to face Barbara. "Jules has been Estella's aide for years. I worked on Estella's campaign for mayor when I was a student in the associate in nursing program at Santa Fe College. I knew Jules was closer to her than anyone. It wasn't fair that the hospital wouldn't give him updates on her condition or let him visit her in the ICU, especially since her husband couldn't be found."

Barbara realized that this aide might be unaware that Nelson disguised in scrubs had been visiting Estella. "Did Estella have any visitors?"

Carol nodded. "The pet therapy volunteer with her dog Bug visited daily but she never stayed long. Everyone knew she had gotten special permission to enter the ICU."

"Anyone else?'

                    J. L. Greger

"Staff who knew her when she was mayor of Santa Fe stopped by."

"How do you know that?'

"I saw a woman physician from another unit once and a man in scrubs a couple of times."

"How do you know they knew Estella when she was mayor of Santa Fe?"

"I asked them." Carol's lips twisted. "You don't realize how nice Estella was to campaign workers and employees. We all loved her."

Barbara asked a few more questions and decided the young woman was naïve and had not talked to others about Jules's calls. If Jules or Abigail had other contacts in the ICU, Carol didn't know about them. She ordered supper from the cafeteria for Carol and asked the security staff to detain Carol in the conference room until any action in room 458 was concluded.

An agent disguised as a diet technician called. "Look at the video I'm transmitting live. Suspect A is getting off the elevator on the fourth floor."

Barbara saw on her phone screen a woman with short, black hair and wearing a white lab coat get off the elevator. The view was partially obstructed by the dietary department tray trolley that the agent was pushing. Barbara said, "Suspect A could be Abigail with a wig."

Suspect A disappeared for a minute while the agent swung the tray trolley around so that the camera mounted on it faced the door to room 458. Then Barbara could see the suspect walking toward room 458 and entering the room without knocking. All the while Barbara had been able to view the two agents in room 458 on the split screen. One was disguised as a patient and lay in the bed with a sheet drawn up to hide much of her face; the other was in the bathroom.

As the suspect entered room 458, Barbara saw the agent disguised as diet tech run to 458 on one side of the split screen.

On the other half of the screen, the suspect picked up a pillow at the foot of the bed. She was about to push the pillow onto the patient's head when the bathroom door swung open and an agent shouted, "Stop or I'll shoot."

Barbara felt like vomiting when on the other side of the screen, Carbonne raced from room 456 to room 458. She should have known Carbonne would not pass up a chance to be in the center of the action. Sometimes she wondered if he had a death wish because he took so many risks.

Carbonne watched as the agent disguised as a diet tech handcuffed the woman and pulled the pillow out of her hands. Carbonne pulled the wig off the woman to reveal long, ash-blonde hair.

Barbara signaled it was Abigail. Barbara couldn't explain why, but she began to sob as the agents arrested Abigail for attempted murder and read Abigail her rights. The tears seemed to release an inner tension and Barbara felt better.

This was a major break in the case. However, other agents would say that Barbara couldn't have done it without Carbonne's help. The worst part was they would be right, but maybe that didn't matter. Barbara knew that unraveling the roles of Abigail, Jules, Nelson, and probably Davita in the murders and attempted murders would be complex. However, results were inevitable and would not require daring exploits but rather patience and dogged determination. She had plenty of both.

Barbara texted Carbonne and slowly walked to room 458 where she found Abigail with a bored look on her face as the fake scene was disassembled. The only words Abigail had spoken to agents were: "I want a lawyer." Abigail didn't call her father but rather one of the best criminal lawyers in New Mexico.

Barbara approached Abigail. "Do you remember me? We spoke through a video conference."

Abigail did not even bat an eyelash.

Barbara drew close, turned on a recorder, and spoke softly. "I am not questioning you tonight. I want you to consider your options. If you provide the right evidence against Nelson Davis, your brother Jules, and even Davita Lopez, the DA might make a deal with you. Remember you have more to lose than your brother. Your medical career is over, of course, but you are still young enough to enjoy your wealth."

Abigail blinked.

"We know your Green Way to Beauty Spas are lucrative. They will not be after my friend Sara and the FDA tear them apart." Barbara smiled. "They will explore every nook and cranny of your businesses and practice and will pile up fines and jail time that will make the punishment for attempted murder look small. Think about it."

Abigail blanched and was even paler than usual.

Barbara figured she had finally scared Abigail. Now was the time for a little drama. She started to walk away. Then she turned and winked at Abigail. "Your lawyer likes to make plea deals, but he cannot if the others sing first. I do not think it will be hard to get your brother to talk."

Abigail looked blank.

"Oh, I forgot. Jules did not have a chance to tell you that the local police arrested him. After spending time in an Albuquerque police holding cell tonight, he can guess what his life in prison will be like. Also, the psychiatrist certified that Nelson is sane. Nelson will have to talk now or face the consequences. My advice is to be ready to talk first tomorrow morning."

Barbara slammed the door as she left room 458.

Carbonne greeted her, "Wow. Lady you've grown…."

"Do not say it. Sara told me I needed to stop being a nice lady and my patience is exhausted."

CHAPTER 23: Sara Makes Progress on Tuesday

Sara was happy. Barbara's email indicated she was through with being a lady and had given ultimatums to Abigail, Nelson, and Jules. Barbara emailed two main orders to Sara:

> *Find all weaknesses in the Green Way to Beauty Spa. I think Abigail counted on her business to provide income even if she was convicted. The loss of her wealth may make her more talkative.*
>
> *Become Estella's best friend. She must know something important because Abigail took a big risk last night to silence her.*

Sara had arranged last week for an FDA compliance officer to meet her at the spa in Santa Fe this afternoon. She and FDA officials thought the best preparation was to visit the spa in Albuquerque first. She guessed the staff in Albuquerque would be more cooperative than those in Santa Fe because they were probably frightened by the death of their manager, Catalina.

She was less sure of how to approach Estella because she hated to undermine Estella's trust in Nelson but knew it was necessary. She thought the first step was obtaining a restraining order so Nelson couldn't visit Estella, just in case the agents at the safe house couldn't control him.

***

Pete was whistling as he tinkered with a computer. "I'm only beginning to assess the contents on Jules's computer. To be honest, his computer may not yield much you can use. However, his messages to and from friends would make most agents blush. Most of his deleted emails to Nelson and Abigail are short. Many contain the phrase: 'will tell you more when I see you.' But he did send a couple of foolish emails last Wednesday."

Sara knew Pete wanted a response before he made his big reveal. "Stop dangling the carrot. What did you find?"

"He cancelled three of Estella's upcoming rallies. The timing is interesting. He did it immediately after his visit to the urgent care clinic."

"So?"

"The clinic nurse didn't tell him that Estella was already in the hospital in Santa Fe."

"You're right. He made a big jump when he assumed she was sick and cancelled the rallies." Sara typed on her laptop. "I suggested to Barbara that she might be able to use this tidbit when she questions Jules later today."

"Good."

"I hate to jerk you from one project to another but the evidence I need first today are items showing Nelson was abusive to Estella. I want to get a judge to issue a restraining order to prevent Nelson from seeing or talking to Estella."

Pete whistled. "Remember on Saturday I showed you an email where he referred to Estella as a 'fat pig'? Is that what you're looking for?"

"Physical threats would be better, but I'll take what you can find in the next hour. While you do that, I'll finish a profile of Nelson I started last night." She turned to leave.

"Come on—don't leave me hanging. My search might be easier if I knew more about him."

Sara turned to face Pete. "He went through majors like rain as he wandered through several colleges in the SUNY system."

"Huh, what's SUNY?"

"The State University of New York. Started in ecology, then switched to psych, then went over to theater with emphasis on acting, and then back to ecology. His grades weren't a problem. He excelled in all his courses. Money wasn't a problem either. His wealthy parents died in an accident awhile he was in college, and Nelson got half of their estate."

"Who got the other half of the estate?"

"A brother."

Pete smiled. "Now that might be useful. Nelson might admit things to his brother that he wouldn't to others."

"Oh, I'd also like copies of Estella's and Nelson's wills."

"Okay. I know I saw wills on one or both computers. I can forward them quickly." Pete winked. "Get out of here before you make more requests."

***

Estella's net worth was impressive with her home, two retail outlets on Canyon Road in Santa Fe, the duplex and land near Crownpoint, the cabin and land holdings in Chama, and her investments in energy properties. Nelson was not listed as a co-owner of any of the properties.

Up to now Sara had assumed Nelson would inherit these properties if Estella died. Sara's case for money as a motive for Nelson harming Estella was weakened when she saw Estella's will and a prenuptial agreement signed by Nelson. Pete noted the documents were on both Estella's and Nelson's home computers. Both were signed photocopies of the original with traces of a notary's seal imprint. Estella's will appeared to have been prepared six months ago. The only property that Nelson would inherit was the duplex and land near Crownpoint. Sara thought—or at least hoped—this might indicate that Estella trusted Nelson less than the scene yesterday at the hospital suggested.

According to Estella's will, Beryl Marks, LuAnn and Bo McCarran together, and Estella's housekeeper would each receive two hundred thousand dollars upon Estella's death. The rest of Estella's property was to be divided among various museums and charities; several were specific to Native Americans. Interestingly, Estella left her clothes to Jules. Obviously, Estella knew about Jules's lifestyle. Sara suspected a smart lawyer had Estella mention Jules in her will so that Jules couldn't claim she had inadvertently forgotten to include him.

Sara was further disappointed as she examined Nelson's financial records. He was much less wealthy than Estella, but he held almost a half-million dollars in stocks, a hundred thousand dollars in easily accessible accounts, and a 300-acre ranch about fifty miles from Gallup but only twenty miles from Estella's duplex in Crownpoint. He had no credit card debt or loans. She couldn't build the case in her request for a restraining order that Nelson was desperate for funds.

Sara finally hit pay dirt when Pete forwarded a copy of Nelson's will. All his stock and cash were to go to his brother upon his death, but the ranch was to go to Abigail Fix Smith. Pete noted that Nelson's will was on his computer, but he had not found Nelson's will on Estella's computer, *until* he scanned her deleted files. That meant Estella knew of Nelson's attachment to Abigail Fix Smith.

Sara concluded that Nelson and Estella were not the perfect couple as they pretended. Now all Sara needed was to find one or two threatening comments by Nelson about or to Estella, and Sara figured any judge would give her a restraining order. She marched back into Pete's space. "Well, what do you have?"

Pete handed her a printout. 'Seems Jules didn't lie. I found this deleted message."

> *Jules,*
> *We need a strategy to make Estella more marketable. Improving her looks and training her to modulate her voice to be less screechy is not enough. I think she'd win sympathy votes if she had a small accident and had to campaign on crutches. It can't be a major illness or her competitors could claim she wasn't capable of being a senator. Any ideas?*
> *Nelson*

"Pete, I could kiss you. I'll have my request off to the judge in ten minutes and I bet I'll have a restraining order within two hours. Now I want you to switch gears. I want any dirt you can find on the Green Way to Beauty Spa—financial mismanagement, inappropriate use of drugs like the botulinum toxin, tax evasion, and fraud or false claims for products."

Pete whistled. "Okay. Winslow already told me the employees at the Santa Fe spa were carnival hucksters."

"If you find useful items, I'll take you along to my meeting at the Green Way to Beauty Spa in Albuquerque in an hour."

"Is that a treat or a threat?"

✳✳✳

Sara drew the curtain around Estella's bed in the ICU and then placed Bug by Estella's side. Estella put her hand on Bug's neck and began to stoke him.

"Estella, I know last night was confusing. You are safe now. We arrested the woman you identified. She's being questioned by the FBI as we speak. Do you know her name.?"

Estella raised her hand and grunted "Ggg."

"Was it Abigail…?"

Estella didn't wait for Sara to finish before she grunted, "Ggg."

Sara guessed she must not have asked the right questions last night. "Do you think Nelson and Abigail are friends?" Sara decided to push. "You know—lovers?"

"Ggg. Ggg."

Sara noticed that Estella had stopped petting Bug. Her hands were in a praying position, and she was exhaling short breaths loudly and quickly—almost like a dog panting. Sara was surprised to see tears drain down Estella's cheeks. "Estella, I don't know how to say this. So, I'll be blunt. Would you glad if Nelson didn't come here anymore?"

Estella raised her hand as she said, "Ggg."

"Okay—you can stop worrying about Abigail, Nelson, and Jules. They can't get into the hospital. The hospital also fired the woman who was watching you for them." Sara knew that wasn't quite true. Carol had been put on administrative leave while the hospital administration worked with police, but Sara thought it unnecessary to worry Estella with that detail.

"Before I leave, I have to ask a few… unpleasant questions."

Sara had thought about her next questions, but hadn't devised any good ones that could be answered with "yes" and "no" responses. She lurched ahead anyway. "Did Nelson want to marry Abigail?"

"Uh," was followed by "Ggg."

"Does that mean you don't know?"

"Ggg."

"Let me put it another way. Did Abigail want to marry Nelson?"

"Ggg."

"I don't mean to be unkind, but need your help as we question Nelson. Did Nelson want to stay married to you because he wanted your money?"

"Uh." Then Estella raised her arm and rubbed her forefinger over her thumb as she said "Ggg."

Sara thought and then duplicated Estella's hand motion. Does that mean a little?"

"Ggg."

"Got it. He liked your money but that wasn't the main reason that he stayed with you?"

"Ggg."

"Did Nelson want to be a senator instead of you?"

Silence.

Sara repeated the question.

More silence. Then the little hand motion and "Ggg." After a long silence. Estella grunted "Ggg" repeatedly.

"Why didn't you divorce Nelson? Did you love him?"

Estella didn't respond.

"Did you like having him around the house?"

"Ggg."

"I'll have a lot more questions for you, but I think the therapists should work with you now." Then Sara realized that if Estella could move her hands, she might be able to write. She handed Estella a pen. "Can you write?"

Estella fingered the pen clumsily and dropped it.

Sara handed the pen to her again, but this time she placed Estella's fingers and thumb as she might hold a pen when writing. Then she rummaged in her purse and pulled out a pad of paper. She put the pad on her closed laptop and laid them on Estella's lap.

Estella began to print. Sara could see it was difficult. First a large *T* appeared. Then a lopsided *H*. Next a character that might be an *A*.

"Are you saying thanks?

"Ggg."

Sara felt tears in her eyes as she hugged Estella. She guessed this was the first time in years that Nelson wasn't terrorizing Estella. "You know Estella, you could get a divorce on the basis of mental cruelty. Pete, an FBI computer technician, found emails from Nelson that would support your case." Sara chuckled. "That would derail Nelson's political ambitions and make it easier for us to get the truth out of him."

Estella was silent.

"Don't answer me now but think about your options. Here's Pete's and my email addresses."

CHAPTER 24: Sara Visits Spas

The nurse at the Albuquerque Green Way to Beauty Spa—Diana Riggs—gulped repeatedly when Sara introduced herself and Pete as investigators from the FBI. She squeaked, "Oh, no," when Wiley Webster introduced himself and his associate as FDA compliance officers. Diana shook and then leaned against the wall as Wiley noted the FDA had received consumer complaints about the spa's home events.

Sara felt sorry for the gray-haired woman but decided this was a time for cool professionalism. "The FBI has reason to suspect that botulinum toxin from the Green Way to Beauty Spa in Albuquerque and/or Santa Fe may have been used to poison food. One death has resulted, and another woman may have permanent injuries. Furthermore, we think your boss, Catalina Herrera, may have been killed because she knew too much." Sara thought a bit and tried to word her next comment carefully. "The FBI might overlook the part you may have played in these events if you cooperate."

Diana stopped trembling. "Just a minute." She walked to the checkout counter, turned over a green flier, wrote *CLOSED TODAY* in large print, taped the sign to the front door of the spa, and locked the door. "I don't know of illegal activities but…" She coughed. "…several strange incidents during the last couple of weeks scared me." She lowered her voice. "I'd rather the clerk stayed here until you're through, but I don't want her to hear my comments. She idolizes the Smiths and is too young to see the obvious."

Sara nodded. "Pete, why don't you let the clerk help you access the store's computers and explain their systems."

Wiley added, "My associate will also need the clerk's help to find records online and to locate all the products in stock, while Sara and I question Ms. Riggs."

***

"I work here because hospital jobs on the floors are for young nurses." Diana waved a strand of hair from her face. The rest was in a tight updo. "After fifty, I couldn't endure twelve-hour shifts standing most of the time. This position gave me good hours except for the crazy home parties. I also get the benefit of free beauty products as I need them." She frowned creating only minimal lines around her mouth and on her forehead. "Dr. Smith makes it a condition of employment that all of us must look like advertisements for our products."

Sara was surprised that Diana had offered an explanation before she had even been asked a question. She guessed Diana knew a lot and would be talkative if she relaxed a bit. "You mentioned that several incidents during the last couple of weeks have scared you. Maybe that's a good place to start.? Tell us about the first incident. By the way, I will record our conversation."

Diana took a deep breath. "Let's see… It was Monday last week that Dr. Smith called the spa. She was annoyed when I told her Catalina had taken an early lunch break."

"Was that typical?"

"No, Catalina generally ate a sack lunch or had her lunch delivered."

Sara realized her question had been vague. "How did you know Dr. Smith was annoyed? Did she raise her voice?"

"Dr. Smith is much too controlled to scream. She said what she always says when she's annoyed, 'I'll send in my brother to sort out the problem.'"

"Is that a threat?"

Diana pulled at the strand of pearls around her neck. "Yes. Jules always apologizes when he arrives and then mentions that his sister will replace the person in question if her demands aren't met. I phoned Catalina on her cell immediately. I was surprised when she put her phone in speaker mode. I heard a man in the background say, 'You made your point' as I hung up."

"What happened next?"

"Catalina returned a half-hour later and made plane and hotel reservations to go to San Diego the next day. All she said was 'the Green Queen'—that's what all of us call Dr. Smith behind her back—wanted Catalina to check on 'those stupid jars for a new product.'"

Wiley leaned forward. "Why was that unusual?"

Diana blinked twice. "Dr. Smith is cheap. She usually insists Catalina book her bimonthly buying trips to San Diego a month in advance so she can get better airfares." She paused. "And Catalina had gone to San Diego the week before."

Sara waited for Diana to say more, but Diana stared into space and fiddled with the pearls around her neck. "Were there other odd incidents?"

"Well, yes. Dr. Smith usually visits our spa twice a month but she called—let's see—last Thursday and announced Catalina must meet her at five that day at the spa in Santa Fe. As usual, Catalina didn't say much except, 'The Green Queen is obsessed about those stupid green jars.'"

"Anything else odd?"

"Dr. Smith called me around four—not long after Catalina left for Santa Fe—and ordered me to be at the shop at eight the next morning because she wanted to review our inventory with me."

"So?"

"I thought it was strange because she always reviewed the inventory with Catalina." Diana pulled at her pearls again. "And… after I learned Catalina was dead… it seemed strange that Dr. Smith anticipated Catalina wouldn't be available. But I'm getting ahead of myself. I was nervous on Friday morning because Dr. Smith had abruptly ended a call more than a week previous when Catalina had suggested a case of our botulinum products was missing. When I arrived, Dr. Smith was rifling through the freezer, which we kept locked. I didn't think she knew where we kept the key. She ignored me until she announced that I didn't need to inventory our botulinum supply. She'd done it and would complete the required FDA forms. Then she stormed out." Diana gave another wrinkleless frown and said, "Strange."

Sara felt Diana might be withholding another detail. "What else was strange?"

"I checked for our freezer key. It was hidden in its usual place. Catalina had always told me that there were only two keys to the freezer— the hidden one and the one on Catalina's key chain."

"I'd like to make an impression of that key. Does your clerk know where it is kept?"

"No, only Catalina and I do… or did."

Sara smiled as she typed a note to Barbara.

Wiley took over the interview as he reviewed the "parties" that Diana had presided over during the last six months. It quickly became apparent that Jules was in charge of the events, which Diana described as "feeding frenzies." "I have to make to make injections so quickly and for so many clients that Jules dilutes the samples for me. He knew I hate the events. He tries to make them more pleasant for me by cleaning up afterwards."

Sara slipped a scribbled note to Wiley:

                                                J. L. Greger

Wiley stood. "I think my associate must have completed the inventory of the botulinum products by now. We will go over the details together with you."

Sara stood too. "Diana, you look like you could use a short break. I want Pete to update me on his activities before you discuss the inventory with the FDA officials."

As soon as Sara and Wiley stepped out of the patient consultation room, Wiley whispered, "I'm glad you said the *FBI* might overlook Diana's possible involvement in this. As an RN, she and Dr. Abigail Smith were responsible for accurate inventories of the botulinum toxin products. Diana also shouldn't have allowed anyone but another nurse or physician to dilute the product and accordingly determine the dosages injected."

"I knew I had to be careful about what I said. That's why I've recorded my interview and hope you will also record your conversation with Diana." Sara noticed Pete was winking at her. "Before you and your associate review the inventory with Diana, we'd better hear Pete's comments. He's an expert at finding deleted files and identifying falsified records. I think he's found something."

Pete quickly made it clear that many files had been deleted from the spa's computers in the last day or two. "I believe Diana was threatened several times, but it would be helpful if Diana and the clerk allowed me to search their personal phones and computers."

"That could be a problem. I have warrants that allow the FBI to confiscate any property belonging to the spa, Jules Smith, Abigail Smith, and Nelson Davis, but that won't cover employees' devices." Sara smiled at Wiley. "Take your time questioning Diana while I talk to my bosses. Also please consider the possibility that Agent Barbara Lewis or Special Agent Paul Carbonne may want to negotiate with the FDA in regard to any charges against Diana Riggs *if* Pete finds what I suspect he will."

Wiley winced. "I had a bad feeling last week when you set up the investigation of these spas." He shook his head. "Sara, you're a known commodity in the upper echelons of the FDA compliance unit. Your cases are always technical nightmares. That's why I brought along my associate from Dallas. He's only been a compliance officer for a few months. My bosses thought this case would be a learning experience for him. I've been instructed to play it by the book with Diana—well all employees." He coughed. "However, I'm sure my bosses will negotiate with the FBI if it becomes necessary. Good luck with your warrants and...."

"I've got to stop her." Pete rushed over to the clerk as she pulled her phone from a pocket in her lab jacket.

Sara was perplexed. She had no charges to level at the clerk but didn't know all that Pete had found. Even a murder suspect had the right to make a call. She followed Pete and held her breath as she listened to his conversation with the clerk.

"Look, I'm no agent, but I don't think you should tell anyone about this inspection until Dr. Sara Almquist talks to you."

The young clerk's pouty lips formed an O. "Oh, but I have to. I'll be fired along with Diana if I talk to you without permission from Jules or Dr. Smith You know everyone wants to steal our products. It's well known the FDA favors our large competitors. Jules reminds me of that every day when he stops by. And he told me the FBI and particularly you..." She pointed at Sara. "...had a vendetta against him."

Sara straightened. "You need to think about the various legal consequences before you place that text. It's your choice."

Pete laughed. "From what I've seen already, I'd guess you won't have this job much longer anyway because this spa is in big trouble."

The clerk burst into hysterical tears but didn't send the text.

Sara called Barbara, but found she was unavailable. She called Carbonne.

***

"I doubt they will be as cooperative here in Santa Fe as they were in Albuquerque. That's why I've asked Hank Snow, the resident FBI agent in Santa Fe, to meet us at the local Green Way to Beauty Spa."

Pete snickered. "Did you rile Davita when you and Carbonne questioned her about her mother's death? Or did you and Winslow insult the nurse there when you visited the spa last week?"

Sara didn't know the answer, but she suspected Pete had guessed right on both counts. "Let's not waste time in fruitless discussions. You know Hank doesn't like to be kept waiting."

Wiley groaned. "I wouldn't call our discussions at the Albuquerque spa 'pleasant,' especially after Carbonne and two other agents arrived."

"Carbonne was annoyed when Diana dithered and was slow to locate the freezer key. His patience has always been limited, but now as the chief of the local FBI office he's particularly annoyed if anyone wastes his time." She saw Hank Snow walking toward them. "By the way, Hank has a short fuse, too. And I'm afraid Pete and I left him in the lurch last week."

Wiley and his associate both inhaled sharply.

Pete extended his hand to Hank. "We've got to stop meeting like this. Winslow told me we're in for a real treat. He thought the clerk and nurse here would give carnival hucksters a run for their money."

Sara stepped forward more timidly. "Hank, I hated to call you at the last minute but after our experience at the spa in Albuquerque, I thought I needed your help." She bit her lips. "And I want to apologize for…."

"No need." Hank deeply lined face crinkled into a grin. "Had a talk with Carbonne. He explained everything. Didn't know you had multiple roles. No wonder the young woman agent was nervous around you."

Sara thought Carbonne must have stretched the truth and inflated her role in helping Sanders. Most of all, she hoped Carbonne hadn't mentioned Sanders's name. On second thought, she was sure Carbonne wouldn't have made that mistake. This wasn't the time for analyses of anything but the current situation. "I'll take the lead because I've questioned Davita before, but feel free to jump in. She's desperate for money. Is probably scared because she knows more about her mother's death than she's admitted. Carbonne thought she might be a blackmailer, but she snowed me." Sara shook her head. "I guess I've read several of the suspects on this case wrong."

Hank nodded. "I'll play the heavy while you play the good cop."

Wiley cleared his throat. "You probably don't have to play the heavy because after what we learned at the other spa, it's pretty obvious this manager knowingly was involved in fraud and misuse of controlled substances."

***

Davita walked up to Sara as she entered the spa. "I talked to a lawyer. I don't have to answer questions about my mother's death. Stop harassing me."

Sara blinked in surprise as Hank stepped forward. "We've got a list of characters who might have poisoned your mother. Up to now, your name wasn't on the list. Don't raise my hackles. I'll add your name to the list of shady characters in this case."

Sara waved her hand between Davita and Hank. "We aren't here to discuss your mother's death. I notified you yesterday that the FDA would inspect your records and inventory today. Here is FDA compliance officer Wiley Webster."

Wiley quickly took control. He insisted Davita close the shop during the inventory and told the clerk to cooperate with Pete as he duplicated all the spa's computer files. He also told the nurse that she must cooperate help his associate with the inventory while he spoke to Davita in a patient consultation room.

Davita screamed, "This is harassment. Get out of here."

Sara handed copies of the search warrants for the spa and for the electronic devices of all employees to Davita and the nurse. Sara stifled a laugh when the nurse turned to Wiley's associate from the FDA and said, "I think you'll find our records are in perfect shape."

The FDA associate shook his head. "I doubt it. I found two cases of botulinum toxin products was missing from the spa at the Albuquerque location." He nodded at Pete. "The FBI's computer expert already identified many files that were altered or deleted from the spa's corporate computer network during the last week. We even know who was logged in during those activities. You were one of the individuals. I think your best option is to convince me that you weren't an individual who deleted and modified files."

The nurse whimpered but her face remained masklike.

Davita slammed the button to open the sliding frosted doors to a patient consultation room. Sara followed Wiley into the room, while Hank remained outside with Pete and the clerk.

An hour later, Hank huddled all the investigators in a back corner of the spa. "What've you got?"

The associate pointed at a quivering mass on a stool by the checkout counter. "It wasn't easy making that uppity nurse see reality, but she has admitted she 'fixed' documents on the usage of the botulinum products under Davita's direction. It seems the records now indicate that she diluted a fresh bottle of toxin each morning and discarded what was left in the bottle each evening when she closed the spa. She actually used the already diluted product until the bottle was empty." He checked his notes. "Then her memory gets fuzzy. She thinks Davita or Jules regularly took bottles of undiluted botulinum product. She assumed they conducted other parties without her."

Wiley asked. "Did she give a reason for not reporting them?"

"Threats from Davita that that the nurse would be fired if she contacted the FDA. She never mentioned Abigail Smith."

Hank turned to Pete. "What've you got?'

"I downloaded all computer files from the spa and the employees' phones and computers and had a pleasant conversation with the clerk. She helped me locate crucial files because as she said, 'Do you think I wear green every day because it's my favorite color? It's easier than hearing the Green Queen and her flunky, Davita, yell at me.'" Pete whistled. "Then it gets better. You'd better listen to part of what I recorded."

The clerk's voice was clear on the recording. "The other FBI technician—I think his name was Winslow—shook me up last Friday. I realized the jig was up here, but I played it cool and watched Davita more. I always thought she went out the back door to smoke in the alley but— no cap—she was talking to Jules. Woke me up to another point. Why were all employees at the spas, but Davita, forced to wear green?"

Pete turned off the recording. "I tried to get her to talk about the nurse. This all I got her to say." He played the recording.

The clerk's voice on the recording was softer this time. "Our nurse is frozen in fear of losing her cushy job. Just like her face is frozen by too many Botox injections."

Hank looked at Sara. "Can you top that?"

"Hardly. All Wiley and I learned was Davita is aware of her Fifth Amendment rights." Then she laughed. "Her legal advisor is Abigail's and Jules's father, Verne Smith."

Wiley whispered to his associate and then announced. "The FDA has enough to file a major case of fraud against the owners of the Green Way to Beauty Spas and Davita Lopez because she cooperated fully with them. We may be able to charge them all under the Controlled Substances Act as dealers. That will mean considerable fines and incarceration. The charges against this nurse will have to be assessed further. Any charges against the two clerks and Diana Riggs are apt to be minor and negotiable."

Sara laughed. "I guess I didn't disappoint you. You'll be working on this case for weeks."

CHAPTER 25: Barbara Negotiates on Wednesday

"A judge released Dr. Smith pending her arraignment and instructed her that she couldn't stay with her brother. The poor woman was forced to stay in a hotel room alone at a time when she needed her family." Abigail's lawyer remained standing as if he expected to leave immediately.

Barbara wanted to gag and knew Carbonne would say "cut the crap." "We have proof that Abigail and Jules Smith talked immediately before Abigail attacked Estella Garcia Davis. The judge did not want them to have an opportunity to adjust their stories before they were questioned initially. Furthermore, Jules was in a holding cell in the city jail waiting for his lawyer father to arrive from Texas." Barbara doubted she should add the next comment but did. "Finally, Abigail is not poor and could afford to stay at one of the best hotels in Albuquerque."

Barbara thought she had responded harshly. She hated to admit it, but she thought Carbonne and Sara might be right. She felt a sense of satisfaction when Abigail showed a slight sign of fear. Her left eye twitched.

The interrogation was slow. Abigail invoked her Fifth Amendment rights when asked most of the questions. After only a half-hour, Barbara announced, "Dr. Smith, you will be arraigned this afternoon at the federal courthouse for the attempted murder of Estella Garcia Davis. The Bernalillo County District Attorney felt you could not get a fair trial in state courts and has asked for the FBI to take over this case because Estella is a candidate for national office and your business is in two states."

Barbara stood and left before the lawyer could protest. Jules and Verne Smith, serving as his son's lawyer, were waiting in another interrogation room.

***

"Your sister was talkative," Barbara said as she breezed into the next room with an Albuquerque police officer. Verne was standing in a corner of the interrogation room in front of Jules. She guessed Verne hoped those in the observation room could not view his private conversation with Jules if he positioned himself correctly.

Jules slunk to the table with his head down. "My sister is never talkative."

Barbara ignored his comment. "We know you called your sister and gave her the room number of Estella Garcia Davis's room in University Hospital last night."

Verne coughed. "You had no right to wiretap his phone."

"We did after we found Catalina's coat in his closet and her green skirt, beige top, and underclothes in a garbage bag in his trash."

Verne coughed.

She did not pause to give Verne a chance to speak. "Catalina's DNA was on all those clothes in spots where only a wearer of those clothes would leave DNA."

Verne spoke. "The garbage bag was in a common garbage collection bin behind several condos."

Barbara reminded herself to be tough. "Jules's DNA was found on the bag and the clothes." She didn't add that Abigail's DNA had also been found on the clothes. "That means we can charge you, Jules, with the murder—or abetting the murder—of Catalina Herrera. The charges against you will depend on how much you cooperate."

She hoped Jules would respond but he sat quietly with his eyes closed.

"We know Catalina and your sister entered the home of Estella Garcia Davis on Thursday around eight p.m. We have a witness. The medical examiner in Santa Fe says Catalina was murdered between two to four a.m. on Friday. A person in a green trench coat was seen leaving the Davis home around six a.m. A woman's olive-green trench coat with your DNA on the inside the wrist areas of the sleeves was in your closet."

Verne smiled. "I believe the witness saw a woman leave."

"Counsel, are you aware your client frequently wears women clothing?"

Jules whimpered.

Verne shook his head. "Agent Lewis, are you harassing my client because of his personal behavior?"

Barbara was glad witnesses were present. "Certainly not. However, we found a number of items of women's clothing in Jules's closet."

"Guest closet."

"Those clothes had Jules's DNA in spots that indicated he's worn the clothing."

Verne coughed. "We plan to charge the Albuquerque Police Department with endangering Jules's life."

The Albuquerque police officer straightened but remained silent. Barbara forced herself to remain calm. "Tell me why you think that."

Jules lifted his head for the first time. "As he led me to the holding cage, an Albuquerque officer asked, 'Do you prefer to be locked up with the men or in administratively segregated housing?'"

"What did you say?"

"With the men. That was a mistake. I should have been warned."

Barbara felt sorry for Jules but thought he was apt to be more cooperative now. "In the future, you can always ask for administratively segregated housing. Now let me explain your options. If you tell the truth and name your collaborators, I will recommend that the judge be lenient with you during sentencing. The case against you is strong for abetting the attempted murder of Estella Garcia Davis in the hospital last night."

Jules returned to his slumped position.

His father said, "My client has nothing to say."

"Fine, Abigail will be arraigned this afternoon in federal court for the attempted murder of Estella Garcia Davis."

Both men gasped.

"We think she is apt to become talkative as we explore with her new evidence about the murder of Catalina Herrera." Barbara wanted to lessen Jules's loyalty to his sister. "She certainly did not have kind things to say about you when we questioned her."

"She never does."

"We have decided not to arraign you until we have a more complete list of charges against you. I suggest you—in consultation with a lawyer who is concerned *only* with *your* interest—think seriously about admitting your guilt and naming others."

Barbara and the police officer left the room.

"Do you think it's wise to wait?" asked the Albuquerque police officer.

"I think he is more apt to think and accordingly talk about his sister if he is not in jail. I also think he is more apt to contact another lawyer if he is not in jail. If he sticks with his father, an appellate judge will throw out any conviction on the basis of inadequate legal representation."

The Albuquerque police officer nodded. "The officer who asked his cell preference in front of others could be in hot water."

"Do not say more and compound the problem." She smiled at the officer. "I am sorry, but I have to check with my FBI colleagues before I talk to the next suspect. I will get back to you after Abigail is arraigned."

Barbara ducked into her own office to check her emails from Sara and Pete. They had provided her with useful points to use as she questioned Nelson, but she doubted Sara's and Pete's time with FDA compliance officers in the two spas would strengthen the case against Nelson. She turned off her phone and drank a cup of tea. Tea didn't seem to irritate her stomach as coffee did lately.

She wasn't sure how to begin the interview with Nelson. Should she scare him immediately or should she build up his confidence before she attacked him? Carbonne had agreed to watch this interview from the observation room because he thought Nelson was the cleverest of the suspects.

***

"Mr. Davis, did you have a relaxing evening with the FBI protecting you?"

He smiled. "Best sleep I've gotten in almost a week."

"Good. I need your help to reconstruct what happened to Catalina Herrera during the last three days of her life. I believe you were with her much of that time." She paused and hoped Nelson would take the bait.

He didn't. Barbara decided not to try to clarify Catalina's and his exit from San Diego because she couldn't endure that discussion again. Why did you stop in the Gallup area? Was it to visit Estella's duplex or inspect your ranch?

He blinked. "What ranch?"

"Mr. Davis, you've been certified by a psychiatrist as sane. You conversed normally with agents at the safe house last night. We've checked your and Estella's property holdings…" She decided to needle him. "…and wills. Please stop your silly games. You can be charged with obstructing justice."

"Are you calling that bit of useless land a ranch?"

"Yes. The FBI agents who visited it reported there were cattle, horses, and two cabins on the land."

"Did my foreman say he saw me?"

Barbara debated internally how to answer Nelson's question. The FBI agent based in Farmington had talked to the ranch foreman and the residents of one-half of Estella's duplex. They'd not seen Nelson last Wednesday or Thursday. However, the foreman's teenage son reported he'd seen Nelson on Wednesday with a woman, but not "the usual one." Barbara avoided the details and said, "You were seen at your ranch cabin with a woman."

Nelson eye's narrowed. "Then why did you ask me?"

"I wanted to give you a chance to cooperate. Why did you stop at the ranch?"

Nelson sighed. "The usual reason. Catalina and I have spent many pleasant weekends there."

"Oh. I was told the woman you are usually with is a blonde. Catalina was a brunette." She paused. "Please stop being creative with your answers."

"I hadn't realized my foreman was a Peeping Tom. We were tired when we reached Gallup. Catalina thought a picnic at my ranch would be fun."

"It does not make sense to drive more than an extra hundred miles for picnic when you're on a seven hundred-mile trek. What was the other reason for stopping at your cabin?"

"I needed to pick up several photos I'd left there. I've taken many of the best shots for my new book around there. Did you know I have a book about to be published?"

The agent had found a file cabinet full of photos in the cabin. Most were of scenes in the region, but the teenager helped the agent locate other photos in boxes under the bed. The agent described these mainly as "raw" shots of a nude blonde woman with a few photos of a blond man in drag. The teenage boy had explained he had at first used the cabin when he felt like getting drunk. After he had accidentally discovered the intimate photos, he had regularly checked for new photos. Barbara didn't want to mention the boy. "Yes, I have seen a draft of your book, but I am more interested in the intimate portraits of Abigail Fix Smith and of Jules Smith that an FBI agent found under your bed in the cabin. How did you plan to use those photos?"

"Why? Do you want to pose for me?"

Barbara hoped that she did not blush. "No. I thought while Abigail and Jules might have enjoyed the photo shoots, they might not want others to see those photos."

She waited for a comment, but Nelson only leered at her and licked his lips.

"We know your relationship with Abigail goes back at least fifteen years and she is listed in your will. Now why did you want those photos bad enough to pick them up last Thursday?"

"I wanted to tease Abigail and Jules and get them to pose for more photos."

"Did you ask Catalina to pose for an intimate portrait?"

"Yes, but she refused."

"Did that make you mad?'

"No, there are lots of brunettes in New Mexico willing to pose for me."

Barbara suspected he was telling the truth about Catalina because the teenage boy had estimated that Nelson and Catalina had stayed at the cabin fewer than twenty minutes. "I think there might be another reason for collecting those photos. It involves Estella."

Nelson stopped grinning when Barbara mentioned Estella. "Estella doesn't know much about Abigail, except that she is the director of the Green Way to Beauty Spas."

"Estella knows a lot. Perhaps even enough to make you afraid."

Nelson shook his head. "You didn't do your homework. I don't need her money."

"I know, but she has something you want."

"Like what?"

"You hoped Estella would launch your political career if she became too ill to run for office."

"Creative idea."

"Did you share that idea with anyone?'

"No."

"How about this email from you to Jules?" Barbara handed Nelson the printout of an email that Pete had found.

"How did you get this?"

"That is not important."

Nelson sighed. "I was desperate to boost Estella's campaign. It wasn't easy."

"And?"

He paused and sighed again. "It's true—my marriage, especially if Estella was disabled, could boost my political career. However, I never wanted Estella dead."

After a long pause, Barbara asked, "Why?"

I'm married to a woman who lets me do what I want. If I divorced her, Abigail would expect me to marry her."

"Why is that a problem?"

"Have you talked to Abigail? She's a control freak. Living with her would be a nightmare."

"Yes. I've talked to Abigail. She can be charming." Barbara decided that keeping Nelson in protective custody last night had been a good investment of FBI funds. He had not learned that Abigail had tried to kill Estella last night, and he'd provided a strong motive for Abigail's action. Barbara knew she should question him more, but she had a splitting headache. "I think we are through for now. I assume you would feel safer in protective custody for another day?"

"Yes, but I won't feel really safe until Abigail and Jules aren't free to threaten Estella and me."

Barbara left the room quickly before she gagged at his fake fears. She paused in the hallway to email the agents manning the safe house.

> *Make sure Nelson sees no media reports on Abigail's arraignment and receives no communications about Estella.*
> *Continue to record all conversations with him.*
> *Goad him into talking about Jules and Abigail. Our best chance of solving this case is if we get the suspects fighting among themselves.*
> *Thanks.*

"You may have what you need." Carbonne winked at her as she walked into the observation room. "But you'll have to act quickly. Play Nelson's last comments to Abigail and her lawyer before the arraignment."

"The arraignment is in thirty minutes."

"I know. A car and driver are at our front door. Abigail's lawyer will be waiting for you at the federal courthouse in Conference Room B. I told him you were coming from a session with Nelson Davis."

CHAPTER 26: Barbara Is Outsmarted

Barbara had expected Abigail to wilt as she listened to the recording of Nelson calling her a control freak. Instead, Abigail had defiantly asked her lawyer, "Why are we wasting time with this woman before my arraignment?"

Less than fifteen minutes later, Abigail looked like a different person. She had messed her hair and smeared her eye makeup. She looked at the floor as she muttered in a weak voice, "not guilty" when the judge asked how she would plead in regard to the charge of attempting to murder Estella Garcia Davis.

While her lawyer claimed Abigail was not guilty by reason of temporary insanity, Abigail had swayed in her chair with her hands uplifted and moaned. The judge had insisted the lawyer control his client.

The lawyer had quieted Abigail and apologized to the judge before he asked for a court-appointed psychiatrist to reaffirm a report from a psychologist he'd hired to examine his client.

***

Barbara felt like a fool as she read the report from the psychologist hired by Abigail's lawyer. She and the U.S. prosecuting attorney had rushed to arraign Abigail. He had thought it would be easy to convince Abigail and her lawyer to provide evidence against Nelson and Jules in the murder of Catalina Herrera when she was facing charges for the attempted homicide of Estella. Now, Abigail was most likely facing a year or less in a psychiatric hospital and the U.S. attorney had lost his leverage on her.

Thus, Barbara swallowed hard before she took the call from the U.S. attorney late Wednesday afternoon He didn't yell as she expected.

"Barbara, we goofed. You and Sara warned me that Abigail Smith was a convincing actress. I should have listened.

The situation now is complicated. Her lawyer can invoke her Sixth Amendment rights if he can show the attempted murder of Estella Garcia Davis and the murder of Catalina Herrera are linked. The local district attorney thinks the cases aren't related; I think an appellate judge might say they were linked. That means I should lead or at least be present when Abigail is questioned in regard to Catalina Herrera's murder."

"Okay, but I doubt her lawyer will allow her to answer any questions."

"Maybe he will, if we set the stage right. We need to make Abigail and her lawyer think it is to Abigail's advantage to answer our questions. One way to do this is to accept she was at diminished capacity *temporarily* when she tried to kill Estella in the hospital. That will make them complacent while we ask for Abigail's help in refuting the claims by both Jules Smith and Nelson Davis that she masterminded the murder of Catalina Herrera. I think she'll talk."

"So, we accept the case against her for the attempted murder of Estella is a bust?"

"Basically, but if we push her through such prolonged sessions with us and our psychiatrist, she either won't be able to keep up the act or she will crack."

"Really?"

"Look at it this way. In my plan a, we'll convict her for her crimes. If we can't, we'll accept my plan b and put her in a psych hospital for as long as possible. She'll be there longer if she's actually sick and not acting. Society will be protected from her for perhaps two years."

***

Barbara was in a funk. Her current case or cases weren't about justice. They were just games of deception by everyone.

Carbonne had lectured her this morning, "Our job in the FBI is to remove dangerous criminals from the population by convictions. That means making compromises—accepting less than perfect plea agreements and getting convictions for crimes that aren't showy. Remember Al Capone was convicted of tax evasion."

Sara had made her feel worse when she stopped by Barbara's office after the arraignment and offered unsolicited advice. "Of our main suspects for Catalina's and Beryl's murders, the one I'd most like to see released on a plea bargain or insanity pleas is Jules. He's the least likely to mastermind another crime."

Barbara understood the wisdom of Carbonne's and the U.S. attorney's comments and agreed with Sara. *However,* she felt Catalina deserved justice. And it was hard to get a conviction for abetting murder when the actual perpetrator wasn't identified and convicted.

Barbara spent an hour making a list of weak points in the cases against all the suspects after reviewing Sara's interviews with Jules and Davita. As usual, Sara had made more progress than she had.

Barbara doubted she was cut out to be an agent. She neither enjoyed interviewing suspects, like Nelson and Abigail, nor negotiating with public officials, like the U.S. attorney. They showed no real emotions, except ruthlessness. It might have been okay if she felt she was gaining justice for the victims, but she doubted that occurred most of the time. As a small town police officer, she felt she was an important part of the community. She didn't as an agent.

She wandered down to her mail slot in the business office. The letter, she was waiting for, hadn't arrived. That probably meant she wouldn't get the position that she had interviewed for three weeks ago. Employers always mailed offer letters before the rejection letters. The new position would make her part of a creative team with constructive not destructive goals.

Barbara bit her lip. She sent a short email to Jim Jung:

> *I want to know whether Abigail could be considered mentally unstable when she tried to suffocate Estella on Monday, but coherent when she lured Catalina to her death last Thursday. I need more than theoretical speculations.*

> *I also need to know Abigail's soft spots. What are ways we can provoke her and undermine her confidence?*

CHAPTER 27: Sara Gets Lucky

Sanders called early—at five-thirty—on Wednesday morning. He immediately asked whether Sara had made reservations for her trip to Boca Raton on Friday. She didn't want to bore him with her current problem. It was unlikely that any of the uncooperative murder suspects in this case would ever be convicted unless one squealed on the others or a miracle occurred. She replied, "Murder investigations aren't easy to force into a scheduled routine. They tend to develop at their own pace. But don't worry, Bug and I will meet you in Miami on Friday morning."

"That bad? I can scrap my plan to rent an airboat on Saturday and tour the Everglades if you're too exhausted to enjoy it."

"Nonsense," she lied. "I'll be ready for action."

***

Sara knew her statement to Sanders could be true if she finished up her major interviews on the case today. Thus, Sara settled Bug into her small office before she began to scan her emails at seven. As she read one from Pete, she thought about their conversation after they and the FDA officers audited the Green Way to Beauty Spa in Santa Fe yesterday.

Pete had said, "I found a number of deleted emails in which Nelson propositioned Catalina on his and the spa's computers. Horny devil also sent a lot of racy emails to Abigail. The exchanges are almost humorous because both women always responded in a businesslike manner. However, I didn't find any suggestive messages to his wife or Davita."

"So?"

He'd whistled. "Davita found a couple of Nelson's emails to Catalina on the spa's computers and sent them to Abigail."

"What did Abigail say or do?"

"Nothing that I can find on the computers, but that's the day Abigail ordered Catalina to go to San Diego."

"What? That doesn't make sense. Abigail had to know Nelson was going to San Diego last Tuesday. She wouldn't throw Catalina into his arms."

Pete smiled. "I think Abigail might be the type of woman who demands a man proves his love for her. The young hotshot in the lab—Winslow—suggested an intriguing idea. Did you ever see the Hitchcock movie *Strangers on a Train?*"

"OMG. That's the movie where two people agree to kill someone the other person wanted gone. But who do you think the two people are in this case?"

"It's obvious. Nelson—he wanted his wife gone or disabled so he could take over her political career—and Abigail—she wanted Catalina gone because Catalina could expose the corruption in the spas and was a threat to Abigail's relationship with Nelson."

"Nice theory, but we need concrete evidence."

Sara stopped remembering their conversation from yesterday and reread an email from Pete. Maybe he'd performed the miracle she needed:

> *Sara,*
> *Catalina had an appointment with a lawyer on the Monday before her trip to San Diego. Here's his phone number. It's the unidentified number which she called three times the following Thursday.*
> *Pete*

***

Sara set up several appointments and started her second diet cola before she called the lawyer Catalina had contacted.

She had to ask twice before the lawyer admitted Catalina was a client. After several questions, he acknowledged, "Someone called Catalina during her second visit to my office. I may have said, 'You've made your point,' at the end of the call." Finally, after five more questions, he admitted, "I debated whether to call the police when I read about Catalina's murder in the newspaper, but I hate the runaround the police always give me."

Sara hid her annoyance. Lawyers took an oath to uphold the law. "Tell me what you know or suspect."

"Catalina called three times and stopped by to see me last Thursday. She approved a letter I prepared for the FDA. It detailed Catalina's allegations against the Green Way to Beauty Spas. I'll fax you the letter."

"Why didn't you send the letter?"

"I was afraid...."

"Of not being paid?"

"No, but I… I can't afford to be involved in long, drawn-out procedures when no reimbursement was possible."

Sara asked the lawyer to fax her the contents of his file on Catalina Herrera and thanked him for his *valuable* time.

When she called Carbonne to ask whether the lawyer could be prosecuted, Carbonne laughed. "That chicken excrement isn't worth trying to prosecute. Send a copy of the letter and his file notes to your friend at the FDA—what's his name?—Wiley something."

***

The interview with Jules started well. He wasn't accompanied by his father but rather by a young, eager lawyer who immediately mentioned Jules was interested in a plea agreement in return for his cooperation.

Sara internally sighed in relief but said, "We'll consider a plea after we ascertain a few facts. I'll warn you I'm tired of playing cat-and-mouse games. I expect full answers." She had debated the previous evening how to start the interview and had decided to start small. She chastised herself because the death of one person was not less important than that of another, but she started small. "I want to explore Beryl Marks's last few days. Did you talk to her in the week before the rally in Clovis?"

Jules's lips formed a fleshy pink O. "Oh dear, I'll have to think. I must have." He bit his lip. "Yes, first to remind her to bring her fig preserves to the rally and then after she and Nelson got into a disagreement."

Sara straightened. This was new. "Why did they argue?"

"Nelson insisted she open a new jar of her fig and nut preserves to check if she'd made it right. Then he'd wanted to take all her preserves to the rally, but she insisted that she would deliver them."

"Did you go to her house?"

"No."

His lawyer taped his shoulder.

"I mean, yes. Nelson insisted I deliver directions for how to get to the rally to her. It was silly because I could have emailed them."

"Then why did you go?"

"Nelson ordered me to do it." He bit his lip. "Look, I might as well admit it. I don't argue with Nelson or my sister. I do what they command. It's easier that way."

"Did Beryl treat you to her canned figs?"

"No, I was there about five minutes." He looked down at the table. "I knew about the recipe she used. I'd given it to Nelson originally as a joke." Jules smiled. "I wanted to show him that he knew less than he

                                           J. L. Greger

thought, but the joke backfired on me—as usual." He shook his head. "It was a bad recipe. I wouldn't have eaten Beryl's fig preserves."

Sara believed Jules. "Thank you for filling in a few gaps, but I still don't understand one point." Sara decided a bluff was better than a straightforward question. "We know—because of lab analyses—that botulinum toxin products from the spas were added to the figs served at the rally. How?"

Jules's full pink lips again formed an *O*. "The preserves were canned with that weird recipe. They formed botulinum toxin naturally."

Sara frowned. "We know botulinum toxin was added. Someone wanted the figs to be contaminated with plenty of toxin."

Jules and his lawyer whispered with their hands shielding their mouths. The lawyer spoke, "He feels uncomfortable answering your question without assurances."

Sara decided to be a bit of an actor, too. She went to the observation room where Hank Snow and Wiley Webster were waiting, "Do you agree with me? I don't think he poisoned Beryl. If he's the one who added the botulinum toxin from the spas to the preserves served at the rally, anyone who became sick can sue him in civil court. Estella is the only one with severe long-lasting symptoms. She's more afraid of Nelson than of Jules. I'm going to offer him a bit of hope."

Hank nodded. "Shucks, yes."

"Try not to preclude the FDA from acting." Wiley's face twisted. "But do what's necessary to get him to talk."

Sara returned to the interrogation room. "Only a district attorney or a federal prosecutor can approve plea agreements, but I think they won't pursue a case against you in regard to what I think you're about to admit. I certainly will recommend that course of action."

Jules's lawyer hesitated before he said, "Go ahead."

Jules blinked back tears. "Nelson ordered me to dump all the preserves Beryl delivered to the rally into a bowl. He even gave me the bowl. Beryl… she argued with me. She thought the jars were pretty enough to put on the table. I did what Nelson ordered and added the toxin from the spa onto the fig preserves and stirred it in." He brushed tears from his eyes. "It wasn't easy without anyone noticing. You know the botulinum toxin is lot more toxic when injected than when fed. I had to add the contents of a lot of bottles to the preserves, but I managed because the churchwomen were too busy to notice me."

After Sara completed questioning Jules about the rally, she spent an hour determining how he siphoned off botulinum toxin products from the spas. He confirmed details that the nurses and clerks at the spas had told her and added several useful tidbits. The plan to "conserve" botulinum product used in the clinics and conduct additional parties without the nurses had been Davita's idea. Abigail had liked the idea and ordered Jules to make it happen. Finally, Jules admitted that he and Davita, who did the injections at these extra parties, each received ten percent of the take from these events, which netted them an additional two thousand dollars each month.

Sara was sure that Wiley was salivating about this new information, but she didn't pursue it further. He could do that himself, later. Instead, she asked, "What about Catalina?"

"She was a problem. Davita and I knew she wouldn't approve. So, we didn't tell her about our way to make extra revenue, but I think she figured it out when I removed two cases of the toxin from her freezer."

"Why do you think that?"

"I found her re-inventorying her supplies on a Friday night after the spa was closed. I guess that was about ten days ago. It scared me and I told Abigail because she was the one who had ordered me to get a lot of toxin for her and Nelson's special project." He shrugged. "I didn't ask for details."

The next half-hour was slower as Sara tried to explore what happened during the last week. Sara kept reassuring Jules and finally said, "I guarantee you'll feel safer when your sister and Nelson are convicted and not threatening you daily. They've kept you in an emotional prison for years."

Jules convulsed into tears. "They call me a disgrace and demean what I say and do because I like pretty clothes."

He cried so hard that he had trouble breathing. Sara was glad that she hadn't shown Jules the pictures of him found in the cabin. She didn't want to join the long list of people who had abused him.

Jules's lawyer couldn't calm Jules. "I think my client and I need to talk privately. When he found me yesterday after you suggested his father wasn't representing him well, he was suicidal. The psychiatrist I contacted thinks he should be hospitalized for his own protection." The lawyer kept his arm over Jules's shoulder. "This isn't a cheap trick. He believes he has to confess in order to survive, but he needs a break."

"I'll send in beverages and sandwiches and check back on you in an hour."

***

Hank stood when Sara walked into the observation room. "Wiley and I are enjoying the rodeo you're putting on. When the action got slow,

J. L. Greger

we reviewed the file you got from Catalina's lawyer. You've handed Wiley everything on a silver platter."

Wiley shook his head. "Not quite. Do you plan to interview the father, Verne? He's the only one on the board of the Green Way to Beauty Spas not being investigated for murder. I'll have to negotiate with him on FDA issues."

"Barbara or I probably should talk to him." Suddenly Sara had a brainstorm. "Hank, you could sit in on Wiley's interview. Verne might make comments pertinent to the FBI cases."

"Can't say I hanker to talk to Verne." Hank scratched his chin. "Figure he must be a real piece of work to have raised two such messed up kids."

Wiley chuckled. "I'd like your help, but first I want to know Sara's plans."

Sara looked at her watch. "Davita is due here in five minutes. I think Jules and his lawyer won't be ready to talk for at least an hour. Barbara and the U.S. attorney are interviewing Abigail now. She's hoping that Abigail will turn on Nelson."

Hank shook his head. "Abby's tough. She won't talk. Now that she's been formally charged for one crime, she has Sixth Amendment rights when she's questioned on another crime—if the crimes are related."

"The federal prosecutor and local DAs are working with Barbara to guarantee no evidence can be tossed on a technicality later."

***

Davita's lawyer didn't give her a chance to speak. As soon as Sara and Wiley entered the room, he said, "Davita knows she should have been more cooperative yesterday at the spa, but you have to remember she feared for her life."

Sara thought for several seconds. She hadn't told Davita a toxin was added to her mother's preserves. Wiley may have threatened her with jail time and fines, but not her life. "What frightened you?"

The lawyer nodded to Davita. "I think Catalina was killed because she didn't cooperate with Abigail and Nelson."

"How do you know that?"

"I… I just do."

"I thought you wanted to cooperative. I know you didn't pick your daughter up after a soccer game Saturday as you told Carbonne and me. Who did you meet at the gym?"

Davita's lips stretched into a thin line. "You had nerve to follow me."

The lawyer put his hand on Davita' shoulder. "Cooperate. You had no way of knowing what would happen."

"I called him…"

"Who's 'him'?"

"I called Jules, but Nelson came to the gym instead after I'd waited for him for over two hours. I told Nelson about your questions."

Sara thought it was too bad Carbonne hadn't had the funds to have Davita tailed for more than two hours. She sighed. Nothing was easy on this case.

The lawyer nudged Davita. "My client has been threatened repeatedly for months and is not responsible for her actions."

Sara found Davita to be unpleasant during the rest of the interview for multiple reasons. Davita didn't regret devising a plan for misusing the botulinum products because she thought FDA regulations were "silly rules." She didn't think she had accepted bribes from Jules and Abigail. "No cap, I deserved the extra cash for arranging extra Botox parties *and* helping them with the books."

Davita had arrogantly explained her actions to target Catalina. "Abigail harassed me because I'm not a size six like Catalina. It wasn't fair. I only leveled the playing field when I forwarded Catalina's emails from Nelson to Abigail."

To her credit, Davita mourned her mother's death, but her grief was less than her excitement over her potential inheritance. She had already called a realtor to estimate the value of her mother's home.

She'd cooperated with Sara and the police during the investigation of her mother's canning methods because she feared those people at the rally sickened by botulism could sue her mother's estate and lessen her inheritance. "I woke up Sunday afternoon. That's when Jules blubbered over his beer and admitted Nelson had ordered him to add Botox to the fig preserves. Then I knew I didn't need to cooperate with you." She'd almost spit the word *you* at Sara before she added, "You know your sweet comments about my mom made me sick. You didn't know her."

Her lawyer had looked at the table during most of the interview, but he put his hand on Davita's shoulder after her last comment. "You've not asked Davita a key question yet. It's frustrating her because she fears you are in league with the real villains in this case."

Sara gasped. "I only want to learn the truth. Tell me what the key question is."

The lawyer smiled. "Davita, what did Nelson say when you met him at the gym?"

"He was furious when I suggested he owed me a favor for my silence. No cap, he said, 'I was lucky I was still alive.'" Davita began to curse.

Her lawyer said, "Since then she's been terrified and angry. Surely, you can see that she didn't intentionally abet the murders and should be kept in protective custody until the real murderers are sentenced."

CHAPTER 28: Barbara Listens to Lies on Thursday

Nelson Davis blinked repeatedly as he read the divorce papers Barbara handed him. "Estella would never request a divorce. She can't talk."

"True, but she can type." Barbara didn't add she too had been surprised when a courier for a Santa Fe lawyer had delivered a packet for Nelson to the front desk of the Albuquerque FBI building. That is until she saw the attached note:

> *Sara,*
> *My lawyer secretly drew up these papers for me six months ago. I didn't have the courage to ask my lawyer to send them to Nelson until today. The lawyer said he couldn't deliver the documents to Nelson personally because Nelson was in protective FBI custody as ordered by Agent Barbara Lewis. Please forward them to Nelson.*
> *Thanks*
> *Estella*
> *P.S. It took me hours to type this note, but I did it.*

Barbara had no idea what Sara had said to Estella, but the shocked look on Nelson's face suggested he might be more cooperative now. Then she returned to reality and recognized that Nelson was incapable of cooperation. However, these divorce papers would strengthen the case against Nelson for attempting to murder or maim Estella.

"Nelson, you have a problem. You admitted that you gave Beryl the questionable recipe for fig and nut preserves and visited her on the Monday before the rally. Jules supplied other details. You argued with Beryl over opening a jar of preserves and you gave Jules a bowl to mix botulinum toxin into the preserves at the rally."

"No jury will believe Jules. He's the one who actually added the toxin to the preserves at the rally."

"I admit my case against you is weakened because it is his word against yours. However, we found you sent dozens of threatening emails to Jules. They will make any jury think you were the mastermind of the poisonings. You also have a motive—your ambition to become a U.S. senator at any cost. Jules had nothing to gain. A jury will convict you."

"We'll see."

Barbara thought she could remove the bored look from Nelson's face. "I have a surprise for you. Abigail tried to suffocate Estella on Monday night. She was arraigned in a federal court yesterday for attempted murder."

Nelson's face lost its bored look. "What? You were supposed to protect my wife. I can sue you for incompetence."

"I guess the best defense is usually a strong offense but not in this case. Think a minute—if Abigail convinces a jury she was mentally unstable when she tried to suffocate Estella, she will walk away with a year in a mental institution and with her fortune intact. She is better at acting insane than you. Remember she played Ophelia while you were only an understudy in *Hamlet*."

Barbara knew she's struck a nerve when she said *Ophelia*. Nelson's shoulders quivered.

"On the other hand, if you provide details about Catalina's last three days, I think the federal prosecutor might turn the case about the poisoned figs over to the Bernalillo County district attorney. That district attorney swears poisoning cases don't yield first degree murder convictions because local juries do not like complicated cases. He might even settle on manslaughter *if* you make the right plea."

Nelson sighed. "I'll talk about Catalina's last three days but you may not like what you get..." He smirked. "...after my lawyer sees statements from the federal prosecuting attorney and the local DA. I believe you'll need to get the cooperation of the DA for Sandoval County because Corrales in in Sandoval not Bernalillo County. And I'll only accept a manslaughter plea."

Barbara kept her lips stiff to keep from smiling. "I'll see what I can do."

The U.S. attorney had been right. He had assured Barbara that Nelson would accept a plea to be tried for Beryl's murder in a state court with reduced charges *if Barbara presented the plan right*. The Sandoval County district attorney had jumped at the U.S. attorney's offer because he thought convicting Nelson for manslaughter would be an easy way to improve his conviction rates and impress voters.

***

Barbara silently asked for forgiveness for the lie she was about to tell when she reentered the conference room. "It wasn't easy to get everyone to agree but the Sandoval County District attorney will accept your plea of guilty for manslaughter in the death of Beryl Marks. Here are signed statements from him and the U.S. attorney."

Nelson studied the signed memos and then smiled triumphantly at his lawyer. He willingly—but perhaps not honestly—began to answer Barbara's questions on Catalina's whereabout during the last three days of her life.

"Abigail is a jealous woman and demanded that I kill Catalina at my ranch." He shrugged his shoulders. "My foreman's nosy son made it impossible."

Nelson's explanation of why Catalina cancelled her flight, rented a car, and drove with him from San Diego was tedious. He insinuated that Catalina found him sexy, but finally admitted Catalina wanted to pump him for information on the Green Way to Beauty Spa and its owners, the Smiths.

Barbara mused the U.S. attorney might have been right on another point. He'd advised her to flirt with Nelson if he stalled the interrogation. She twirled a few strands of her long black hair around her fingers and licked her lips. "It must have been embarrassing when Catalina told you were too old and turned you down at the ranch."

The nostrils of Nelson's nose flared.

"What did you talk about on the drive to Albuquerque after she refused to have sex with you at the ranch?" Barbara leaned toward him but couldn't force herself to touch his arm.

Nelson snorted. "We didn't talk. She dropped me off at a motel in Gallup and drove back to Albuquerque alone. Then she had the nerve to call me and ask that I not tell Abigail about her suspicions."

Barbara thought Nelson was angry enough that he might slip and make another honest comment. "Is that when you ordered Abigail to lure Catalina to your home in Santa Fe?"

Nelson stared at her. "About then."

Barbara's phone pinged. She hurried to the observation room. Jules had admitted to Sara that Nelson had called him from Gallup on Wednesday and instructed him to buy "working-girl clothes in sizes six and fourteen" and deliver them to Estella's home in Santa Fe by ten on Thursday evening.

Sara reminded Barbara that both Abigail and Catalina were small women but Davita would probably fit into a size fourteen. "Originally I thought our lady's man planned to knock off all three women, but Jules insisted he was told to buy clothes for only two women." Sara looked like she might cry. "So, Beryl's death saved her daughter's life."

Armed with these additional details, Barbara walked briskly into the interrogation room where Nelson waited. "Were you disappointed when Abigail was unable to lure Davita, as well as Catalina, to your home in Santa Fe?"

"One has to be flexible."

Barbara thought that was as much of an admission as she would get from Nelson. "Where did you stay after you returned from Gallup?"

"I spent most of Thursday in *my* house. That's how I know what Abigail and Jules did, but they didn't see me."

Barbara doubted his statement. The house had no attic nor basement. The murderer—or murderers—had obviously been in most of the rooms in the house. She decided it best to lure Nelson into bragging. "That was clever of you. No one saw you enter even though the woman across the street saw two women enter your home around eight in the evening and a single woman leave around six in the morning."

Nelson smiled. "That old bat doesn't notice anything. She only noticed anyone entering and leaving *my* home because I called her and told her to look out her front window."

"Why didn't she recognize your voice?"

He sat straighter and assumed a poor French accent. "I disguised my voice and used a throw away phone. Bet she didn't admit the calls."

Before Barbara could text anyone, Sara had emailed her. That was one way that Sara showed her age. Sara definitely preferred emails to texts.

> *Hank got a neighbor yesterday to admit she'd received calls both times before she looked out her front window. She didn't recognize the man's voice.*

Barbara decided to encourage Nelson's ego trip. "Why don't you tell me what you saw and heard Abigail do in your home?"

"Abigail gave Catalina a rosé wine with knockout drops. Then Abigail used Catalina's own green silk scarf to strangle her before she called Jules. I could hear her order him to buy hooker clothes in a small size and get to Santa Fe fast."

Barbara could hardly disguise her disgust at his story. "How did you get close enough to hear her?"

Her question must have sounded too skeptical because he leaned back and seemed to think a bit. "Abigail was excited—almost gleeful—when she called Jules. She yelled."

Sara emailed:

> *There was one call from a phone in Estella's home around nine. At least one bounced off a nearby tower.*
>
> *Jules swore his sister never mentioned the clothes when she called around nine to tell him to hurry. Only Nelson ever mentioned the clothes and that was when Nelson called him from Gallup on Wednesday.*

Barbara decided to not press Nelson on the obvious gap in his story and leaned toward him. "What did Abigail do next?"

"She was careful and put on gloves before she wiped all surfaces in the living room and kitchen." He licked his lips. "She also removed all Catalina's clothes and stuffed them in a garbage bag." He shrugged. "Jules got there around ten."

Sara sent another email:

> *Winslow looked carefully throughout the house. He didn't find Abigail's fingerprints. Of course, many prints were badly smudged. He found two dirty wine glasses in the dishwasher. One had Abigail's DNA on the rim. I'll have the lab check the glasses for a sedative.*

Barbara forced herself to look at Nelson without showing her revulsion. "What happened when Jules arrived?"

"They dragged Catalina up the stairs. Only half-way up, she gurgled. Jules ran to the kitchen for a knife while Abigail sat on Catalina. Then Jules stabbed Catalina repeatedly."

Barbara didn't correct Nelson. Hank had told her that there was no sign anyone or anything had been dragged across the living room carpet. He had opined that neither Jules nor Abigail were strong enough to carry a limp body alone. Barbara also doubted Nelson's comment about the knife. It had been found in the master bath, not the kitchen. Barbara guessed Nelson had been snacking upstairs while he waited for Abigail to

J. L. Greger

sedate Catalina. No one but Nelson would have known the knife was there. She texted Sara.

Sara appeared within a minute. "I'm the one who supervised the lab work and I've got several silly questions. How did Abigail and Jules keep blood from getting on the steps? We had to look to find traces in the crevices of the stairs."

Nelson sat back and squinted. Barbara guessed he didn't like Sara's direct style. She was also probably too old for his taste.

Sara must have recognized his negative reaction to her because she sat at the table near him, gently slid her index finger across the table toward his hand, and rubbed her finger on his fingers. Barbara couldn't believe how Sara batted her eyelashes, but Carbonne always said Sara was a ham. "I appreciate good workmanship. How did they contain the blood?"

"They dragged Catalina up the stairs in a blanket."

"Do you know what happened to the blanket?"

Nelson frowned. "I think Jules stuffed it in a box in the garage."

Sara slid her finger down his arm. "You have a good memory. What did Abigail do before she left? By the way, when was that?"

"She helped Jules carry the body to a guest bedroom and cleaned the knife. She left around one."

"How about Jules?"

"He worked hard staging the stairs. You know when he left—around six in the morning."

"When did you leave?" Where did you go?"

"I left after Jules by the back door. I took the Roadrunner train to Albuquerque."

Sara nodded to Barbara and stood. "I don't believe you, Nelson. I've caught several places in your story where lab evidence contradicts what you've said. Good luck in convincing this young agent that you've told the truth. If not, your plea agreement won't be valid."

Nelson glared at Sara.

Barbara thought she should be able to wring a bit more of the truth out of Nelson now, but it didn't matter. The plea agreement wasn't valid if Nelson was caught in a lie. Then too, she now had points to goad Abigail. The U.S. attorney's plan might work.

CHAPTER 29: Several Plans Fail; Others Succeed

Abigail's lawyer wanted to start the interrogation period with a statement from Abigail. Barbara was surprised when the U.S. attorney agreed. The statement was ridiculously saccharine.

In essence, Abigail admitted she'd been in love with Nelson Davis for fifteen years, despite her two failed marriages. She claimed she established the Green Way to Beauty Spas in Albuquerque and Santa Fe because they gave her excuses to see Nelson regularly. There was one semi-interesting point in her statement. Abigail rendezvoused with Nelson at his cabin near Gallup on weekends and in Jules's condo while Jules was leading spa parties.

When Abigail finished reading the statement, Barbara asked, "Why did you insist Catalina go to San Diego on business when you knew Nelson was there?"

Abigail emitted little squeaks, like a frightened mouse. "Nelson wanted me to."

Barbara realized Abigail was still into acting, but played along. "Why?"

Abigail's lawyer whispered into her ear.

Abigail nodded. "He loves me and wanted to make me happy."

"How?'

"By making Catalina magically disappear."

Her lawyer announced, "My client is too fragile to not answer any more questions about Catalina."

The U.S. attorney ignored the lawyer's comment. "I doubt Nelson killed Catalina in Santa Fe because no one saw a tall man in the neighborhood on Thursday evening. The masked person who turned off the security system in the house didn't appear to be as tall as Nelson. Was that you in heels?"

This time it was Abigail's lawyer, not Abigail, who emitted a slight squeak. Barbara surmised Abigail had not told him that detail.

When Abigail began to cry, Barbara noticed Abigail shed few tears but yowled loudly. Finally, Abigail muttered, "I was confused. Nelson had promised… I couldn't believe… he failed. When Davita rushed away, I was left with just Catalina. We hadn't expected that, but I wanted to give Nelson one more chance. I took Catalina to his house, like he ordered me to do."

Barbara thought she spotted Abigail taking a peek at the U.S. attorney during her performance.

Instead of yowling, Abigail now emitted a mewing noise. "He'd told me to sedate Catalina and he'd take care of the rest. I did and left her on the sofa in the living room. I left immediately."

Barbara realized Abigail was lying. Both Nelson and Jules had said Abigail helped clean up the blood after Catalina's murder. "We know your brother received a call from a burner phone in Santa Fe about nine. It was transmitted through a tower not far from the Davises' home. Did you make that call before or after you left the house?"

Barbara thought she saw anger on Abigail's face before she looked down. "You couldn't… I mean… I don't remember."

Abigail's lawyer stood abruptly "My client is unable to answer further questions. She may never recover from this trauma."

The U.S. attorney frowned. "I expect Abigail will agree to be examined further by Dr. Jim Jung, a psychiatrist on contract with the FBI."

***

After Jim Jung asked Abigail a few key questions, he knocked on the window to the observation room. An aide carried a bloody, plaid blanket into the conference room.

Abigail took one look at the blanket and began to shudder. She screamed, "No."

"Close your eyes." Abigail's lawyer stepped in front of the aide "You don't have to look at it."

Abigail pushed him aside and fixed her gaze on the blanket.

Barbara was glad she was in the observation room not the conference room as she brewed another cup of tea for herself. "Abigail is about to do her Ophelia routine again."

The U.S. attorney studied the scene through the window to the conference room. "Maybe not. She seems mesmerized by blanket."

Abigail spoke slowly. "I'd never seen Nelson like that before. After I'd removed Catalina's clothes as he asked, he picked up her green scarf and pulled it slowly between her legs and up her torso to her neck. He became excited as he tightened and tightened a double loop of the scarf around her neck."

Abigail seemed to come out of her trance. "I wanted it over and handed him that blanket and told him to carry her up to a guest bedroom. Then everything… fell apart."

Abigail paused and her lawyer said, "You don't have to go on."

"Catalina began to gurgle. Nelson dropped Catalina—right there on the stairs—and told me to sit on her." Abigail's face contorted as if to scream, but she didn't. "I don't know where he went." She stared at the ceiling. "I waited… waited. When he returned, he pushed me away…. He pinned Catalina down with his knees and stabbed her repeatedly."

Abigail had become more and more hysterical as she told her story until she shrieked, "Blood. More blood—I didn't think I'd ever get it all off the stairs." Suddenly she stooped screaming and said quietly, "Until Jules came and helped me. You know he's a great brother."

***

Sara's walked out of the observation room as Abigail began to babble about how wonderful Jules was. "I'll clean up all the details with the Davita and the FDA while you two figure out what to do with Abigail."

"You know what I want. Make it happen." The U.S. attorney smiled. "We'll probably proceed with my plan b in regard to Abigail." He glanced at Barbara. "Sara, you may have to do the final interview with Nelson because you're tougher than Barbara."

Sara slammed the door. He might a good prosecuting attorney but he was not a nice man.

***

Sara decided the best way to deliver the goods on Davita was to make her angry. Accordingly, she summoned Wiley Webster to join her and told Davita the truth: Nelson had ordered Jules on Wednesday night to purchase "working girl" clothes for her as well as Catalina.

Sara's plan worked. Davita was livid. When Davita began to detail the shady business practices of the Green Way to Beauty Spas, Wiley Webster took over the interview.

Sara knew the U.S. attorney had decided not to charge Davita for blackmailing Abigail for months because he doubted any jury would convict Davita out of sympathy for her mom's murder. On the other hand, Wiley Webster insisted that the FDA would charge Davita and Jules

J. L. Greger

with fraudulently mishandling botulinum toxin and endangering the lives of clients at the in-home parties. He thought they would both be imprisoned for several years because federal juries were seldom lenient with drug dealers *and* botulinum toxin was considered a controlled substance.

Next, Sara and Wiley Webster met with Hank Snow. Hank and Wiley had done a good job of frightening Verne Smith, but all they had learned was what they'd already guessed. Verne was not a loving father. Although Verne liked the income from the Green Way to Beauty Spas, he had intentionally avoided knowing much about the business. Wiley opined that the FDA could fine Verne because he was on the board of directors, but Verne would not be subject to incarceration like Jules and Davita.

Sara knew the U.S. attorney would be pleased. As a prosecuting attorney, he would have no more work to do in regard to Davita. Although he had agreed to let Jules plea for a suspended sentence in abetting the murder of Catalina Herrera and the attempted murder of Estella Garcia Davis, Jules would be incarcerated for several years, albeit in a low security prison, for his illegal and dangerous activities at the Green Way to Beauty Spas. Any guilt Barbara felt for originally offering a plea deal to Jules for abetting murder would also be assuaged.

***

Sara watched nervously as Abigail's lawyer joined Barbara and the U.S. attorney in the conference room. After listening to Jim Jung's report on Abigail's mental health, the U.S. attorney was sure his plan b would work. Neither Sara nor Barbara shared his confidence.

The defense lawyer leaned back and said, "You saw today how quickly Abigail slipped into hysteria when she was forced to remember Catalina's murder. That's what I saw after Barbara's visit before the arraignment and that's why I claimed Abigail was innocent because of insanity. Today, I think you pushed my client too far again. She is now incompetent to stand trial until she gets psychiatric help. She may need years of treatment." The defense lawyer folded his arms in front of his chest and glared at Barbara and the U.S. attorney. "My client should have all charges dropped, pending her admission to a psychiatric facility."

Sara noticed Barbara flinched.

The U.S. attorney showed no emotions. "I've listened to our psychiatrist. Your client knew the difference between right and wrong when she plotted the murder of Estella Garcia Davis with botulism toxin and recklessly endangered the lives of a hundred others. She was sane when she plotted and participated in the murder of Catalina Herrera, even though she may be incompetent to stand trail now. She is a menace to society and deserves two homicide charges." He shook his head. "Then too, she's already been charged with the attempted murder of Estella on Monday. That evidence is indisputable."

"Don't be obstinate." The defense lawyer's face flushed a dull red. "Abigail is mentally incompetent to stand trial for any of these charges now or in the foreseeable future."

The U.S. attorney leaned forward and folded his hands on the table. "I will accept a plea that Abigail is guilty of attempting to murder Estella Garcia Davis in the hospital but mentally ill. I will ask the judge to stipulate Abigail must receive treatment in a mental institution until a psychiatrist certifies her as sane. Rather than serve time in prison afterward, she will be placed on probation for ten years and must give up all her medical licenses."

"Acceptable."

"I'm not through." The U.S. attorney smiled slightly. "I will also accept a guilty but insane plea by your client for abetting the murder of Catalina Herrera *if* Abigail is treated in a mental health facility at least a year and *if* she testifies against Nelson Davis."

"She can't. She might not recover if Nelson's defense lawyer forced her to tell certain details."

"The deal is a good one considering that she also participated in planning a poisoning that could have killed dozens of people with botulism. Think of all the charges I could pile up against her. Think of all the possible civil suits by those poisoned."

Sara noted the U.S. attorney had not mentioned any charges the FDA might bring against Abigail. Wiley had opined the charges against Abigail would be similar to those against Davita and Jules because Abigail as their boss had approved their activities. He'd also noted the FDA would require several months to prepare their charges.

"I have to talk to my client and her psychologist."

***

"I cannot do this. I am so nauseated," Barbara whispered to Sara as they and the U.S. attorney walked into a room where Nelson and his lawyer were waiting.

"Don't worry I'll trot out the new evidence and the U.S. attorney is itching to play the heavy."

Sara remained standing after she entered the conference room. "Nelson, we know you lied in regard to the murder of Catalina Herrera. We have more evidence against you now than when we spoke earlier."

Nelson studied Sara as she spoke "I like the young female agent better. You don't blush."

Sara wanted to say: *Be glad you got me, not Carbonne.* She decided it was better to ignore Nelson's comment. "The testimonies of Jules and Abigail are consistent."

The defense lawyer raised a finger and whispered in Nelson's ear.

"We have not allowed any contact between Abigail and Jules since Monday. You can't claim collusion in regard to their testimonies." Sara continued as if there had been no interruption. "You stabbed Catalina Herrera to death after you failed to kill her by strangulation. The lab data supports your cohorts' statements." She pointed at the bloody, plaid blanket, which she had placed on the table. "Only your and Catalina's DNA are on the blanket or the box containing the blanket. Technicians have located your email correspondence with Catalina, which supports our theories on your motives."

The U.S. attorney said, "Consistent with our prior agreement, you will be arraigned in a state, not a federal, court. However, the agreement is invalid if we catch you in a lie. It's time for you tell us honestly what happened after Catalina entered you house on the day of her death."

Nelson didn't ramble much as he told his story. Not because he didn't try, but because every time he began to ramble or made a questionable statement, Sara of the U.S. attorney said, "Remember your agreement won't be valid."

As soon as Nelson admitted he stabbed Catalina, the U.S. attorney knocked on the window to the observation room. A Santa Fe police lieutenant and the Santa Fe County DA entered the conference room.

"Nelson Davis, I will accept your guilty plea for the second degree murder of Catalina Herrera in Santa Fe," said the Santa Fe County DA as the lieutenant placed handcuffs on Nelson.

"The agreement was all charges would be only manslaughter," said Nelson's lawyer.

The U.S. attorney smiled. "Consider yourself lucky. I planned to allow her—the Santa Fe County DA—to charge you with murder one. Remember you and your lawyer didn't ask the Santa Fe DA to sign the agreement. But this DA and this agent..." He pointed to Barbara. "...thought I might have misled you when you signed the earlier plea bargain."

CHAPTER 30: Sara on Her Way on Friday

Sara pushed a treat into Bug's wheeled pet carrier which was underneath the seat in front of her on the plane. His little tongue licked her fingers, but he didn't whimper in the claustrophobic space. She sat back in her seat and thought about the blur of activity during the last two days.

Sara and Barbara had scurried among interrogation rooms extracting details from Abigail, Jules, Davita, and Nelson as if they were conducting a silent auction. Each confession had upped the ante for the next person questioned.

They couldn't have done it without help. Hank and Winslow raced to Santa Fe and literally opened dozens of boxes in Estella's garage. They found a bloody, plaid blanket in a box under a heap of other boxes and trash. The box was the only one that the tape on it had not turned yellow and brittle with age. Wiley Webster, Jim Jung, and local DAs had cooperated as the U.S. attorney pursued his plan to force Abigail to provide evidence to convict Nelson—even if it meant pushing her over the edge psychologically.

Sara guessed justice had occurred even if several of the decisions, in isolation, seemed unfair. The look on Nelson's face when the U.S. attorney and the two DAs explained after he signed the pleas agreements that he would have to serve the time on each of his pleas, consecutively, not concurrently, had been satisfying. However, the best part of the week was the proud looks on Pete's and Winslow's faces when Sara had six pizzas delivered to the lab crews.

***

The flight into Miami was late. Sara sprinted through the airport pulling Bug's carrier. She didn't see Sanders until he stepped directly in front of her as she darted toward the flight information display in the baggage area.

He placed his hands on her shoulders. "Slow down." After she stopped gasping for breath, he gave her a long slow kiss. Thoughts about the Green Way to Beauty Spas disappeared. All that mattered now was Sanders and Bug.

They chatted about their flights and Sara didn't ask any of her burning questions until the three of them were seated in their gray rental car. "Did I interpret your jungle message right? Did my comments help your boss?"

"First, I have a gift for you." He pulled from his briefcase a three-inch gold frog.

Sara squelched a gulp and tried to smile. She hoped he'd not wasted much money on this… ugly, useless paperweight. She turned it over. It was brass with gilding and probably not that expensive. "It's interesting."

Sanders laughed. "You must have gotten plenty of sleep last night to be so tactful. I know you hate junk like this, but I couldn't resist. I thought you could put it on your desk in the FBI building and say it's me."

She looked at him quizzically. "What?"

"When a princess kisses a frog, isn't the frog supposed to turn into a prince? This is the reverse."

"Enough of the bad jokes—answer my questions."

He seemed to ignore her. "We're meeting a friend who is sailing in on his yacht."

"I know it's classified but can't you tell me anything about your jungle message. Did I guess right?"

He winked. "You're fishing for compliments. Didn't you hear that a drug kingpin in a major Columbian-based drug cartel was arrested in Boca Raton last Saturday?"

"It rated only two inches in the *Albuquerque Journal*. I couldn't figure out why such a small amount of drugs was mentioned." She studied his face carefully to see if he flinched slightly at her next comment. "Unless the *drug* was extracted from the skins of golden poison dart frogs. By my calculations, that amount of batrachotoxin could kill twenty-thousand people."

Sanders's upper lip quivered. "Time for us to be on our way." He turned the radio to a salsa station and upped the volume. "You'd be surprised how carefully the drug cartels monitor each other's activities. Our embassy was notified by a member of a rival gang that the man arrested was the nephew of a particularly ruthless drug lord who is taking over the cocaine market along the East Coast. The embassy information officer thought the cartel's base of operations is in the upper Amazon."

Sara suspected the rival had supplied these tips before Sanders's trip up the Amazon. "So, were my guesses correct?"

He hummed along with a song blasting from the radio for a few bars. "You underestimated the potency of the toxin."

"Oh."

He turned the radio off. "I'll never get used to modern renditions of traditional Latin American melodies. The originals are subtle and more interesting." He paused only briefly to tune the radio to another station. "We're meeting a wealthy Brazilian physician who wants to be elected to be the president of Brazil. He wants to unofficially talk to a high-ranking State Department official."

"So, I assume your boss will also be in Boca Raton."

"Yes, both she and the Brazilian will join us tomorrow morning as we tour the Everglades on an airboat. I don't think Bug should accompany us and have arranged for a dog sitter to take care of Bug and the secretary's dog."

"Thanks. As I remember, airboats are noisy." She thought but didn't say: *He doesn't want anyone to overhear their conversation.* She filled the next several minutes with idle conversation about Bug's success in the hospital with Estella. When Sanders had finally cleared the traffic around Miami, she said, "I checked on the toxicologist who disappeared in the Amazon region of Brazil about a year ago."

"How?"

"Looked up old issues of *Science* and St. Louis newspapers. He was a toxicologist at the St. Louis Zoo for years."

"What have you confabulated?"

Sara disliked when he was dismissive of her ideas, but recognized he might be worried that she was getting too close to the truth. That meant this might be her last chance to learn about his mysterious message of a week ago. "What if the missing toxicologist didn't drown in the Amazon as assumed? What if he was kidnapped by a drug cartel and forced to work for them? You asked me a strange question before you took your post in Brasilia."

He sighed. "I asked if there was a way to increase the potency of the toxins in the skin of the golden poison dart frog. You said you didn't know. That's the end of the conversation."

"I was thinking. The missing toxicologist could have found an answer to your question. Are you going to rescue him?"

"Stop." Sanders's jaw was set as if he was ready to grind his teeth.

                                             J. L. Greger

It was time to change the conversation. "There are several parks and nature reserves between Boca Raton and Miami. Let's visit one on Sunday."

"Good idea. We can talk about our plans after my posting in Brasilia ends." He patted her shoulder. "I've only one more special assignment to complete and I'll be nominated for a promotion."

Sara hated to think what the next special assignment would be. She was sure his trip up the Amazon had been a lot more dangerous than he'd admitted. "Don't take too many chances. I'd rather have you as a live chicken than a dead duck."

Sanders snorted. "Any updates from Carbonne?"

"Yes, Barbara accepted a new position yesterday. She will be a regional supervisor of FBI minority recruitment efforts in the Southwest. Her work will focus on working with minority youth and helping them to understand the importance of a college education and a clean criminal record if they want a career in law enforcement. Barbara said she took the job because she was 'tired of acting counter to her native American heritage.'"

"It's a good career move for her and solves Carbonne's problem. Federal agencies are tightening their enforcement of nepotism rules."

"Mmm. I think nepotism and cultural clashes weren't the real reasons for Barbara's decision. I'd bet money that she's pregnant and doesn't want to take physical risks. She showed signs of pregnancy— grumpiness, tiredness, and an upset stomach which she tried to assuage by constantly chewing soda crackers. Anyway, she and Carbonne are getting married."

"You know my offer to marry you still stands."

Sara thought quickly. "I'll compromise. I'll revise my refusal to consult in Brazil and agree to consult on one case if I don't have to spend much time in Rio."

"You don't know what compromise means."

THE END

THE SCIENCE BEHIND THE STORY

Natural toxins are murder weapons in *Fair Compromise*s. Sara Almquist tracks the sources and uses of botulinum toxin, while her friend Sanders suspects potential uses of the toxin found in the skin of the golden poison dart frogs of South America. Maybe, you'd like to check the facts on both poisons.

Botulinum Toxin

Botulinum toxin is a neurotoxic protein produced by Clostridium *botulinum*. This toxin prevents the release of the neurotransmitter acetylcholine and thus prevents muscle contractions. The early symptoms of botulism poisoning are double or blurred vision, tiredness, and trouble speaking due to paralysis of muscles in the face. The effects may progress to the paralysis of larger muscles in the arms and then the legs. In the past, deaths due to the paralysis of muscles involved in respiration occurred in fifty percent of cases. Now deaths occurs in about five percent of cases because of the use of an antitoxin, ventilators, and antibiotics (*Botulism*. Centers for Disease Control and Prevention. https://www.cdc.gov/botulism/index.html).

Toxicologists consider botulinum toxin to be the most potent natural poison with nanogram (one billionth of a gram) quantities sufficient to kill a human. It has been studied extensively as a bioterrorism factor.

Problems with canned foods

Clostridium bacteria are spore-forming bacteria. These spores survive for years naturally in unfavorable environments. However, the spores can grow and produce a toxin in anaerobic (oxygen-free), nonacidic, and low-sugar and low-salt environments. These conditions exist within improperly canned, nonacidic foods, such as most vegetables and meats. The *USDA's Complete Guide for Home Canning*

(<u>https://www.nifa.usda.gov/about-nifa/blogs/usdas-complete-guide-home-canning</u>) offers this advice:

- Nonacidic foods (meats and vegetables) during the canning process need to be heated in a pressure cooker, where temperatures exceed 212 degrees Fahrenheit, to kill any *Clostridium* spores.
- If consumers fear the safety of canned foods, they can denature any *Clostridium* toxin (but not kill the spores) by boiling the food for an additional ten minutes after the cans or bottles are opened.
- The acid in tomatoes and most other fruits cause the spores to be more sensitive to heat. Thus, boiling water baths are an acceptable way at home to can tomatoes and other acidic fruits.
- Pureed or mashed pumpkin, squash, and potatoes generally should **not** be home canned.

Although Cooperative Extension Service offices in every county in the U.S. have offered free brochures on proper home canning methods for the last seventy years, the most common cause of botulism in adults is improperly home-canned vegetables and meats. The information that Sara Almquist provides in this novel is consistent with USDA guidelines.

<u>Other forms of botulism</u>

Botulism sometimes occurs among two- to eight-month-old infants when *Clostridium* spores grow in babies' immature intestinal tracts, often after the infant is fed honey contaminated with botulinum spores. Rarely, patients develop botulism when a wound becomes infected with *Clostridium*. (*Botulism*. Mayo Clinic. <u>https://www.mayoclinic.org/diseases-conditions/botulism/symptoms-causes/syc-20370262</u>).

<u>Botulinum toxin as a therapeutic agent and cosmetic</u>

Botulinum toxin is used cosmetically to reduce facial wrinkles. It is used medically to treat muscle spasms in neurological disorders, eye conditions such as lazy eyes and uncontrolled blinking, dental problems such as grinding of teeth, bladder dysfunction, and chronic migraines (*Botox*, WebMD. <u>https://www.webmd.com/beauty/cosmetic-procedures-botox</u>). The recent use of botulinum to treat depression is still controversial (*Science*. [25 June 2021] 372, 6549:1376).

Often cosmetic botulinum toxin is called "Botox" because it was the name of the first injectable botulinum product. However, several brands of the toxin are now available.

The lethal dose of botulinum given orally is probably about a thousand-fold more than the lethal dose of injected botulinum (*Botox injections*. Mayo Clinic https://www.mayoclinic.org/tests-procedures/botox/about/pac-20384658). Thus, the murderers in this mystery had to accumulate relatively large amounts of the injectable botulinum toxin in order to poison individuals at Estella's rally.

Toxin in the Skin of the Golden Poison Dart Frog

Golden poison dart frogs (*Phyllobates terribilis*) live in the jungles of the Pacific coast of Columbia (not the Amazon jungle) and can be yellow, green, or orange. They are arguably the most poisonous animals on earth. Each wild frog contain about ten milligrams of poison, enough to kill ten to twenty humans.

Batrachotoxins (a type of neurotoxin) in the frogs' skins are derived from toxins in the insects, probably beetles, consumed by the frogs. Those frogs grown in captivity eventually lose the toxins in their skin when not fed their native diet (https://en.wikipedia.org/wiki/Golden_poison_frog).

New Techniques

The equipment and techniques used by the FBI in this novel reflect those in modern forensic laboratories. Thus, Sara and the FBI agents have access to rapid DNA testing, although they use the results of more traditional DNA testing in court.

TOF-SIMS (time-of-flight secondary ion mass spectroscopy) is a new technique that allows forensic scientists to date fingerprints through the diffusion of fatty acids during the first four days after the print is made (*Analytical Chemistry* [2015] 87, 16:8035-8038).

Isn't science amazing?

ABOUT THE AUTHOR

J. L. Greger is a biology professor and research administrator from the University of Wisconsin-Madison turned novelist. She lives in New Mexico. The pet therapy dog Bug in her mystery/thriller novels is based on her own Japanese Chin. She includes tidbits about science, the American Southwest, and her international travel experiences in the Science Traveler Series.

The Flu Is Coming - In the first book in the series, a woman scientist traces the spread of a deadly new flu virus among the frantic residents of a quarantined New Mexico community. (New Mexico/Arizona Book Award Finalist)

Murder…A Way to Lose Weight - A dean in a medical school helps police discover whether an ambitious young "diet doctor," disgruntled patients, or old-timers with buried secrets are killers. (Winner of the 2016 Public Safety Writers Association contest and New Mexico/Arizona Book Award Finalist)

Ignore the Pain - A woman scientist learns too much about the coca trade and too little about a sexy new colleague while on a public health assignment in Bolivia.

Malignancy - A woman tries to escape the clutches of a drug lord and accepts a risky assignment as a science consultant in Cuba. (Winner of the 2015 Public Safety Writers Association contest)

I Saw You in Beirut - A woman's past provides clues for the extraction of a nuclear scientist from Iran. The author's experiences as a science and education consultant in the United Arab Emirates and Lebanon are featured.

Riddled with Clues - A homeless man and a woman scientist are targeted by drug gangs after she listens to the strange tale of an undercover drug agent about his war experiences. The memories of an actual CIA agent in Laos during the Vietnam War are featured. (New Mexico/Arizona Book Award Finalist)

A Pound of Flesh, Sorta - The police and a woman scientist can't decide whether a package contaminated with the bacteria that causes the bubonic plague is a plea for help by a whistleblower or a threat from gang leaders awaiting trial. (New Mexico/Arizona Book Award Finalist)

Dirty Holy Water - A woman who usually serves as a science consultant for the FBI learns there is a thin line between being a victim and being a villain when she becomes the chief suspect in a bizarre murder case. (New Mexico/Arizona Book Award Finalist)

Games for Couples - Did lethal compounds in a cultured meat product—meat made in a test tube—kill a man in a clinical trial? Or did a toxic competition between biotechnology companies and the spite of battling couples cause his death? (New Mexico/Arizona Book Award Finalist)

Fair Compromises - Sara Almquist and her FBI colleagues rush to find the culprits who endangered the lives of a hundred attendees at a political rally by poisoning the food with botulism toxin in order to kill their target—a woman candidate for the U.S. Senate.

See more at https://www.jlgreger.com.

www.ingramcontent.com/pod-product-compliance
Lightning Source LLC
Chambersburg PA
CBHW021334190726
48288CB00003B/1104